Snow Bells Christmas

De-ann Black

GW00469500

Published 2018

Snow Bells Christmas

ISBN: 9781720182986

Also by De-ann Black (Romance, Action/Thrillers & Children's books). See her Amazon Author page or website for further details about her books, screenplays, illustrations, art and fabric designs.
www.De-annBlack.com

Romance:

The Sewing Shop
Heather Park
The Tea Shop by the Sea
The Bookshop by the Seaside
The Sewing Bee
The Quilting Bee
Snow Bells Wedding
Snow Bells Christmas
Summer Sewing Bee
The Chocolatier's Cottage
Christmas Cake Chateau
The Beemaster's Cottage
The Sewing Bee By The Sea
The Flower Hunter's Cottage

The Christmas Knitting Bee
The Sewing Bee & Afternoon Tea
The Vintage Sewing & Knitting Bee
Shed In The City
The Bakery By The Seaside
Champagne Chic Lemonade Money
The Christmas Chocolatier
The Christmas Tea Shop & Bakery
The Vintage Tea Dress Shop In Summer
Oops! I'm The Paparazzi
The Bitch-Proof Suit

Action/Thrillers:

Love Him Forever.
Someone Worse.
Electric Shadows.

The Strife Of Riley.
Shadows Of Murder.

Children's books:

Faeriefied.
Secondhand Spooks.
Poison-Wynd.

Wormhole Wynd.
Science Fashion.
School For Aliens.

Colouring books:

Summer Garden. Spring Garden. Autumn Garden. Sea Dream.
Festive Christmas. Christmas Garden. Flower Bee. Wild Garden.
Faerie Garden Spring. Flower Hunter. Stargazer Space. Bee Garden.

Embroidery books:

Floral Nature Embroidery Designs
Scottish Garden Embroidery Designs

Contents

Chapter One

Snow fluttered down outside the windows of Marla's office in New York. The city looked like a winter wonderland. It was a week before Christmas and the home decor company, who specialized in their own range of fabric, was getting ready to finish up for the holidays.

Marla sat at her desk and studied Sylvie's new fabric designs on her laptop. The office was tidy with clean, elegant lines and a calm but efficient vibe. Sylvie waited while Marla evaluated the new patterns. If approved, the fabric would be made into everything from bed linen to table covers and sold by the yard in stores as quilting fabric.

Sylvie stood patiently and gazed out at the wintry morning view of the city. Her reflection in the window showed an attractive young woman wearing pale gray separates that were a fair match for her eyes. Her caramel colored hair fell in soft waves to her shoulders, but her expression was tense. She was hoping Marla liked the new designs. She'd taken a chance using her floral watercolors as the basis for the artwork. She'd aimed for light, pastel patterns for summer with delicate daisy and rose prints. Her previous spring collection had been brighter and bolder, so this was a change from her usual style. She liked it and was mentally crossing her fingers that Marla would too.

The hardest thing for Sylvie was designing out of season. Now that the summer prints were finished, she had to focus on ideas for the fall. It was as if she was always living ahead of the curve, out of step with everything. Here she was at Christmastime creating summer fabrics. Sometimes she thought this contributed to what was wrong with her life for the things she wanted, really wanted. A happy, settled life with a man she could trust, love and rely on. Someone to share things with, especially during the holidays when everyone she knew had family or were part of a couple.

Sylvie glanced at Marla. She was still concentrating on the designs. Sylvie couldn't tell what Marla thought about the new floral prints she'd created. This was always a nail–biting part of her work, and it seemed even more so because the holidays were almost upon them.

Most of her patterns had already been approved by the company, but these new designs were still to be accepted as part of the latest collection. Sylvie was in her early thirties, several years younger than her boss, and the two of them were friends as well as business colleagues. Despite their friendship, she knew Marla would be honest with her when it came to business.

Sylvie watched the snow fluttering down and wished she was far away from the constant pressures of work and business in the city. She'd always loved Christmas, but hadn't had time to celebrate it properly these past three years as she'd put her career first. Working hard had paid off, but it had also cost her. All she ever seemed to do these days was work. Frankly, the holidays couldn't come fast enough for her and she couldn't wait to enjoy her down time. She had something special planned.

Marla eventually looked up from the laptop and smiled. 'Your fabric designs are amazing.'

A huge wave of relief washed over Sylvie. 'I'm so glad you like them.'

'Like them? This is your best collection yet. They'll look wonderful as part of our summer fabric line. The softer tones are beautiful.'

Marla stood up and walked Sylvie to the door. 'Any plans for Christmas?'

Due to the pressures of their busy schedules, they hadn't had a chance to catch up on what they'd both planned for the holidays. Sylvie worked from home, a studio apartment in the city, and popped into the office regularly to give Marla updates on her designs.

Sylvie's expression showed her excitement. 'Yes, I have. I'm treating myself to something special this year. It's my Christmas gift to me.'

'Whatever it is, you deserve it. You've worked hard on the new designs for months.' Marla's eyes sparkled with curiosity. 'So, what is it?'

'A trip to one of the cutest small towns up north — Snow Bells Haven. I'm getting away from the city, as much as I love it here, and heading to a quaint town that pulls out all the stops for the holiday season — at least according to their website. The stores are all done up for Christmas, snow is guaranteed and they have lots of festive celebration events including a Christmas Eve party where Santa arrives on his sleigh.'

'Like living the Christmas dream?'

'Exactly. I've rented a house there during the holidays and I plan to relax, sip mulled wine in front of a real log fire, eat gingerbread cookies, listen to Christmas music and enjoy the whole season.'

'It sounds great.'

'What about you? What are your plans?' said Sylvie.

'I'm spending it with Peter and the family. My parents are coming over, same as every year. Tradition.'

'I love tradition.' She just hadn't nailed it yet, especially when it came to relationships.

'I'm sorry about you and Conrad. Splitting up is hard enough without having to be on your own during the holidays.'

Sylvie's smiled faded.

'Sorry, I didn't mean—'

'No, it's fine. It was never going to work. Conrad was a mistake. Big mistake. Huge.'

'You're better off without him. We all thought he was so handsome and charming.'

'Conrad had us all fooled, especially me. The charm was fake.'

'Have you seen or heard from him recently?'

'No, I haven't had any contact with Conrad since I yelled at him over the phone that he was a lying, no good weasel.'

Marla pressed her lips firmly together. The less said about Conrad the better. Marla brightened. 'Maybe you'll meet someone wonderful in Snow Bells Haven?'

Sylvie held her hands up. 'No, I don't think so. I'm stepping off the dating treadmill during the holidays. No romance, no entanglements, no broken hearts. Nope. I plan to enjoy eating cookies and chilling out.'

'And no work.'

'Well... perhaps a little bit of work. I've got a few ideas for designs that I may put down.'

'While you're sitting roasting chestnuts by the fireside?'

Sylvie smiled. 'You know me, I'm always sketching down ideas. I'm taking my laptop and artist's pad with me, but apart from that, it's nothing but having fun in a real life snow globe.'

'It seems very adventurous of you.'

Sylvie nodded firmly. 'Yes, it is. I don't know if it's the sense of excitement of the holiday season, but I'm really in the mood for some adventure.'

Sylvie's adventure began with the drive up north. The further north, the more snow she encountered which was just fine by her. She listened to Christmas music and sang along to her favorite festive tunes with gusto. She was halfway through one carol when a sign on the roadway read: Welcome to Snow Bells Haven.

She pulled the car over with the intention of taking a photograph of the sign to prove to everyone, including herself, that she'd done what she'd set out to do. Finishing her designs within a tight schedule was one thing, and she'd never missed a deadline for work, but doing something totally for herself was something else. She wanted lots of pictures of the whole experience to look back on when she returned to her apartment in the city.

She stepped out of the car and felt her boots sink into the deepest snow she'd trudged through in years, perhaps ever. It touched the furry trim on her boots, and although it wasn't snowing, she put the hood of her warm coat up against the cold, early evening air.

She snapped a few pictures of the sign with her phone, and then stepped back to capture the full scenic view of the snow covered countryside and the town, aglow with lights, set in the heart of it.

Perhaps it was a rut in the snow or that she was looking at her phone, but she stepped backwards and tumbled into a deep drift and emerged as if she'd been dipped in icing sugar. A human sugar cookie.

Struggling to her feet and keeping a tight grip of her phone, she brushed the excess snow from her clothes and hair as a car pulled up and a guy got out.

'Are you okay?' His voice was filled with as much concern as the expression on his handsome face. His stunning blue eyes scanned her for damage. 'I saw you stumble.'

'I'm fine, thank you.' She tried to sound perky while inwardly squirming. 'I'm not usually a klutz.' She glanced down at her fur trimmed boots. 'It's probably my boots. They're way too big.'

He nodded and grinned. 'We'll blame the boots.'

She smiled up at him. He had a tall, broad shouldered, rangy build, though it was hard to be precise as he wore a warm jacket that added a touch of bulk to his physique. In his early thirties, he wasn't much older than her with dark hair swept back from his sculptured, clean–shaven features. He was a handsome one, no doubt about that, but past experience warned her to be wary and trust her instincts. To be fair, there was nothing about this man that made her feel anything other than safe — just a thoughtful guy making sure she hadn't hurt herself.

She kept her guard up anyway, emotional and otherwise.

He looked around. 'Can I ask what you were doing?'

'I was taking photographs of the sign.' She showed him her phone still clutched in a tight grip.

'Why?'

'I wanted proof that I was here, in the snow, at Christmastime, doing what I'd set out to do.'

He didn't quite understand, but he was trying. She gave him ten for effort. 'And what is it you set out to do?'

'To get away from New York and enjoy a vacation in a little town like this.' She spread her arms out wide. 'Do something I've wanted to do for a long time. Be more adventurous.'

His firm lips broke into a smile.

'What's so amusing?'

He looked down, shook his head, still smiling. 'Nothing.'

'No, not nothing.' Her tone was insistent.

He shrugged. 'It's just that... people I know leave small towns and go to the city to be adventurous. But you do things the other way around.'

'The story of my life,' she muttered.

'What do you mean?'

She hesitated before telling him. 'I'm a fabric designer. I've just finished designing a range of prints for the company's summer collection. My boss approved them this morning. I've been working on those all through the fall and into December, creating light, warm, summery floral designs in the midst of the autumn and then into the winter. Now I'm about to start sketching patterns for a fall collection. I'm never in the right season. I'm always out of step with everything that's going on around me.' She paused and looked at him. 'And here I am, doing something I never do — explaining myself to a complete stranger.'

He smiled warmly, and there was something in his expression, like he understood. He extended his hand. 'I'm Zack.'

'Sylvie.'

They shook hands and smiled.

'So, where are you headed in town? Are you staying at the lodge?'

She pulled a piece of paper from her pocket. 'No, I've rented a house. This is the address. Do you know it?'

He read the address. 'I do. I'm heading home. This is on my route. You could follow me if you want. It would save you driving around looking for it.'

'Great. My sat–nav is wonky.'

'Wonky huh?'

'It was working fine until I got near here, then it seemed to start being out of whack. Maybe the signal isn't so strong here.'

'That happens sometimes. Cell phone reception and online connections are fickle.'

She dusted some more snow from her coat and straightened her shoulders. 'All part of the adventure,' she said chirpily.

He looked at her for a moment and was about to tell her something, but she brushed his concern aside and went to walk towards her car.

'Let me help you,' he said. 'I think you should—'

'I can manage to walk to my car.'

'Yes, but—'

Again, she ignored him, misinterpreting his concern. She pulled up the hood of her coat and gasped as a hood full of snow tumbled on to her hair and face.

'That's what I was trying to tell you.' He tried not to smirk as she spluttered and shook the snow off.

Pretending to be unfazed, she continued to her car. 'I'll follow you.'

He buttoned his lips, got into his car and the two of them drove into the center of the town. Stores were lit with twinkle lights and decorations. Garlands stretched along the road from the street lamps. There were ornamental Santa Claus with sleigh displays and everything looked just like she'd imagined it would.

She almost wished she hadn't agreed to follow Zack because she'd have driven up and down looking at everything — twice. But it was getting dark and her tummy rumbled in need of something to eat. The snowflakes were also melting on her hair and dripping down her neck. She planned to change into dry clothes and venture out for a meal, or buy groceries and cook dinner herself.

She was still thinking about this when his car indicator signaled her to pull up at one of the prettiest houses just off the main street. The property sat in the middle of a snow covered garden, surrounded by a white picket fence, with similar houses on either side. Christmas tree lights glowed in the window of the front lounge in an inviting gesture.

With excitement bubbling inside her, she parked the car and got out, as did he.

'Here you are,' he announced. 'If there's anything you need give me a shout.' He thumbed behind him. 'I'm not far away.'

'We're next door neighbors?'

'Nearly. I'm a couple of houses along.'

She started to unload her luggage.

'Let me give you a hand with those.'

'I can manage,' she said, but he'd already picked up the bulk of her cases and carried them to the front door. She followed with the rest of her bags.

He put the cases down. 'I hope you enjoy your stay.' He started to walk away, then paused. 'Oh, and the key is usually tucked above the door ledge.' He waved and continued on his way.

A festive garland of greenery and winter berries was draped around the doorway. It was covered with snow. Sylvie stood on tiptoe and reached up to the lintel to feel for the key.

He stopped and glanced back at her.

Anticipating he was about to offer to help her reach it, she overstretched to grab the key, knocked the garland and sent a flurry of snow tumbling down on her head. She sucked up the urge to let out a yell.

He didn't say anything, but he was smirking.

7

'There's a grocery store nearby that should have everything you need.' He pointed in the direction of the store. 'It's between the cafe and diner.'

She smiled tightly. 'Thanks for your help. I appreciate it, despite the smirking.'

He gave her a sheepish grin. 'I didn't mean to smirk.'

'I'm sure you didn't.'

'Just being neighborly. You'd be surprised how many city folk aren't familiar with small town life. Some of them don't even know how to light a log fire.'

'Really?' She suddenly realized she was one of them, but how difficult could it be? She'd look it up online if she got stuck.

'Yes. Though I'm sure you're quite capable and won't go burning the roof down.'

Had he read her expression? Did he suss out that she'd never lit any fire in her entire life?

As he headed away she called after him. 'Wait, perhaps you could give me a few tips on how to light the log fire here. Not that I couldn't figure it out, but I'm not silly. I wouldn't want to cause any damage to the property.'

He walked back to her, kicked the snow from his boots and accompanied her inside the house, lugging her cases for good measure and putting them down in the hallway.

The house was everything she could've hoped for. The photographs she'd seen online of the lounge with its log fire and comfy couch, colorful rugs on the polished wood floor and traditional, homely decor were an accurate portrayal. The only thing missing from the pictures was the Christmas tree and decorations that the owner had thoughtfully added as a welcoming bonus.

Sylvie stood mesmerized for a moment. 'This looks amazing.'

'Pretty house. The folks who own it always do it up real nice.'

'You know them well?'

'Nate and Nancy are neighbors. They're organizing the chestnut roast event this year. We tend to know each other around here. Everyone helps out.'

'Real neighborly.'

He crouched down and started to build the fire in the hearth. 'Unlike the city.'

'You ever lived there?'

'New York? Yes, I did, for a year. I rented out my house, but city life wasn't for me. I missed my home town and moved back. I've no intention of leaving again except for the occasional business trip. No offence to where you come from.'

'None taken. Each person to their own choices.'

He showed her how to build the fire using kindling and adding logs. She watched his strong but elegant hands break the kindling with ease, arrange it for maximum airflow and set the logs on top. He knew fine she hadn't a clue what to do but didn't make her feel inadequate. His method was straightforward and she reckoned she could handle it by herself next time.

The fire sparked into life bringing warmth to the lounge. The scent of the burning logs mingled with the fragrance of the real pine Christmas tree near the window.

He put a fireguard in front of the fire to contain the sparks. 'Make sure you keep this up if you have to pop out,' he advised her. 'If you get cold and don't want to build a fire, there's a switch in the kitchen to activate the central heating.' He went through to the kitchen to show her where it was.

She followed him. 'You seem very familiar with the layout of the house. Have you ever lived here?'

'No, but I have been here lots of times over the years visiting Nate and Nancy,' he explained. 'Besides, most of the houses in this street have similar architecture. Great houses.'

The central heating switch was near the stove. On the wall hung a selection of gleaming copper pots and pans that added a glow to the room.

The yellow and cream decor made the kitchen feel inviting on a cold winter's night. She imagined it would feel equally lovely in the summer with warm light pouring in like liquid sunshine.

The designer in her took in the prints on the fabrics used throughout the lounge and kitchen. Modern vintage is what she classed it as. A look she'd always liked. While the kitchen colors ranged from buttermilk to golden vanilla, the lounge had rich tones of burgundy and cherry brandy. She tended to think of colors as flavors, scents and seasons.

'Thank you for being so helpful.' She took her coat off and hung it over the back of a kitchen chair to dry. She shook her hair that still retained flakes of snow, and couldn't wait to get changed and freshen up.

He took the hint that it was time to leave. 'I'd better get going. I've got someone waiting for me.'

She didn't doubt it. A personable guy like him was bound to have someone special in his life, though the fleeting pang of disappointment she felt that he wasn't single took her aback. She wasn't here to get involved with anyone. Maybe she was just overtired and overexcited, a jarring combination that was sure to mess with her emotions.

He headed out. She accompanied him to the front door and watched him walk away to his car. He got in, turned it around, drove a couple of houses along from her and parked outside his property.

She stood for a moment with her arms wrapped around herself against the cold night air and breathed in the wonderful atmosphere.

Gazing up at the deep, velvety sky, she smiled. She'd done it. She was actually here. Then she went inside, started to unpack, hung her clothes in the closet and changed into something dry and comfortable.

The house had two bedrooms, a lounge, kitchen and bathroom. She chose the bedroom at the front with a view of the tree–lined street. She peeked out the window. The trees had a scattering of twinkle lights, and all the houses were lit with festive decorations with many having a Christmas tree in their garden in addition to one inside. It was like looking at a traditional Christmas card with all the pretty houses set amid the snow.

Her tummy rumbled as she checked the food situation in the kitchen, opening cupboards and the refrigerator to find that basic supplies had been left for her, including coffee, sugar, fresh milk and butter, but she needed to stock up on her own food groceries.

She put on a warm jacket, woolly hat, wrapped a scarf around her neck and headed out.

The grocery store was nearby. She enjoyed the walk there, breathing in the scents of the snowy evening. She gazed at the Christmas lights draped along the main street and stores ablaze with festive decor.

Delicious aromas wafted from the cafe and the diner on either side of the grocery store. The cafe and the diner were busy, and benefited from having menus that complemented each other rather than competed for trade, resulting in both businesses thriving. Although she was tempted to pop into them, having read the menus in the front windows, she decided to buy her groceries first.

Her phone rang outside the grocery store. She was pleased to see it was a call from Marla.

'How's life in the snow globe?'

'Snowy.'

Marla laughed. 'Is it everything you hoped it would be?'

'It is, and the house is even prettier than I imagined. I'm out buying groceries and then heading back to make dinner and eat it by the fireside. I've even learned how to build a real log fire.'

'I'm impressed. I've always wanted to do that but wouldn't know where to start,' said Marla.

'Neither did I, but I've got the hang of it now.'

'Did the owners leave instructions?'

'No, one of the neighbors, Zack, showed me.'

'Zack, huh?' Marla didn't disguise the underlying tone in her voice.

'No, it's not what you're thinking. He was just being neighborly. That's what they do around here.'

Marla fished for details. 'Is he a looker?'

'That has nothing to do with it.'

'So, he's handsome.'

'I didn't say that, Marla.'

'The tone of your voice said it. You sound... perky.'

'It's not because of Zack. Besides, I think he's taken. He said he had someone waiting for him at home. However, he's been very helpful since I arrived.'

'I'll just bet he has.'

'He seems like a nice guy, but I have no intention of getting involved with anyone while I'm here, and certainly not with a man who doesn't like the city and is a real homebody.'

'Could he be any more perfect?'

'Yes, he could stop smirking every time I do something dumb or look like I'm clumsy.'

'You're not clumsy, Sylvie.'

'I seem to be since I arrived here.' Sylvie went on to describe what happened at the road sign and the trail of events with Zack.

11

Marla listened to every detail. 'Well, the human sugar cookie thing doesn't seem to have put him off. I think he's interested in you. I have a nose for these things.'

'No, Marla, your nose is way off the scent.'

'No it isn't, and I think you're interested in him.'

'I'm not.'

Marla laughed. 'Oh I think you are. He could be single.'

'Even if he was unattached, I am determined not to get romantically involved with anyone during my Christmas vacation.'

'The guy was in your house tonight building you a log fire. It took Conrad three weeks and five dinner dates before you let him into your apartment.'

'With Conrad I was just being careful. You know I'm the careful type.'

'That's exactly what I mean. This Christmas adventure of yours is great, so don't make rules for yourself that you're reluctant to break. Besides, Conrad was a no good weasel. You said so yourself. Give Zack a chance,' Marla advised. 'He sounds promising.'

Sylvie sighed. 'I'm here to relax and think up ideas for my new designs.'

'What does Zack do for a living?' Marla asked.

Sylvie realized he knew plenty about her but she knew very little about him. 'I don't know what he does.'

'I'm an architect.'

Sylvie jumped and looked round to see Zack standing there with a bemused expression on his face.

'Wow!' said Marla. 'An architect. Impressive.'

'Thank you, Marla,' said Zack.

There was a tense pause and then Marla whispered over the phone to Sylvie. 'Can he hear me?'

'Oh yes, Marla,' Zack replied as Sylvie squirmed with embarrassment.

'But how...?' Marla's voice sounded shrill.

Zack pointed to Sylvie's phone. 'Speakerphone.'

Sylvie immediately jabbed at the buttons on her cell trying to switch the speakerphone function off, but couldn't work the touch screen well with her gloves on.

'How much of the call did he hear?' Marla asked Sylvie.

12

Sylvie glared at Zack who was happy to recap the salient points he'd overheard. 'Apparently Conrad is a no good weasel. Oh and, I'm single, but I really was just being neighborly.'

'And nosy,' Marla called through to him.

'Unintentional I assure you,' Zack said in his defense. 'But it's difficult not to get involved when you hear two women talking about you in a less than private phone call.'

Sylvie glared at him. 'You could've made your presence known. You could've let me know I was accidentally on speakerphone instead of eavesdropping.'

Zack held up his hands. 'Guilty as charged. But I did interrupt before you said anything else about dating me.'

'I didn't mention anything about dating you,' Sylvie objected.

'Not specifically, but it was hinted that you might be interested.'

Sylvie looked at him defiantly. 'I'm definitely not.'

'Fine. Enjoy the rest of your evening, Sylvie,' said Zack. 'Goodnight, Marla,' he called out as he walked away.

'That was totally embarrassing,' Sylvie said to Marla, having finally switched off the speakerphone.

'Try to think of it as part of your adventure. The night we got caught talking about a guy as a potential love interest.' Marla was still laughing as the cell phone signal cut out.

Sylvie sighed, put the phone in her pocket and headed into the grocery store.

Chapter Two

A handful of customers were inside the grocery store and a cheerful woman in her fifties was serving behind the counter. The shelves were stacked with tinned goods, and fruit and vegetables were well displayed. There was a deli counter with a tasty range of cheese, and a bakery section with fresh baked items ranging from bread to bagels, cupcakes to cookies and pancakes to pumpkin pie that also sold bags of flour and other items for home baking.

Sylvie filled her basket with a selection of items, including vegetables, fruit, bread, eggs, cheese, pizza and iced gingerbread cookies and took them up to the woman.

'Do you have any logs for sale?' Sylvie asked as the woman dealt with her purchases and packed them into bags.

'Logs? No, I'm sorry we don't actually sell those.' She called through to the back of the store. 'Nate, do we have any logs to spare?'

'I don't want you to go to any trouble for me,' said Sylvie.

The woman smiled. 'No trouble.'

'Be right there, Nancy,' Nate called to her.

'You're Nate and Nancy?' Sylvie asked.

'Yes... are you...?'

'Sylvie.'

Nancy's face lit up. 'Welcome to our town. Sorry we weren't there to greet you, but we've been so busy with the store this time of year.'

'And getting ready for the chestnut roast,' Sylvie added.

'Yes, that's right. I hope you'll come along. It's a heap of fun.'

'I will. I'm planning to enjoy all the festivities.' Sylvie plucked a leaflet from the counter listing all the celebratory events and put it in her pocket.

'Let us know if there's anything you need,' said Nancy, and then she frowned. 'Though I thought we had a pile of logs out back at the house.'

'I haven't checked. I've only just arrived. I'm still getting my bearings,' Sylvie explained.

'There should be a stack of logs outside the kitchen door.'

Sylvie nodded her thanks and paid for her groceries.

Nate, a sturdy looking guy similar in age to Nancy wandered through, smiling. 'So you're our Christmas visitor? Zack mentioned you'd arrived.'

'He did?' Had he mentioned about her looking like a sugar cookie?

'He said you were delighted with the house. I'm glad you like it. We try to make folks welcome.' Nate glanced at Nancy. 'My wife gets all the credit for the Christmas decorations and homely touches.'

Nancy smiled at Nate and then at Sylvie. 'Zack says you're a fabric designer and will be working on new designs while you're here. I trust you won't be working too hard and missing out on all the holiday fun.'

'It's really a vacation,' Sylvie explained, 'but I'll be sketching some ideas while I'm here for my next fabric collection.'

Nancy nodded. 'For the fall. Zack mentioned you have to work seasons ahead.'

Sylvie tried to smile. 'Zack's certainly been talking a lot about me.'

'All flattering,' Nancy assured her. 'So if it's of any help to you, there is a photograph album in the dresser drawer in the lounge beside the Christmas tree and it's packed with pictures of the garden, the town and surrounding countryside at various times of the year. There are plenty of pictures of the trees in the garden during the fall.' Nancy shrugged. 'Maybe they'll help inspire you, not that I think you need it being a New York designer.'

'That's very helpful. I'll definitely take a look.' Sylvie picked up her bags and went to leave the store.

'Zack's a great guy,' Nancy called after her.

'I'm sure he is,' said Sylvie and then stepped out into the cold night carrying her groceries.

She walked back to the house, enjoying the atmosphere of the town, feeling it wrap itself around her. Festive music drifted from a couple of stores and she found herself humming along to one of the tunes. Despite the embarrassing incident with the phone call, she was determined to make the most of her vacation. Although Zack lived two houses down from her it didn't mean that she'd see him again, and after hearing what she'd said to Marla and then to his face, it wasn't likely he'd want to deal with her again either. No, they could go about their business as if they'd never met.

As she walked past his house she quickened her step, looked ahead and pretended not to notice him chopping logs in his garden at the side of his house.

Putting on a spurt of speed, even though her boots had a tendency to slow her down, she was soon inside her house and placed the groceries down on the kitchen table.

She looked at the selection of items she'd bought, wondering what to cook for dinner. Something easy to make, so she could sit down and relax for the remainder of the evening. The log fire had almost burned itself out, but she had the main heating as backup if adding more kindling and logs didn't spark it up again. Or... she could take the real easy option and pop along to the cafe or the diner.

As she hadn't even taken her boots, jacket, hat or scarf off, option B got her vote. Besides, she was free to do as she pleased. There were no work deadlines or restrictions on her time. She could make her own schedule and that included venturing out rather than staying in. If she was in New York, she'd be in her apartment eating dinner, probably at her desk, and then working all evening on her designs. It had become such a familiar pattern of her life that she was determined to head out into the snowy night.

She picked up her purse from the hall table, opened the front door and jumped when she saw Zack standing there with an armful of freshly cut logs.

'Nancy called and asked me to top up your log supply.'

'Oh, thank you. She told me there were logs outside the kitchen door but I haven't checked yet.'

She stepped aside and he walked through to the lounge bringing the scent of a Christmassy night in with him.

'I'll put these at the side of the fireplace. It'll save you lugging them through.' He stacked them up neatly. 'That should keep you going for a couple of days, and I'm sure there's plenty out back.'

She sensed an awkwardness in him that hadn't been there earlier. Clearly the phone call to Marla had changed things between them.

He wiped the remnants of firewood from his hands and looked at the fire.

'I'm letting it burn out,' she said before he could criticize it.

16

He pressed his lips firmly together and nodded as if it was none of his business what she did.

'I thought I'd go to the cafe or diner for dinner,' she piped up.

'I can certainly recommend both, but I think there's a special menu on at the diner tonight. Not sure what it is, but their specials are always delicious.'

She tried to sound perky, pretending that things between them were totally fine. 'I'll definitely check it out.'

He headed out and so did Sylvie, wrapping her warm scarf around her neck as he strode away.

'Thanks again for the logs,' she said, locking the front door.

She glanced round at him but he'd disappeared to the back of the house. She hurried after him.

'What are you doing?' she called to him.

'Checking your log supply. I promised Nate and Nancy I'd make sure you had enough.' He looked at the log storage where the firewood was kept dry and aired. 'Yes, there's plenty here.'

A lantern hung above the kitchen door illuminating the fenced yard. She'd thought that the front garden was lovely but this was beautiful. Trees and bushes were iced white with snow and the ground glittered all around. This was a garden someone cared about and had landscaped with little niches including a seated area with an overhanging tree bough, an ornamental beehive sparkling as if encrusted with crystallized sugar, and a small pond frozen solid that she had the urge to slide on just for the fun of it. But she didn't. Instead she stood and gazed around her in wonder.

'This is magical,' she gasped.

He looked over at her. 'It is.'

For a moment she thought he was going to break the ice between them, to say whatever was on his mind, but instead he walked back round to the front of the house.

She did the same, keeping her thoughts to herself.

He paused at the gate, and she saw his breath in the cold air as he let out a reluctant sigh. 'I'm heading down this way. I'll walk you along.'

They walked together, neither saying a word until Sylvie finally couldn't stand the tension.

'Listen, Zack, there are obviously things we need to say to clear the air between us.'

17

'I think plenty has already been said, don't you?' He continued walking.

She kept pace with him. 'Fine, we'll leave things on an awkward note.'

He was quiet for a moment before letting go a torrent of issues. 'This is the thing about relationships. There's all the drama that goes with it.'

'We don't have a relationship, Zack. And I don't like drama any more than you do. I had that with my ex. Not going there again. Never, ever.' Her determined tone rang out clearly in the crisp night air.

'With Conrad the weasel?' he said, letting her know that every word of that phone call still resonated in him.

'Yes. Some people like the drama. They think it keeps things exciting, but I just find it draining. Dating Conrad was hard work, and it shouldn't be like that.'

'Is that why you split up with him?'

She nodded. 'I realized that Conrad was no good for me. He had no real interest in anything I did. And the fake charm... I couldn't put up with that. Conrad was such a fake.'

'You still sound angry with him,' he remarked.

'I'm angry with myself for letting a guy like him fool me.'

'So you won't be missing him at Christmas?' There was a hint of hope mixed with sarcasm in his tone.

'No. I won't be missing anyone.' The anger in her voice was calmed. 'I've no family to spend the holidays with, and any friends are part of a couple so...' Her voice trailed off and she shrugged. She didn't want to say the words that she was on her own for Christmas. She had no intention of sounding downcast. Okay, so it would've been great to spend the holidays with someone she loved, but life hadn't worked out that way. Maybe one day things would be different, but for now she intended to enjoy her vacation.

'You're here to get away from everything?' he said tactfully.

'Yes, but I've always wanted to enjoy the perfect cozy Christmas. Ever since I was a little girl I've thought wouldn't it be great to celebrate the holidays in a small town that looks like it belongs on a Christmas card. After the break–up with Conrad and finishing the fabric designs, this was the ideal time to get away from the city and do what I'd always dreamed of even if I was on my own.'

'You certainly came to the right town,' he said, then paused outside his house. 'This is my stop.'

'Nice house.'

She admired the substantial property and surrounding garden. The exterior had a grander styling than others nearby, but it still retained a homely quality. This was a family house, made for a couple to build a life together, raise some kids, maybe even get a dog. It was a house that would accommodate the seasons. In the heart of winter, iced with snow, it was the perfect festive family home. She pictured it in summer, bathed in sunlight with the trees providing shade in parts of the garden and the porch ideal for relaxing in the warm air with a tall glass of cold lemonade. In the spring, the trees would be covered in pink blossom, and the house with its white painted eaves would look like the setting for a bridal brochure. And in the fall, everything would have an autumnal glow of copper, bronze and gold.

'It's really lovely,' she said, snapping out of her faraway thoughts.

'Thank you. My grandfather built it and I've renovated parts of it, including the porch and extension out back.'

'Have your family always lived in this town?'

'Yes, and I was born and raised here. My parents used to live on the other side of the town, but I lost them a few years back and moved in here when I inherited it.'

'It's handy that you're an architect and can make changes to the house. I like the design of the porch,' she said, imagining what it would be like to sit out front and watch the world go by at an easy pace.

'I haven't changed the structure too much. The design was great. I've just added a few little touches and kept up with repairs. I didn't want to alter the traditional style of it. I like tradition.'

'So do I.'

He nodded thoughtfully and smiled.

'What?' she asked him.

'Nothing.' He looked down, hands thrust in his jacket pockets.

'Come on, tell me,' she insisted.

'When I first saw you I thought... she looks like a modern city girl in the wrong zone. Even though you did look like a sugar cookie.'

'You really heard a lot of my conversation with Marla didn't you?'

He grinned. 'But now I think you look like you could belong in a small town.'

'You think so?'

He held his hands up. 'I'm not trying to—'

'That's okay,' she interrupted before he made some awkward excuse that he wasn't coming on to her. She didn't think he was anyway and she wanted to know what had changed his mind about her. 'So why do you think that now?'

'It was the log fire moment,' he told her.

'The log fire moment?'

'You really looked like you wanted to learn how to build that fire.'

'I did want to learn.'

'I know, and that's when I started to think, okay, she's from New York but maybe she's a small, home town type at heart.'

For some reason this made her feel quite emotional. She blinked and tried to hide her reaction.

His gorgeous blue eyes looked right at her. 'Are you okay?'

'Yes, I'm fine. I'm just...' she sighed. 'It's been a long, crazy day and I'm in need of something to eat. I should get going.'

He nodded and smiled. He had such a nice smile she thought as she walked away. She wasn't certain what she liked most about it — the way his lips looked so inviting or the fact that it reached right up to his eyes. A genuine smile. Not like Conrad with his fake charm.

She paused for a moment and called to him. 'How do you do that?'

'Do what?' he called back to her.

'Get me to tell you all these things about myself? I never do that.'

He shrugged and spread his arms out. 'I don't know.'

She gave a tight–lipped smile and continued on towards the diner.

The scent of chestnuts roasting wafted in the air. Someone had set up a stall near the grocery store and several people were waiting to buy a bag of freshly cooked chestnuts. If she hadn't been enticed into the diner for a Christmas turkey dinner, she would've bought a bag for herself. Another night perhaps. No, she quickly corrected herself. Another night for sure.

Sylvie was welcomed into the diner by a friendly waitress in her late twenties with a name badge, Ana, and seated at one of the windows with a view of the main street. Colorful Christmas lights decorating the street lamps reflected off the window and made her feel cozy inside the diner.

The staff were cheerful and busy dealing with lots of customers. Most people were ordering the evening special — a pre–Christmas turkey dinner with all the trimmings including buttery mashed potatoes, herb stuffing, gravy and cranberry sauce.

Sylvie ordered the special which was served up with a generous portion of fresh baked bread. She knew she was hungry when she started to tuck in, but the taste was superb and she was surprised how much she'd needed a good meal to help settle her.

'Pumpkin pie?' Ana offered her a slice as she cleared away her empty plate and topped up her coffee cup.

'I don't think I've got any room left for pie,' Sylvie confessed with a smile. 'That meal was delicious.'

'I'll wrap up a slice for you to take away,' Ana insisted. 'It's part of the special, and believe me, you don't want to miss out on a slice of our pumpkin pie.'

Sylvie left the diner with her slice of pie and headed down the main street to walk off some of that great meal and to explore the town. Driving along the road earlier behind Zack, she'd admired all the decorations and the store windows aglow with lights. However, seeing them up close was far more exciting. It was like walking through a scene from a Christmas card. Her heart felt fit to burst with joy. She gazed at the twinkling lights on the trees as she walked under the branches and loved the feel of the glistening snow beneath her boots. There were enough people around to make it pleasantly busy.

A group of carol singers were gathered near the largest Christmas tree in the heart of the town. They were dressed from a bygone era and held old fashioned lanterns to complete the look. Their voices rang out clear in the wintry air and people were encouraged to stop and join in.

Sylvie watched them from nearby, but then went over when some of them waved, beckoning her to join them. With her bag of pumpkin pie in one hand and a lyrics sheet in the other, she sang her heart out amid the group of strangers who made her feel so welcome.

She gazed around her at the cheerful faces and sang along with everyone. This felt like Christmas. It really did. Her first night in town and here she was feeling well fed and festive. Not bad for a city girl, miles from home. No, not bad at all, she thought, as she joined in the next carol before walking back to the house to get a good night's sleep.

After getting changed for bed, she padded into the kitchen wearing a pair of warm socks. She heated a cup of milk and carried it through to the lounge. The lights of the Christmas tree created a welcoming glow and the atmosphere of the house made her feel safe and secure. On her own and far from the city, she felt more at home here than she had in a long time.

She thought about some of the things Zack had said to her. Could a city girl belong in a small town? She'd coped well with her life in the city, building a career and working from a studio apartment. New York didn't overwhelm her but it never nurtured her either.

Her reflection in the window didn't look like a modern city girl, especially with her messy ponytail, cozy nightwear and sipping a cup of hot milk in the midst of a traditional, homely setting.

She looked at herself in the glow of the Christmas tree lights and wondered... is this what Zack saw in her?

Finishing her hot milk, she went to bed, keeping snug and warm under the covers, and settled down for the night.

Sylvie had always been an early riser and woke up at her usual time having slept well. She hadn't stirred since climbing into bed, and she did mean climbing. The bed wasn't like the one in her apartment. No, it was a big old fashioned bed with a substantial mattress topped with a lovely patchwork quilt that someone had expertly hand made in a traditional style. The type of bed you had to climb into and snuggle down, and were reluctant to emerge from its comforting depths without a lot of coaxing.

Sunlight streaming through the bedroom window and glistening off the fresh snow that had fallen overnight was all the coaxing she needed to get out of bed, shower, dress and get ready for the day ahead. She hadn't anticipated just how excited she'd feel at the prospect of an entire day without any commitments. She couldn't remember the last time she'd had the luxury of one of those. Certainly not for a long time.

She rustled up breakfast and ate it in the kitchen while gazing out the window at the back yard. The winter sunlight created a blue white glow and the snow sparkled like thousands of crystals. This was the first time she'd seen the garden in the daylight and it looked incredible.

She opened the kitchen door and stood there sipping her coffee, admiring the freshness of the day. The quietude was something she welcomed. Even at this early hour the sounds of the New York traffic and buzz of the city would be humming in the background of her apartment. But here there was calm and only a few sounds from a sleepy little town slowly stretching awake. She loved the unhurried atmosphere of it.

She breathed in the early morning air and felt the tension that had gripped her shoulders over the past few months ease a little more. This vacation was just what she needed, she thought, admiring the view. Everything in the back yard was iced white with a fresh layer of snow. But then she noticed something — wait a minute! There were paw prints in the snow. A dog had obviously been bounding around in her back yard.

No sooner had this thought crossed her mind than she heard something move near the log stack. She glanced over and saw a pair of adorable brown eyes peering out at her from behind the logs.

Her heart fluttered with excitement and she smiled at the dog. 'Well, hello. What are you doing here?' Not that she minded. She loved dogs, but had never actually owned one. Work had always taken priority.

Hearing her friendly tone, the cutest chocolate Labrador emerged, tail wagging, from his makeshift hiding place and padded right up to her for affection. She crouched down and welcomed every bit of it.

Her fingers felt the silky softness of his fur that gleamed like rich chocolate velvet. He looked fit and healthy and very well cared for.

She glanced around, but there was no sign of the dog's owner. She reckoned he was a neighbor's dog, and he definitely knew his way around her garden. Full of fun, the dog had bounded off down

23

the yard, picked up his chew ball from the ground, came running back with it in his mouth and dropped it at her feet. The expression on his face said it all.

Sylvie picked up the ball and threw it for the dog to fetch. He loved this game and raced back and forth for several minutes playing this with Sylvie, his new found friend.

'Okay,' she gasped. 'You're in better shape than me.' She sat down on the back step and the dog joined her, resting his head on her knee in the hope that she would pat him, and she did.

Minutes later she heard someone calling out a name — 'Cookie! Here, Cookie. Where are you, boy?'

The dog immediately ran and hid behind the log pile. There was no sense of fear from the dog, just a look of sheer mischief, hiding out, all part of the game.

Zack was startled as he peeped round the side of Sylvie's house and saw her sitting there on the back step.

He wore a cream sweater and jeans. The shoulders she'd thought owed some of their width to his warm jacket were apparently part of his naturally fit physique. His dark hair was still damp as if fresh from the shower and sleeked back from his face. A few unruly strands refused to be tamed and fell across his forehead. In the winter sunlight his blue eyes looked like aquamarines. Her heart squeezed a little just looking at him.

'Oh, hi,' he said. 'I'm looking for my dog. Have you seen him?'

She flicked a glance at the dog, then at Zack. The dog's expression was clear to her. Please don't shop me. I'm only playing. Shh! Don't rat on me.

'A dog?' It was a question, not a denial she told herself.

'Yes, Cookie.'

'Cookie as in chocolate cookie?'

'Yeah.' Zack nodded but kept looking around. Several times his gaze panned across towards the logs but the dog snuck down even further, and then peered out again when he looked the other way. If ever a dog had a grin on his face, it was this one.

Guilt clutched at Sylvie's heart. She wouldn't dream of putting the dog in any harm by not telling Zack where he was, and yet... adorable brown eyes peered out at her, imploring her not to tell.

She was torn, but before she had a chance to point to Cookie, Zack turned and walked away. 'Sorry to have bothered you.'

She hurried after him. 'I'm sure your dog will turn up safely back at your house,' she assured him, especially when she glanced over her shoulder and saw the dog disappear through a gap in the fence heading home. It seemed like Cookie had worked out a secret route from his back yard, to the next garden and then into hers. She was sure the dog looked back at her with a grateful expression.

She took a deep breath. Okay, she scolded herself, if the most adorable chocolate Labrador visited her again she'd fess up to Zack. Definitely, absolutely... probably she would.

As Zack walked away she sighed, wishing his dog had been able to stay and play a little longer. In her back yard there was nothing left except paw prints in the snow. Zack hadn't even noticed them. He'd seemed distracted. Maybe he had a lot on his mind?

Zack tried not to think about Sylvie as he walked back home. He'd promised himself he would not compromise her at all. He'd been awake during the night wondering if he should ask her to have dinner with him. The sleepless night had resulted in a conflicting list of do it versus don't even think about it. Things such as — Sylvie had made it clear she was on vacation and did not want to date anyone while she was here. Okay. Fine. He wouldn't even try to persuade her.

Then there was the Conrad issue. That bad apple had spoiled a heap of trust in her heart. He didn't blame her that she'd decided not to date during the holidays. He understood that feeling only too well. His last relationship had come to a fiery end when the woman he'd intended proposing to claimed she didn't love him anymore. No, he didn't blame Sylvie for preferring no romance versus the risk of yet another wounded heart.

And yet... she'd looked radiant in the morning light. He would've liked to have asked her to go sledding with him today. But he wouldn't pressure her. No way.

Inviting her to the sledding event had been the second choice on his list instead of asking her out to dinner. Sledding was fun, out in the fresh air, whereas dinner was more personal and sort of like a date. Other ideas on his list included asking her to accompany him to the party in the community hall after the chestnut roast, however that could also be construed as a date. He sighed with exasperation. He was running out of ideas and his lists were getting longer.

Cookie's welcoming bark shook him out of his mental list checking.

He smiled as the dog came bounding over the snow covered lawn. The trees in the front garden were encrusted with snow, and some of the branches were frosted together, creating an icy canopy over the garden.

The dog's eagerness to reach him showed in the flurries of snow his paws kicked up.

'Where have you been, boy?' Zack patted the dog's head reassuringly.

Cookie's mouth gaped open, and he swore that dog could smile. His happy expression was one of the reasons he'd picked him out from the rescue center. Cookie had sort of picked him too, jumping up for attention. Zack had taken him home two years ago and now couldn't imagine not having a friend like him around.

Chapter Three

Sylvie walked along the town's main street. The winter sunlight made everything look bright and fresh. Her intention was to browse through the stores that morning, but a friendly Santa bearing a leaflet advertising a fun filled sledding event nearby waylaid her.

'We're having a sledding day to help raise funds for local charities,' said Santa. 'Hope you'll come along and join in the fun.'

Sylvie studied the leaflet depicting someone smiling while sliding down a snowy slope. 'What do I have to do?'

'Nothing except have a load of fun.'

'But I don't have a sled.' Or experience in sledding. None whatsoever.

'You don't need one. Folks bring their own but there are plenty of sleds to spare.' He glanced up at the clear blue sky. 'A fine day for enjoying yourself. The slopes have a fresh layer of snow this morning. What do you say?' He gave her a broad smile.

She couldn't resist an offer like this from Santa. 'Okay, where do I go?'

'Just down there,' he said, pointing nearby. 'People are already heading over so follow them.'

She folded the leaflet and tucked it into her jacket pocket. 'Thanks,' she said, giving Santa a cheery wave and following the sounds of laughter.

She arrived at an area of snowy slopes, most of them gently meandering down the hillside and only one that seemed to be steep and more challenging. Quite a few people were sledding and she reckoned she'd give it a go. She was casually and warmly dressed in dark pants, boots and a cream woolly hat. Her hair tumbled to her shoulders and she swept a couple of strands inside the front of her hat. She had a pair of gloves in her pocket and thought she'd wear them to hold on to the... whatever it was you held on a sled. A rope of some sort to steer the thing, or maybe she didn't need to steer it? Perhaps she could just sit on it and hold on tight like she saw kids and adults doing? Line it up at the top of a slope and then simply slide down until it slowed at the bottom.

Yes, she thought, this would be fun. Outdoors, in the fresh air, exercise, no pressure of work. The longer she considered it, the more eager she became to join in.

Stalls were set up serving coffee and hot chocolate. Donations were requested rather than a fee paid. It was up to each individual to drop a few dollars into the collection tins.

She was putting her money in one of the tins when a familiar voice startled her.

'Morning, Sylvie. I'm glad you're joining in.'

She spun around to see Zack standing there gazing at her. He had a event helper badge pinned to his stylish blue ski jacket that emphasized the color of his eyes. Her heart squeezed when she saw him. Could he be any more handsome?

She paused. Wait a minute. Ski jacket?

'Isn't this a sledding event?' she asked.

'It is,' he said, glancing around as if it was obvious.

'What's with the ski jacket?'

He looked like this hadn't even crossed his mind. 'Just a practical jacket. It's a nice day, but after a couple of hours standing around, the cold can get to you.' He grinned, seeing the relief on her face. 'Don't worry, you won't need to take the black run slope.'

'Very funny, Zack.'

He leaned back on his heels and evaluated her capability. 'So, what type of sled would you like? I take it you haven't got one with you.'

'No. I'm sledless.'

'Hmmm. Okay, let's find one for you.' He walked to where several sleds were sitting near the top of the highest slope. She went with him.

'Do you help out with a lot of things like this?' she asked him.

'Eh, yes, I volunteer when I can. Most capable folks take part in the town's fundraising activities during the holiday season. This year I'm involved in the outdoor activities such as this, one of the festive dinner dances in the community hall — setting up the tables, lifting and shifting, that sort of helper. And I'm assisting with the Christmas Eve party. Those were my three tick boxes this year.'

'A busy man.' And a nice guy, willing to give his time to help the local community.

'Yeah, well, I'm lucky that I can make my own hours when it comes to work, unless I have a specific deadline for a project,' he explained.

'Your architecture work?'

He nodded.

'What exactly is it you design?'

'Houses. New houses and renovations for traditional property where the design work has to fit in with the original structure.'

'Like you've done with your house?' she asked, remembering what he'd told her.

'Yes. I enjoy doing both. A lot of my time is spent drawing and redrawing until I get the design the way I want it. Working from home suits that type of framework. Often I'll get inspiration late at night and draw right through until the dawn. I make my own hours.' He gestured around him. 'It allows me to do stuff like this.'

Sylvie nodded. 'I work from home too. I pop into the office to discuss final design selections, but ninety percent of my fabric designs are finished at home.' She admired the beauty of her surroundings. 'But I don't have something like this right on my doorstep.'

'So what do you do when you're not working on your designs?' he asked.

She sighed and gave him an honest reply. 'I work.'

He pressed his lips together, something she noticed he did fairly often when he had a comment on the tip of his tongue but thought best not to say anything. It drew her attention to his mouth, his good looking features, and she sensed how easy it would be to let her feelings for him wander. Zack was handsome, and she was attracted to him, but she kept those feelings on a tight rein. Zack was heartbreak material. She'd no intention of risking that.

They arrived at the sleds and he brushed a handful of snow from the seat of one. 'This would probably suit you for size.'

Sylvie looked down at the sled, quickly trying to figure out how she was supposed to sit in it without letting him know this was her first time. Should she sit near the front or position herself further back?

He was looking at her, wondering why she was pausing. It was a sled. He thought he'd selected a nice one for her.

29

'Something wrong with it?' he said. 'I can get you another one if you prefer.'

'No, no, it's... a fine sled.' She forced herself to sit on the wooden seat, wedged her feet on the edges and grabbed hold of the... steering? Was the rope attachment capable of steering this thing? Or was it there just to get a grip of it?

Now he was looking down at her curiously and she knew he was about to ask her—

'Have you ever been on a sled before, Sylvie?'

She smiled up at him. Why didn't she admit this was her first time? But stubbornness took hold of her senses. She'd already felt foolish tumbling into a snow drift, having a hood full of snow, knocking more snow down on herself reaching for the house key, and then being clueless when it came to lighting a log fire. No, she could do this. How hard could it be? If kids could do it, she could do it. She just wished Zack wasn't standing over her. She would've preferred to get comfortable on her own, try it out a little bit without being watched, especially by him.

Nearby she saw a brown dog that looked like Cookie bounding around in the snow and almost let slip her secret.

She pointed towards the dog and said to Zack, 'Oh, did you bring—' She stopped short of uttering the word — Cookie. It was just as well because when she looked again she noticed it wasn't his dog. He'd told her he had a dog called Cookie, but he hadn't revealed it was a chocolate Labrador.

Zack frowned at her. 'Did I bring what?' He glanced in the direction she'd pointed wondering what she was talking about.

'Eh, nothing,' she chirped, and in her urge to avoid further explanation and scrutiny regarding her lack of sledding skills, she pushed off hard and let the sled take off down the slope. The high slope. Not the one she'd intended at all, however the need to get away from Zack took priority.

She heard him shouting after her as she held on to the rope thing with a grip of steel. The cold air whipped her hair back but her woolly hat was pulled on firmly giving her a clear view of her route.

Zack might have been joking about calling this the black run, but from the low angle she was traveling fast and picking up speed. Thankfully, no one was in her way. She'd no idea how to steer the sled or if altering the direction would send her soaring off course and into yet another snow drift.

She'd watched people sledding before in Central Park. Okay, not often, but they seemed to come to a natural stop at the bottom of a slope. All she had to do was hold on tight and give the impression that she knew what she was doing.

Judging by the rousing cheer that went up when she finally drifted to a halt way beyond the bottom of the slope, she'd achieved her aim. And she hadn't come to an abrupt halt or fallen off it. She stood up, trying to look casual as if this was exactly what she'd intended to do.

Several people came running over to her including Zack. He must've bounded down that hill.

'Wow!' he gasped, wide eyed and smiling at her in amazement. 'I'm sorry if I underestimated your ability. I thought you had no idea how to sled.'

She smiled tightly at him, hoping he couldn't tell that her heart was still racing as fast as she'd hurtled down that slope.

Nancy from the grocery shop gave her a hug. 'That's got to be the fastest time so far today.' She smiled proudly at Sylvie. 'I think you've got the winning time.'

'Someone timed me?' said Sylvie.

Zack held up a stop–watch. 'That was *fast*.'

Ana, the waitress from the diner joined in. 'I'm never going to beat that time.'

There was no hint of competitiveness in their voices or resentment that an outsider like her had done so well. Their genuine smiles and praise was heartwarming.

'I hadn't realized it was a contest,' Sylvie told them.

'It's all just for fun,' Nancy explained. 'But there are prizes for the fastest sled runs of the day. The three fastest times. Nothing fancy, simply little tokens of appreciation donated by local stores and businesses.'

Ana chimed–in. 'The diner has given a meal for two for the fastest on the slopes today. I reckon we'll be seeing you and Zack later for dinner.'

Sylvie was taken aback. 'I, eh...'

'Going for a second run?' Zack asked her.

'No, I think I'll quit while I'm ahead.' Sylvie glanced over at one of the stalls. 'But that hot chocolate looks tempting.'

Nancy swept her along to the stall. 'With or without marshmallows?'

'With.'

Zack took charge of the sled and pulled it back up the slope.

The fun continued while Sylvie sipped her hot chocolate and chatted to Nancy.

'I'm glad to see you and Zack getting along,' said Nancy, while preparing more warm milk. 'It's been a while since I've seen him so interested in a girl.'

Sylvie clutched her drink with one hand and held up the other. 'There's nothing going on between Zack and me.'

Nancy stirred a fresh pot of hot chocolate. 'Hmmm, not yet perhaps, but he's definitely interested. I'm not the only one that's noticed. He's never spoken so much about anyone since... well, since all the heartbreak.'

Sylvie took a sip of her drink, then peered over the rim of the cup. 'What heartbreak?'

Nancy glanced up the slope to check that Zack was out of earshot before she explained what happened to Sylvie. 'Zack isn't a philanderer. He's a steady guy. But sometimes guys like him can have their trust broken so badly. He'd been dating a young woman and thought she was the one for him. He bought an engagement ring with the intention of asking her to marry him. He planned to surprise her with the ring, flowers, all those romantic things. But when he arrived at her house she told him she didn't love him anymore. Later, she left town.'

'Oh, that's awful.'

'That was a couple of years ago, but it took Zack a while to get over it. Not that anyone blamed him.'

'Where did she go?' Sylvie asked.

'She moved to Los Angeles. She's never come back to this town and I doubt she ever will.'

'Zack must've felt really upset. I split up recently with my boyfriend, so I can understand his heartbreak. Thankfully I've had my work to keep me occupied.'

Nancy noticed Zack heading back down the slope. 'Don't let on I told you,' Nancy whispered. 'I just thought you should know. I'm sure he'll tell you in his own sweet time, but he'll probably play it down.'

'I won't say anything,' Sylvie whispered back. 'Thanks for telling me.'

'Is there a cup of that hot chocolate going spare?' Zack said, smiling as he approached them.

Nancy started to pour one for him. 'There sure is.'

Zack saw the marshmallows in Sylvie's drink. 'I'll have what she's having.'

Nancy added a lavish sprinkling of marshmallows to his chocolate.'

'Thanks, Nancy.' He smiled and took a sip.

Nancy's phone rang. 'Hi Nate.' She paused. 'Oh, right, I don't know if I can. Hold on a second.' She spoke to Zack. 'Nate's extra busy at the grocery store and there's been another delivery of stock. He needs me there to help with the customers, but I don't want to leave the hot chocolate stall unattended. I won't be back for over an hour.'

'No, you should go,' Zack told her. 'I'll find someone to help cover the stall.' He glanced around. 'Where did Ana go? She was here a few minutes ago.'

They saw Ana whizzing down one of the slopes on her sled, having fun with some of her friends.

Zack bit his lip. 'I suppose I could...'

Nancy shook her head. 'No, you're in charge of the sleds and timing folks.'

Sylvie wondered if she should volunteer. 'I could watch the stall for an hour,' she said hesitantly.

Nancy gave her a huge hug. 'Thank you, sweetie.' She picked up her purse.

'What do I have to do?' Sylvie asked quickly. 'I mean, how much do people pay for the hot chocolate and—'

Before Sylvie could ask anything else, Nancy pointed to a list of ingredients on the table. 'The list tells you how much milk and hot chocolate to use. It's easy.'

Sylvie's eyes were wide, speed reading the method. 'Okay, I can handle that.'

'Extra bags of sprinkles are under the table along with plenty of paper cups,' said Nancy. 'People make a donation as payment. They drop their money in the donation tin, so you won't even have to handle the cash.'

Sylvie straightened her shoulders and tried to sound confident. 'Just make the hot chocolate. I can do that.' She didn't feel half as confident as she sounded, but she'd made chocolate for herself plenty of times. This was for fun, for charity. It wasn't like she was working in a cafe and having to deal with customers who may not be happy with the frothy consistency of their delicious hot drink.

Nancy gave Sylvie a wave and hurried away leaving her standing with Zack.

'This is very kind of you,' he said, sounding grateful that she was helping them out. Then he paused and looked thoughtful. 'There's just one thing.'

Sylvie's heart tightened. 'What's that?'

He held out his cup. 'Do you think I can have more marshmallows?'

Sylvie grinned at him and sprinkled extra on top of his hot chocolate. 'There you go.'

He smiled broadly at her and walked away, sipping his drink, to attend to his duties.

She watched him go, and her heart ached at little, knowing what had happened to him in the past with his ex–girlfriend, and concerned what else would happen if she dropped her guard and let him into her heart during Christmas. What would happen when it was time for her to leave and go back home to New York? That's if she let herself enjoy a bit of flirtation. She didn't have to become heavily involved with him. Maybe they could have dinner at the diner and simply enjoy each other's company?

She sighed as she looked at him. There was a lot at stake for both of them. Perhaps it wasn't worth the risk. She took a long breath of cold fresh air to clear her thoughts. No, she decided. It was better, for now, to leave things as they were.

A family came over, brushing snow from their clothes and laughing from the fun of sledding. The wife had teamed up with the daughter, a little girl of around seven years old. The husband and ten year old son had partnered up. From the hearty laughter and jibes, it seemed like they'd been about even in their sled races and were in need of a break for a warming drink.

34

The husband tucked a handful of dollars into the donation tin. 'Hot chocolate for four please,' he said to Sylvie.

'With sprinkles,' his wife added cheerfully.

The little girl grinned up at Sylvie. 'And marshmallows.'

Sylvie kicked into serving mode. 'Coming right up.'

Nancy sent someone to take over the stall after Sylvie had manned it for an hour. A customer at the grocery store gladly volunteered their time.

The way people helped each other in the little town community impressed Sylvie. She thought how great it must be to be part of something like that.

She'd enjoyed being in charge of the hot chocolate and the time had whizzed by. It helped that she had a legitimate reason for standing there at the stall watching Zack run around tending to the sledding. Occasionally, he'd waved over to her and she'd waved back, as if they were friends.

While he was busy, Sylvie headed up to the main street to browse the local stores. As she passed by the grocery store, Nancy waved to her, beckoning her to come in.

'How did you get on with the stall?' Nancy asked her while stacking a shelf with fresh bread and rolls.

'Fine, and thanks for sending one of your customers to take over,' Sylvie told her. 'It was great being outdoors in the fresh air and seeing the fun people were having sledding.' And watching Zack, of course. That was a definite bonus. The way he smiled at her and waved made her heart flutter. Even thinking about him now sent a wave of emotion rippling through her.

Nancy glanced at Sylvie over her shoulder. 'All that fresh air has certainly brought a glow to your cheeks.'

Sylvie gave a tight smile. Zack may also be partially responsible for the blush in her cheeks, though she had no intention of admitting to that. 'I spend so much of my time indoors, sitting at my desk, working on designs. I really enjoyed being outside. I should do things like that more often.'

Nancy stacked another shelf with rye and whole wheat bread. 'What are you up to now?'

'I thought I'd take a look around the main street and do some shopping,' said Sylvie. 'The shops are so pretty and I love seeing the Christmas decorations.'

'There's a little quilt shop further along that you might be interested in, with you being a fabric designer. They sell lovely fabric and their quilts are beautiful,' said Nancy. 'I bought a couple for the holiday house.'

'The patchwork quilt?' said Sylvie, referring to the one on her bed.

'Yes, the one with all the lovely prints and colors. It's hand quilted by Jessica. She owns the shop and helps run the local quilting bee.' Nancy paused. 'In fact, why don't you come along and join us this evening. We meet in the community hall at seven to stitch together.'

'Oh, I wouldn't want to intrude,' Sylvie said, though the idea appealed to her. She loved to sew and often made things with samples of the fabric she designed. It helped her to make her prints better, sewing with the fabric, seeing what worked and coming up with ideas for other designs.

'No, we'd love to have you join us. I don't think we've ever had an actual fabric designer at one of our quilting bees. Come along. The ladies would love to meet you. And we have coffee and cake.'

'Okay, I'm in.' Sylvie smiled and a rush of excitement went through her. 'I've never been to a quilting bee.' She'd seen plenty of people talk about them online.

'Do you sew?' Nancy asked her.

'Yes, I enjoy sewing.'

'What about quilting?'

'I've made a couple of quilts. I've also started sewing another two mini quilts, though I haven't finished them. They're back home in New York. I didn't bring any of my sewing with me.'

'We have plenty to share. You don't need anything. Just come along.'

'I will. See you at seven.'

Sylvie left the grocery store and headed along to the little quilt shop. The front window was edged with sparkling twinkle lights and filled with Christmas quilts. Sylvie stood under the shop canopy gazing at them before going inside. One of the quilts had a poinsettia design edged with tiny Christmas trees. Another comprised of pretty blocks of holly. However, the one that caught her eye was sewn from hexies, little hexagon shapes stitched together like patchwork, in shades of icy blue with a snowman print.

Sylvie went inside. Two customers were buying fabric and thread and chatting to the owner, Jessica, a woman in her forties wearing a hand knitted sweater.

Jessica smiled at Sylvie. 'I'll be with you in a moment.'

'I'm just browsing,' said Sylvie, taking a look around. It was such a lovely shop and had shelves stacked with cotton fabric suitable for quilting. A thread display offered an assortment of colors and there was a haberdashery area with everything from thimbles and pincushions to ribbons and trims. It was the type of shop Sylvie could happily spend hours in just looking at all the fabric.

'Take your time,' said Jessica. 'If there's anything you want to see unrolled, just holler.'

Sylvie nodded and smiled while Jessica continued to serve the customers. She had a look around the shelves, and then was drawn to the fat quarter fabric bundles piled up on a table. The pre–cut bundles had pieces of beautifully coordinated cotton fabric that were ideal for quilting. One of the bundles had the snowman print along with other prints of snowflakes, and Christmas tree designs all in shades of blue and white with matching solid colors. Sylvie picked it up immediately. This was perfect. Then she saw another bundle in festive reds and green that she couldn't resist.

The two customers left and Jessica came over to assist Sylvie.

'I'll take these two bundles.' Sylvie handed them to Jessica. 'And I'll need thread.'

Jessica selected some thread for her. 'These colors of thread work well for blending with the prints, though I'd recommend a couple of other tones too for contrast if you're going to hand quilt them.' Jessica held the threads close to the fabric to show how nice they looked.

'Yes, I'll take those,' Sylvie said, feeling the urge to start sewing.

Jessica wrapped her purchases. 'Is there anything else you need?'

'I'm not sure. I'm going to the quilting bee tonight. Nancy from the grocery store invited me.'

'That's wonderful. Are you a quilter? Are you here for the holidays?'

'I'm here on vacation, and I'm a fabric designer.'

'Really?' Jessica's eyes brightened. 'It'll be great to have you join us at the bee.'

'I love sewing and quilting, but I've never joined in with a bee. I'm looking forward to learning new techniques.'

'You'll pick up plenty of tips from us tonight — and we'd love to hear how you actually create your designs.'

Sylvie nodded and agreed she'd bring some sketches with her to show the ladies at the quilting bee.

Sylvie wandered over to the window to study the quilts on display. 'I'd like to make a quilt from hexies, like the one you've got in the window.'

'Then you'll need some paper templates and a pack of needles. We've got cutting mats and rotary cutters you can use when you come along tonight.'

Jessica put Sylvie's purchases in a couple of bags and handed them to her. 'See you later.'

Feeling like she was kitted out for her evening of quilting, Sylvie smiled and waved as she left.

Outside the shop Sylvie peeked inside the bags and viewed the colors of the fabric in the December sunlight. They were lovely.

Sylvie spent the remainder of the day in town shopping, and popped into the cafe for lunch. Staff dressed as Christmas elves were busy dealing with customers. A man, the only one not wearing an elf costume, welcomed her. He was in his thirties with a fit build, light brown hair and dark brown eyes with a mischievous twinkle.

'Hi, I'm Greg. There's a seat over here.'

'Thanks.' Sylvie sat down, picked up the menu and saw his name on it. 'You're the owner?'

He smiled warmly and nodded. His smile was his winning feature.

'Can I suggest you try the soup of the day served with crusty bread? I baked it myself.'

'Sounds delicious.'

Greg went through to the kitchen to get her order, casting an admiring glance back at her.

Within minutes, he served up her soup and bread, then ran around serving customers at the busy little cafe. Most of the customers were local people, but a few were passing trade and holidaymakers.

After lunch, the time flew in, and she started to walk back to the house to get ready for her evening at the quilting bee.

'Sylvie,' Zack called to her, running across the road.

He looked at the shopping bags she was carrying and smiled. 'Been busy?'

Sylvie held up the bags and shrugged. 'I've been fabric shopping. Nancy invited me to the quilting bee at the community hall tonight.'

He nodded, taking in what she'd said. 'I wanted to give you this.' He handed her a ticket. 'You won the fastest time for sledding — and a meal ticket for the diner.'

She read the wording on the ticket. 'You have won — dinner for two. Congratulations on winning the day's fastest sledding time. Well done! Come and enjoy dinner at the diner — and bring a friend.'

She tried to hand the ticket back to him. 'No, I can't accept this.'

'Why not?'

'It was a fluke that I was so fast.'

'A fluke?'

'Yes, I'm not experienced in sledding. This should go to someone who deserves to win. Give it to whoever was second fastest.'

Zack smiled and gazed right at her. 'You won, fluke or not. This is just a nice gesture. We don't take things as seriously here as you might think.'

He refused to take the ticket.

She read the wording again. 'Bring a friend, huh?'

He raised his broad shoulders and grinned at her.

'Where am I going to find one of those?'

'Perhaps at the quilting bee?' he suggested lightly.

She played along. 'I could. Or... there's this guy I know...'

They smiled at each other, and she guessed she had a dinner date with Zack.

Chapter Four

Zack walked Sylvie back to her house, insisting on carrying her bags for her.

'I never thought fabric would weigh so much,' he commented.

She thought she caught a glimpse of a wry smile from him. 'Okay, so I may have bought more fabric than I intended to, but that quilt shop was far too tempting.'

'I'm like that with the art supply store,' he admitted. 'I'll go in to buy graphic paper and I come out loaded with other stuff — new pencils, watercolor brushes and paints.' He shook his head. 'I have more than enough of those in my studio, but I just love all those things. I can get lost in a store like that. It's near the quilt shop, so you may want to look the other way when you're walking past it.'

Sylvie smiled. 'It sounds like my kind of shop too. I only brought my sketch pad with me. I wish now I'd packed my artist's case with my watercolor pencils and gouache paint, but I was trying to make this more of a vacation than about work.'

They approached his house and he thumbed over at it. 'You're welcome to cherry pick anything you need from my studio while you're here.'

'Thanks, I might take you up on that, depending on how things go at the quilting bee. I promised I'd bring some of my sketches to show the ladies how I design my fabrics.'

'Sounds interesting. If I could sew I'd come along to see your design process.'

'I'm pretty sure the ladies wouldn't mind if you joined us.'

Zack shook his head. 'Nooo, I recently popped in to help set up tables for one of their festive fundraisers and it was... happy chaos with numerous ladies and a lot of fabric being cut into little pieces and sewn together again.'

'Quilting.'

'Yep. I was with another couple of guys and we were plied with chocolate cake, coffee and quilting.'

'But luckily you managed to make your escape,' she joked with him. 'After eating the chocolate cake.'

'It was home baked with chocolate frosting. How could I refuse?'

She laughed, and by now they'd reached her house. He carried her bags up to the door and held them while she unlocked it.

He handed her the bags. 'Enjoy yourself at the quilting bee.'

'Thank you. I'm looking forward to it.' She waved him off and then hurried inside to jump in the shower and get ready for the evening quilting.

Her mind was racing with all the things she wanted to take with her, including her sketches and laptop so she could show them designs she'd worked on. It would be nice to share these. Due to her busy work schedule she didn't have many close friends in New York. She worked on her designs on her own most of the time. She really only shared them with Marla. It was quite a solitary lifestyle.

Conrad certainly hadn't been interested in her work. Though to be fair, she knew as much about his stock market career as he did about her fabric designs. She sighed and tilted her face up to let the water wash away the feelings of resentment that threatened to overwhelm her whenever she thought about Conrad.

She'd just emerged from the shower, dried her hair and thrown on a silky dressing gown when her phone rang. She picked up.

'I have some great news for you,' Marla announced.

A rush of excitement went through Sylvie. 'What is it?'

'The company want to make your new collection the leading range for our summer fabric line.'

'Wow! That's brilliant. Thank you.'

'It's all your hard work and taking a chance with those floral watercolor prints. We're confident these are going to be really popular. I've contacted several of our regular buyers and their reaction was instant — they love them and have placed substantial pre–orders. So, merry Christmas, Sylvie. I am now officially on vacation. Peter and the kids are making dinner and then I'm going to relax and watch a family movie. I hope I didn't disturb your relaxation, but I simply had to tell you the news.'

'No, I haven't actually started to unwind and relax yet,' said Sylvie.

'Really? I pictured you with your feet up eating cookies beside the fire.'

'Nope,' said Sylvie and began to summarize what she'd been up to. 'I had dinner last night at the diner, left with the largest slice of pumpkin pie and joined in with carol singers. I went into town this morning to do some shopping, but a guy dressed as Santa suggested I go sledding.'

'Sledding?' Marla sounded surprised. 'I didn't know you were into that.'

'Neither did I. Anyway, Zack was there helping out to raise money for local charities, and I thought I saw his dog.'

'Zack's got a dog? This sounds like progress.'

'His dog, Cookie, is the cutest chocolate Labrador. He's totally adorable, but...' Sylvie went on to explain about Cookie being in her garden.

Marla started laughing. 'Zack doesn't know his dog was in your garden?'

'You had to see the look in that dog's eyes. I couldn't rat him out. I think he has a little secret route through the gardens until he reaches mine, and he made his way back safely.'

Marla was still laughing as Sylvie continued. 'So I nearly gave the game away at the sledding when I saw a brown dog that looked like his, and in my haste to avoid explaining I went sliding down the steepest slope at such a speed that I won first prize for the fastest time for sledding.'

'You won a prize? What did you win?'

'A free meal ticket. Dinner at the diner, and they do great food. It said to bring a friend, and I've sort of invited Zack.'

'Now that's what I call a prize. A dinner date with Zack.'

'It's not a date. Definitely not a date. Just a... dinner for two friends. It's okay to be friends with Zack, but it doesn't have to be any more than that.'

'Friends with potential?'

'No potential. It would never work.'

'He's an architect. He could easily move to New York to be with you.'

Sylvie was adamant it wasn't feasible. 'He's a home town kind of guy. He has this great house that he's renovated.'

'That's too bad, Sylvie. He ticks all the right boxes.'

'The man who ticks all the right boxes doesn't exist. Except for your Peter. But for me, he's just a piece of wishful thinking.'

'At least you're thinking about it.'

'I'm not. Really I'm not. So tonight I'm going to the local quilting bee. They want to see how I create my fabric designs. They have this great quilt shop that sells fabric and I bought some so that I can start to make a new quilt.' Sylvie went on to elaborate about the shop and the fabrics she purchased.

'Would you like me to add the quilt shop to our promotional list?' Marla offered.

'Yes, do that.'

'Let me look it up online. I'll add it right now, so that I don't forget after the holidays.'

'It's the only quilt shop in town,' Sylvie told her. 'I'm not sure of the exact name.'

'Here it is. Owned by Jessica?'

'That's the one.'

'Okay, I've added her shop to the list.'

'I'll tell her tonight,' said Sylvie. 'Speaking of which, I'd better get ready.'

There was a knock at the front door.

'Someone's at the door, Marla. I have to run. Thanks again, and have a wonderful relaxing Christmas.'

'You too, Sylvie.'

'That's the plan,' Sylvie said as she finished the call, jumped into a pair of fluffy slippers, pulled her silk dressing gown around her and ran through to the hall to answer the door.

She wrenched it open to find Zack standing there. When he saw what she was wearing, he smiled and then tried to avert his gaze, while having an admiring peek.

'I can see you're pushed for time, but I brought you these watercolor pencils and paper. I thought they may be useful tonight at the quilting bee.' He handed her an artist's tin of pencils along with two pads of watercolor paper. 'I wasn't sure what type of watercolor paper you use, so I brought smooth hot pressed and slightly textured cold pressed.'

Sylvie accepted them gladly, while keeping a grip on the front of her dressing gown to protect her modesty. 'These are so useful. Thank you, Zack.'

He smiled, pleased he'd done the right thing. Then he handed her a bag containing a selection of gouache paints and brushes. 'I popped some gouache paints and brushes in a bag just in case you could use them while you're staying here.'

She peered inside the bag. 'You really do frequent that art store, don't you?' she said lightly.

'I've got to be one of their top customers.' He sighed heavily and stepped back. 'Well, I'd better let you get dressed. I'm glad the paints are useful.'

'More than useful. And very thoughtful of you, Zack.'

He smiled, nodded awkwardly, clearly affected by her, and waved as he left.

Sylvie got dressed quickly in a soft blue sweater and navy pants, packed the items she needed along with the fabric she'd bought, and got ready to head out to the bee.

Cookie stretched out in front of the log fire in Zack's studio. Zack was busy drawing, trying to concentrate on his latest assignment, working on an architectural design, but he kept thinking about Sylvie. He liked her, really liked her. However, after Christmas she'd go home to New York and he'd probably never see her again. He pushed the feelings he was developing for her deep down, and told himself there was no point in falling in love for nothing.

He sat in the midst of his studio, steeped in his work. The studio walls were cream, like a blank canvas, that allowed him to think creatively without distraction. The scatter rugs on the polished light wood floor matched the cream decor. No clutter. His stylish architect's drawing desk took pride of place and the finish on it was smooth like white glass. Any bumps could ruin a finely drawn plan. It extended to a glass drafting table with built–in lighting for tracing, and adjustable drawing positions for sitting and standing while working.

The traditional fireplace and glass lamps provided a comfortable warmth to the studio. He'd always done his best work here and had no plans on leaving. His ex–girlfriend hadn't liked his taste in decor. She hadn't liked his taste in anything really. Why he thought she was the one for him eluded him. He'd loved her. That was all. He'd thought that would be enough, but clearly it wasn't.

He sighed and continued drawing. But she was in the past and he'd put all that behind him. He hadn't felt attracted to anyone special in a long time, not until Sylvie stepped into his world. He smiled to himself when he pictured the first time he saw her — the prettiest human sugar cookie he'd ever seen.

Cookie suddenly jumped up, ran over to the window, nudged the curtains aside and peered out, tail wagging.

'What are you looking at, boy?' Zack asked, going over to peek out.

The only person he saw was Sylvie on her way to the quilting bee. She walked past, carrying her bags, and didn't glance over at his house.

Zack patted the dog's head. 'That's Sylvie. You like her, huh?' He sighed again. 'So do I. I'll have to let you meet her. Though I'm not sure if she's a dog loving type of person. Hopefully she is, and she'll be pleased to meet a sweet guy like you.'

The dog lapped up the affection lavished on him, and then lay down again by the fireside while Zack continued drawing.

The community hall was situated on the main street. A Christmas tree stood outside the front entrance, lit with colored lights. Sylvie heard the sounds of activity and chatter as she approached the hall and went inside.

Tables were arranged around the main floor area. There was a stage set up with festive scenery that Sylvie assumed was part of the forthcoming Christmas Eve party and dance.

Decorations adorned the hall, and around twenty ladies, members of the quilting bee, were seated at two long tables, some with sewing machines, but most were hand stitching their quilts and chatting happily. The layout allowed everyone to share everything from fabric scraps to cutting mats and rotary cutters, and to exchange quilting tips and gossip. The atmosphere was warm and welcoming, and although Sylvie wasn't especially confident about joining them, she didn't feel intimidated either.

Jessica saw her walk in and hurried over to greet her, as did Nancy.

'Come in and meet the ladies,' said Nancy, linking arms with Sylvie, leading her over to the hub of the bee, delighted she'd joined them.

'They've been so looking forward to meeting you,' Jessica added.

'This is Sylvie, the fabric designer from New York I was telling you about,' Nancy announced to the ladies of the quilting bee.

She was greeted with smiles all round.

Jessica indicated a vacant seat. 'We've kept a seat for you here beside us.'

Sylvie sat down between Nancy and Jessica and quickly took a moment to tell Jessica about her shop being added to the company's list.

'Oh, that's great,' said Jessica. 'My little shop has never been part of a big city promotion before.'

'They'll send substantial free samples of all of my fabric from the new summer collection,' Sylvie explained. 'It won't be for a few months yet, but your shop will be one of the first to have them available.'

All the women were delighted.

'How did you get started in this type of work?' Jessica asked Sylvie.

'I'd always been interested in textile design,' said Sylvie. 'I started printing my own fabric with floral designs. A home decor company in New York saw my work online and invited me to join them. Now I design fabric for them.'

'That must be so exciting,' one of the ladies commented.

'It is,' said Sylvie. 'I'm so lucky, and my boss Marla has become a dear friend.'

'You mentioned you work on your collections seasons ahead, designing patterns months in advance of their release,' Nancy prompted her.

'I'm perpetually working on designs ahead of the seasons,' Sylvie confirmed. 'I try to anticipate what's going to be popular and keep an eye on the trends. And I rely on making traditional floral prints as they never go out of style.'

'Did you bring some of your design work with you?' Nancy asked.

'I did.' Sylvie set up her laptop, turning it so that the ladies could see the screen. 'The new designs are top secret as you can imagine and won't be released until nearer the launch date. However, I can show you glimpses of the original watercolor floral artwork that I used to create the designs.'

The women were eager to study the images, and Sylvie opened her sketch book to let them view more of her artwork. 'These are a few of the original sketches. Everything starts with a pencil drawing. Then when I'm happy with that, I'll draw it again to finished artwork level and paint it. I usually use gouache paint, a sort of opaque watercolor, but for my latest summer collection I used watercolors in soft pastel tones. Most of my designs are floral and nature prints.'

The sketches were passed around and handled carefully.

'These are beautiful, Sylvie,' Nancy commented. 'Such lovely artwork.'

'Thank you, Nancy.' Sylvie brought out the pencils and paper Zack had given her. Using a glass of water, she demonstrated how she created the floral art. She also let them try their hand at it. Several members were delighted to give it a go.

'How do these become patterns on the fabric?' one of the ladies asked.

Sylvie was happy to explain using a flower print as an example. 'Once I have all the floral artwork finished, I scan it into my computer and start to make it into a repeat pattern.'

The ladies watched as Sylvie demonstrated the process on her laptop. 'This design was created using a half drop repeat pattern. I adjust the design until the pattern matches seamlessly.'

'Thank you so much for showing us your work, Sylvie,' said Nancy.

The ladies gave Sylvie an enthusiastic round of applause. Then it was on to the business of quilting. A couple of the women were professional quilters and most of the others had been quilting for many years. Sylvie was surrounded by a wealth of experience.

'I'd like to make a Christmas theme quilt for my apartment,' Sylvie told them. 'I was thinking of fussy cutting some of these little Christmas tree prints.'

There was heaps of advice from the bee, and they helped Sylvie cut her fabric to make hexies for a quilt. They also cut one of her fat quarter bundles of fabric into small squares so she could make a patchwork quilt. Soon she was sitting amongst them, hand basting her hexies, while listening to all the local gossip and their plans for finishing their Christmas quilts.

Nancy was hand stitching the binding on her quilt. 'How are things going between you and Zack?'

A slight hush fell over the bee as the women looked at Sylvie.

'Well, he loaned me these watercolor pencils and paper,' Sylvie began, feeling a blush rise in her cheeks. 'He's been very welcoming, as has everyone I've met in town.' She hoped this would satisfy their curiosity, but it only whetted their appetite for further details.

'Zack is such a sweet guy,' Jessica remarked.

Sylvie nodded and continued sewing.

'Handsome too,' one of the ladies added.

There was plenty of agreement on that score.

'He's a looker all right,' said Nancy. 'It would be great if he could find himself a nice young woman to settle down with.'

Sylvie felt herself blush rosy pink as several sets of eyes focused on her.

'No, I'm not getting involved with anyone while I'm here,' said Sylvie. 'I've put romance on hold for the holidays.'

Jessica frowned at her. 'Can I ask why? Did something happen?'

Sylvie gave them the short course on her disastrous mistake dating Conrad.

'It sounds like you're really better off without him,' said Jessica. 'But surely you want to meet someone else?'

Sylvie tried to concentrate on her stitching. 'I do, but just not yet. I came here to give myself a break, to enjoy a cozy Christmas away from the city. The last thing I want or need is all the drama of a relationship.' She found herself repeating part of Zack's phrase, hoping this would put an end to the conversation.

'I'm no expert when it comes to romance,' Jessica admitted. 'However I wouldn't put any chance of love and happiness on ice because of a smooth talking guy like Conrad.'

The women nodded in agreement.

Nancy snipped the thread on her binding having finished the final stitches. 'Now we don't want to upset Sylvie,' she told the ladies. 'It's up to her how she deals with her love life. If she's not ready for romance, then that's up to her.'

'Sorry, Sylvie,' said Jessica. 'We don't mean to interfere.'

'That's okay,' Sylvie said, sensing that they meant well.

'I got lucky with my Nate. He's such a sweetheart,' said Nancy. 'But the guy I dated before Nate...' she shook her head. 'He could've ruined everything. He kind of reminds me of Conrad's type. So charming, and yet I kept feeling he was stringing me along. Turned out I was right. Thankfully, I ditched him, but I thought my heart would break. I thought I loved him and I guess I sort of did. But he was no good for me, no good for any decent young woman.'

'What did you do then?' Sylvie asked.

'I avoided romance for a while, a whole winter and spring,' Nancy continued. 'Then I went to one of the summer dances in town with a group of girls I was friends with. I didn't know Nate. He was from another town and had turned up with some of his friends. I'd been up dancing with the girls and was tuckered out. I was sitting with them chatting when this big bear hug of a guy approached me and asked me politely if I would dance with him. I nearly said no, but the girls encouraged me to dance with the guy. And so I did. He took my hand and led me on to the dance floor and we fell into step right away. We've been in step ever since, and I believe we always will be.' A frown puckered her brow. 'Sometimes I shudder to think what would've happened if I'd said no. Nate didn't have a lot of confidence with girls and I don't think he would've asked me again. I'd have missed out on the love of my life.' She looked at Sylvie. 'Not that I'm saying you should do what I did. I'm just sharing a little bit of experience.'

'You and Nate really seem to get along,' said Sylvie.

'We do. Folks thought we'd get tired of each other working together at the grocery store and then being together all the time at home,' said Nancy. 'But it works for us and I've never tired of his company. As I say, I got lucky with Nate.'

'I assume he was happy to move from his town to this one,' said Sylvie.

Nancy nodded. 'Yes, and we've lived here ever since. Of course, he came from a small town and it's not far from here.'

'What would you have done if Nate had been from the city?' Sylvie asked her.

'Probably the same as Jessica and her husband did. We'd have found a way to be together no matter what,' Nancy assured her. 'I've always thought it's important where you live, but who you're with matters more.'

Jessica agreed. 'This town has everything I could ever wish for, and then some. I think there's often more going on here with our fundraisers and functions, true friends and family, than I could need. I don't care much for the city. I'm always hankering to get back home, but that's where I met my husband. I'd gone to New York to attend my first quilt show with a couple of other quilters. At the

49

event I got talking to one of the security guys, and it was kind of like Nate and Nancy. We clicked right away.'

'Tell Sylvie what happened when you got back home,' Nancy encouraged her.

'He came here to visit me one weekend, and take me dancing in this community hall. It was the harvest dance. He told me he wanted to date me properly and was prepared to drive back and forth from New York to visit me on weekends. And he did.' Jessica smiled. 'Then one weekend he asked me to marry him and I said yes. He moved here and now he's the town sheriff.'

Sylvie brightened. 'The sheriff?'

Jessica smiled proudly. 'He sure is. A great guy.' Then she confided. 'The thing is, he nearly didn't take the security job that night at the quilting event, and I almost didn't go because I wasn't keen on the city. I guess you could say we met by chance on both our parts, and sometimes things work out better that way.'

Sylvie nodded thoughtfully.

Nancy folded her quilt and stood up. 'Well, I think it's time we had our coffee and cake.'

Several ladies got up to help her.

Sylvie felt the pressure ease from them trying to pair her with Zack. The atmosphere sparked up a gear as the ladies continued quilting while others prepared the coffee and cake.

Nancy brought coffee for Sylvie and a selection of cake. 'Would you like a slice of mocha cake or vanilla cream sponge?'

'Hold the mocha and vanilla,' a man's voice interrupted.

Everyone turned to see Greg had arrived with a tray of chocolate brownies and cupcakes. He smiled at Sylvie and offered up the alternative selection.

Sylvie reached up and picked a cupcake swirled with pink buttercream and sprinkles.

'Great choice,' said Greg in a cheerful tone. 'There's a hint of pink champagne in those. Perfect for a night of celebration.'

'What are we celebrating?' Nancy asked him, not in a curt way, just curious.

Greg grinned down at Sylvie. 'This fine young fabric designer joining our bee tonight of course.'

The women smiled, seemingly used to Greg's playful manner.

'This is Greg,' Nancy said to Sylvie.

'We've met,' he said.

Nancy gave Sylvie a questioning glance.

'I had lunch at Greg's cafe,' Sylvie explained, though she wondered how he knew she'd be here.

'I heard you'd been invited to our bee,' he told her.

'Greg is our only male quilting member,' said Jessica. 'He's a great quilter and an accomplished baker.'

'I'm impressed,' Sylvie said, joining in the friendly banter.

Greg grinned. 'My plan worked then.'

Nancy shook her head and smiled at Greg. 'He is incorrigible at times.'

Greg pulled up a chair and sat down beside them. He looked at Sylvie's sewing. 'What are you making with those hexies?'

'A Christmas quilt. I love to sew and I'm learning new techniques from the ladies.'

Greg continued to be entertaining and charming for the rest of the evening. Sylvie was impressed by his quilting expertise, but slightly wary of his charm as it reminded her of Conrad. The ladies seemed to feel at ease with Greg, so she finally set aside her reservations about him. They'd surely know if he was a weasel.

At the end of the night everyone helped to clear things away, packed up their quilting and started to head home.

Outside in the snow Nancy and Jessica gave Sylvie a hug and thanked her again for joining them.

Nate came ambling along to walk Nancy home and carry her sewing machine for her. Jessica and her machine were picked up by the sheriff's car waiting nearby.

Although they were heading in the opposite direction to where Sylvie was going, Nancy and Jessica offered to make sure she got home safe.

'Thanks, I'm fine,' Sylvie assured them. 'It's a lovely snowy night. I'd like to take it all in.' She waved them both off.

'I'm going to my cafe. I'll walk part of the way with you,' Greg offered. 'You're staying at Nate and Nancy's holiday house, is that right?'

'Yes, but you don't need to escort me,' said Sylvie.

'It's on my route. Come on,' he insisted.

He carried her laptop bag as they walked along.

'I have a confession to make,' he said, giving her a sheepish glance.

'What about?'

'I wasn't intending going to the quilting bee tonight until I heard you were going to be there. I'm busy baking Christmas orders for the cafe and should be in there right now frosting cupcakes.'

'I thought you were a regular member of the bee?'

'I am, but I planned to skip it tonight and work late at the cafe. Then I changed my mind when I heard Nancy had invited you.'

'Why?'

'Because I wanted to meet you, be properly introduced. Not just be the guy from the cafe.'

'I'm not a well known fabric designer,' she was quick to explain. 'I do quite well, but—'

'That's not why I wanted to meet you socially,' he said.

'Then why?'

'When you came into my cafe I thought — she's lovely. I'd like to meet her, get to know her.' He glanced at her to gauge her reaction.

Before she could respond she saw Zack walking towards them. He looked taken aback when he saw them together.

Greg stepped closer to Sylvie but she moved away. She felt Greg was trying to give Zack the impression that they were together, and didn't like the feeling that Greg was somehow trying to manipulate the situation in his favor. She started to wish he hadn't insisted on walking her part of the way home.

'Zack, hi,' she said, giving him a cheerful smile.

She saw Zack's eyes flick from her to Greg as he replied. 'Hi.' He tried to sound casual but the muscles in his jaw were tense.

'We had a great time at the quilting bee,' Greg told Zack. 'Didn't we, Sylvie?'

'Eh, yes, I enjoyed myself, and I've started sewing my Christmas quilt,' she said to Zack. 'Thank you for letting me use your watercolor pencils. They were so useful. I could drop them off at your house tomorrow or give you them now if you prefer.'

'Keep them,' said Zack. 'I have plenty. Make use of them while you're here, which obviously won't be long.'

'No, that's too generous of you, Zack,' she said.

'Not at all.' Zack forced a smile and started to step away, continuing on to wherever he was supposedly going, leaving them together. He gave them a curt nod. 'Goodnight.' Then he walked away.

Greg didn't miss a beat and continued as if Zack hadn't interrupted them. 'Would you like to come into the cafe for hot chocolate?' he asked Sylvie.

Sylvie blinked. 'No, I'm heading home.' She took charge of her laptop bag. 'Nice to meet you at the bee, Greg.' She smiled politely and began to walk away.

'Drop by the cafe anytime, Sylvie,' Greg called after her.

'Thanks,' she said without turning around and continued on her way, trying to figure out what just happened there.

Zack trudged through the snow, hands thrust in his jacket pockets, mentally kicking himself, hoping he hadn't come across as a jealous fool. He wasn't like that at all, but he hadn't expected to see Sylvie with Greg. Of all the guys in town... Greg had a reputation for being charming, and although a harmless flirt with the ladies, maybe he'd end up dating her. Wouldn't that be typical. Guys like Greg had a knack for being very persuasive. Greg could be making a move on Sylvie right now and there was nothing he could do about it.

Zack had been restless at home and decided to go out for a walk. Okay, so he'd deliberately taken the main street route in the hope of accidentally on purpose bumping into Sylvie and walking her back home safely from the bee. Boy, had that plan backfired, he thought. Now she probably had him pegged as the possessive type. Dinner with her at the diner was likely to be cancelled. He wouldn't blame her if she made up an excuse why they shouldn't have their dinner date. No, not a date, he scolded himself. It definitely wasn't a date and it never had been. It was nothing more than wishful thinking on his part. She'd been totally upfront about not wanting to get involved with anyone here while she was on vacation. He needed to respect that, and he would.

He stopped, took a deep breath, turned around, scrunching his boots into the snow, and headed back home.

Chapter Five

Sylvie unpacked her bags when she got back to the house and tried not to think about Zack, which wasn't easy. She kept picturing his face when he'd seen her with Greg.

No, she scolded herself. She wouldn't think about Zack anymore tonight. She was too tired and not sure how she felt about him.

Instead, she thought about lighting the fire in the lounge, but then reconsidered. Probably by the time she got it going, it would be time for bed. So she planned to light it in the morning. Tomorrow was going to be a relaxing day, she promised herself. The type of day she'd planned when coming here. She'd relax by the fire, sew more of her quilt, maybe even use the watercolors and gouache Zack had given her to paint a few new designs.

She pulled open a dresser drawer and saw the photo album Nancy had mentioned to her. She hadn't even had time to flick through it or sit by the fire toasting the marshmallows she'd bought. All these things were on her agenda. No sledding or running around town impulse shopping. A mellow day, feet up, chilling.

She could feel herself start to relax just thinking about it. A day in. A snow day. Whatever she wanted to call it.

She put her sewing down on a table in the lounge and the art supplies beside her laptop on a makeshift desk near the fireside.

Next, she went through to the kitchen to check the food situation. She opened the refrigerator and cupboards. She had plenty of supplies including fresh milk and bread. No need to pop out to buy groceries. She could stay in all day.

Then she remembered — the not a dinner date with Zack. This caused her to think about Zack again. She hadn't agreed on an exact time for dinner, but kind of assumed it would be tomorrow night. It would've been this evening if she hadn't gone to the quilting.

She wondered what to do. It would be awkward to cancel and she didn't want to do that. She did want to have dinner with Zack. So what did this mean? She couldn't even begin to contemplate this scenario. Falling for Zack? No she couldn't let that happen.

She leaned on the kitchen table and sighed. There she was thinking about Zack again. She shrugged off the unwanted thoughts, made herself a hot malted drink, went through to the bedroom and climbed into bed. Things would look more mellow in the morning. They would, she told herself. They definitely would.

She sipped her drink and gazed out the window. Snow was starting to fall, fluttering down, sprinkling the houses and trees with a new layer of sparkling flakes. She tugged the patchwork quilt around her, cupped her hot drink, and admired the wintry scenery. Some people loved the summer, others preferred the spring or fall, and although she enjoyed the seasons for the individual beauty they created, there was something special about a snowy night like this at Christmastime. Everything was so quiet and calm, as if the snow muffled the sounds of chaos. She continued to gaze out the window, thinking how fortunate she was to be here, and how she'd miss it when it was time to go back home to New York.

Zack couldn't sleep for being annoyed with himself. He lay in bed gazing out at the snow, wondering what Sylvie thought about his reaction earlier.

Cookie was sound asleep in his cozy basket in Zack's bedroom, snuggled into his blanket with his favorite soft toy.

Zack recalled the first night he'd brought Cookie home from the rescue center. Although the dog had liked him right away, it had taken time for him to truly settle, to understand that he was in his real home. The first few nights he'd had to reassure Cookie that he was safe, sitting up with him, keeping him nearby.

It had taken a couple of weeks to build the dog's complete trust in him and his new home. Now Cookie slept happily every night, and enjoyed snoozing during the day between bursts of bounding activity. Maybe that's why they got along so well — their lifestyles kind of matched. As Zack was free to make his own hours, he could sleep when he wanted and work all hours when he was on a roll and inspired to finish a project. That didn't mean he couldn't yearn for a settled life with someone to share it with, to be married and hopefully raise a family.

His life was full of lots of things, yet empty of the things that really mattered to him.

He leaned back on his pillows, gazed outside at the snow and hoped Sylvie would still have dinner with him.

Sylvie was up early to enjoy the day. She ate scrambled eggs on toast for breakfast in the kitchen, and looked out the window at the garden. Everything was covered in snow, glistening and bright.

Wearing a warm sweater, pants, scarf and boots, she went outside to breathe in the cold morning air. She snapped several pictures with her phone. That's when she noticed Cookie sneaking into the garden through a gap in the fence that separated her from the property next door — the house that stood between her and Zack's home.

When Cookie saw her he perked up and came running over to her, all excited, tail wagging.

She crouched down and gave him a welcoming hug. 'Hi, Cookie. Does Zack know you're here?'

The dog nuzzled into her, pleased to feel welcome.

Sylvie stood up and looked across the fence to see if Zack was in his garden, but there was no one around.

She shook her head at the dog. 'You're going to get us both into trouble.'

But Cookie wasn't bothered about any of this. He was ready to play chase and fetch games in the garden with her.

'Okay, but then you're going straight back home,' she told the dog.

Cookie had found a stick and came galloping over, dropped it at her feet and then waited eagerly for her to throw it so he could fetch it.

Sylvie picked it up and threw it down the garden near the trees.

A chocolate brown bundle of energetic fun bounded after the stick, found it in the snow, fetched it, came running back to Sylvie and dropped it again at her feet.

She picked the stick up and threw it again, and again. The dog loved this game. His mouth was open in a smiling expression that was hard to resist, and his trusting brown eyes were gazing at her.

She continued playing games with Cookie until she saw Zack appear in his garden. She immediately ducked down out of sight, and the dog did the same. So there they were, side by side, hiding behind the bushes at the fence, watching Zack. She hoped her white sweater helped her blend into the snow, and barely moved, except to glance at Cookie. Up close that dog's big brown eyes were filled with

56

mischief. He knew what they were doing. Hiding from Zack. He knew.

'We're in big trouble if Zack sees you here,' she whispered anxiously, but his only response was to give her face a loveable doggie kiss.

As it was early morning, Zack had the manners not to shout the dog's name to disturb the neighbors. Some of them were still asleep in bed. But she saw him look around, obviously wondering where Cookie was.

She waited until Zack was looking the other way and then encouraged Cookie to go home. 'Okay, run now. Go home to Zack.'

On her command Cookie found the gap in the fence, squeezed through and ran full pelt to his own garden.

She watched the dog make his way back, but that dog was smart. He emerged from the trees at the bottom of Zack's garden as if that's where he'd been hiding.

In the clear, still air she listened and heard Zack talking to Cookie. 'Oh, there you are.' The two were reunited happily and went inside the house.

'Phew!' Sylvie gasped and stood up.

By now it was starting to snow and she stood there feeling the light, icy flakes fall around her. She welcomed the fresh snow to cover the evidence in her garden. It was clear that a dog and a playful person had been running around in the snow leaving trails of paw and footprints everywhere.

She took a full breath, tilted her head back and let the flakes fall gently on her face, then she went inside to attempt to light a log fire, on her own.

After clearing out the ash and debris from the previous fire, she set up the logs and tried to follow the method shown to her by Zack. It worked. Soon she had a crackling fire going, heating up the lounge where she intended spending most of the day.

One of the first things she did was flick through the photo album. She thought how pretty the house and garden looked in summer with lots of flowers. Beside some of the photos were notes, presumably written by Nate and Nancy. Two different styles of handwriting detailed what was in the pictures. One note stated — planting more cornflowers and roses in the garden. Later, there were pictures of the trees taken in the fall and several close shots of burnished leaves and autumn flowers.

Sylvie was immediately inspired to sketch the flowers and leaves. She used the watercolor pencils and paper to create an autumn color palette ranging from warm maple to hazelnut and rich gold as part of her next fabric collection.

Normally once she started designing she'd work for hours, but instead she put the artwork aside after a little while, determined not to make her snow day a work day.

She listened to cheerful carols, and took time to admire all the baubles and decorations on the Christmas tree in the lounge. She loved the sparkling reindeer ornaments and the shiny Santa baubles. Nancy had decorated it beautifully and draped silver tinsel around the base.

On the windowsill was a snow globe ornament with a miniature house and Christmas tree inside it. Sylvie gave it a gentle shake, held it up and watched the white glitter create a miniature snow scene. Glancing outside the front window, she felt like she was living in a real life snow globe.

While she was watching out the window, she saw Zack leave his house and walk away towards the main street. He was well wrapped up in a warm jacket. Her heart skipped a beat when she looked at him, and she hadn't felt lonely in the house until she'd seen him walking away.

He was the one thing she hadn't accounted for in her plan to enjoy Christmas in a small town. In New York, everything had seemed so simple. Even though it was an adventure to do this on her own, to go somewhere no one knew her, to venture away from the city, she hadn't thought about romance. When Marla had suggested she might meet someone wonderful here, she'd been adamant that she was not dating during the holidays. No romance, no entanglements. And most of all, no broken hearts.

She shook the snow globe again, put it down, and watched the flakes swirl around inside the glass. Then she started to sing along to the Christmas music, while wandering through to the kitchen to make herself a hot white chocolate drink topped with whipped cream.

Carrying it carefully through to the lounge, she snuggled up in front of the fire to watch a festive movie. This is what a snow day was all about.

She'd just finished her drink when Nancy knocked on the front door. Sylvie flicked the sound down on the movie and let her in.

'Good morning, Sylvie. I brought you this sewing basket. I thought it would come in useful when stitching your quilt.'

Sylvie accepted the basket and invited Nancy into the lounge.

'I can't stay long. It's going to be another busy day at the store. We've had our delivery of Christmas cakes and customers will be coming in this morning to pick up their orders. If you'd like one, I'll put it aside for you.'

'Yes, please.'

They sat together by the fire.

'I managed to build the fire myself.' Sylvie tried not to sound too proud of herself.

'It's handy once you know how, and there's something so comforting about a real log fire on snowy days like this.' Nancy glanced around. 'Are you settled in okay? Is there anything else you need?'

'No, everything's perfect, thank you, Nancy.' She opened the sewing basket. Inside it was lined with pink satin and had a wooden drawer filled with thread, a pin cushion and thimbles. The drawer lifted out to reveal a selection of scissors and other items for sewing. 'This is great, but don't you need it for yourself?'

'I have two, so I thought I'd pop round with this one.' She stood up and went over to a cupboard in the corner. 'There's a sewing machine in here if you need it, though I know you're sewing most of your quilt by hand.' Nancy opened the cupboard. 'It doesn't do any fancy stitches, but it's reliable and sews easily. I keep it in here in case visitors want to use it, though few have, but I thought you may find it handy.'

'Yes, it's very handy. I love the patchwork quilt that's on my bed and it's put me in the notion of making one with some of the fabric I bought. That's something I could stitch up easily using the sewing machine.' She went on to talk about enjoying her evening of quilting with Nancy and the other members. 'I had fun at the quilting bee last night.'

'It's the last one before the holidays. The hall is going to be busy now with the Christmas events. It's a shame you only got to attend one bee, but you never know, perhaps you'll extend your vacation and stay in town a little longer.'

'I'd love to, Nancy, but I can't. I have to get back home to work.'

'You'll be attending the Christmas functions won't you?'

'Oh yes.'

'The chestnut roast is tomorrow night. We gather in the town center at the Christmas tree.'

'I wouldn't miss it.'

'Later that night there's a party at the community hall.' Nancy smiled. 'The first of many. I hope you'll come along.'

'I'd better look out a dress, or what should I wear? Is it casual?'

'Wear whatever you want, Sylvie. I'm wearing a skirt and top and shoes I can dance in. No fancy high heels for me.'

'I'm sure I have something I can wear.'

'You don't need a partner,' Nancy was quick to add. 'Everyone just turns up and those on their own soon partner up for a bit of social dancing. Zack may invite you of course. Or Greg.'

'I'll probably turn up on my own.'

'Greg was asking me all about you. I didn't tell him anything private,' she assured her.

'There's something about Greg that I'm not entirely comfortable with.' She told her what happened with Greg and Zack.

'Greg shouldn't have given Zack the wrong impression. Sometimes men are such fools when it comes to courting. And I know that sounds kind of old fashioned.'

'I like old fashioned. I love the idea of romance and tradition. It just never matches up to the real world.'

Nancy stood up and got ready to leave. 'Sometimes it does. You've got to be willing to give it a chance.'

After Nancy left, Sylvie felt unsettled.

She peered out the window and a surge of excitement encouraged her to throw a scarf on over her sweater and head out into the wintry day. She didn't go far. In fact, she started to build a snowman in her front garden. There was a load of snow on the front lawn area.

Wearing mitts, she started by making a snowball and then rolling it across the garden until it became big enough to make the body of the snowman. Then she repeated the process to create the head. This was fun. This was exactly what she needed. No moping around indoors thinking about Zack, or trying not to think about him.

Cupping handfuls of snow, she packed it on to the snowman, adding to his build. It was snowing all around her, getting heavier by the minute, and made her feel less noticeable especially as she was wearing a white sweater. If anyone was watching her from their windows they'd only see a soft focus version of her playing around. The woman with a pink scarf and mitts building the first snowman she'd made since she was a little girl and loving every carefree moment of it.

Zack had arrived home with fresh groceries. He was unpacking them in his kitchen and making coffee when Cookie scooted past him and ran to the front study window.

He followed the dog through and they both peered out. Flurries of snow swept past the window.

'We're in for a real snow day,' Zack commented to Cookie, but it wasn't the snow that the dog was excited about.

Cookie pressed his nose against the window and looked further along the street towards Sylvie's house, and that's when Zack caught a glimpse of a woman wearing a pink scarf building a... snowman? In this freezing weather? She was wearing a sweater and scarf. Didn't she know she was underdressed for a day like this?

He threw his jacket on and hurried out. Someone had to talk some sense into her. He had to try, even if she didn't want to take advice from a guy who'd acted like a jealous nincompoop.

Cookie watched from the warmth of the study as Zack trudged through the snow towards Sylvie.

'What are you doing?' It seemed like the dumbest question in the world, but Zack's voice was filled with concern.

Sylvie looked round to see Zack walking purposefully towards her.

'I'm building a snowman.' As if it wasn't obvious. She hadn't got around to sticking a carrot in for his nose, but she'd jammed two stones in for his eyes and twigs for arms. For someone who hadn't done this in years, she was making a fine job of it.

Zack spread his arms out. 'In this weather? It's snowing.'

Sylvie stopped and put her hands on her hips. 'Isn't that the ideal weather for making a snowman?'

Zack pressed his lips together, stifling a comment that might have offended her, but she caught the look anyway.

'What am I doing wrong now, Zack?'

'I didn't say you were doing something wrong,' he said firmly. 'I didn't say anything.'

'Your expression said it loud and clear.'

The snow was starting to become heavier.

He sighed and reeled off the things she was doing wrong. 'You're not dressed warmly. A sweater isn't enough. You're not even wearing a hat. People usually build snowmen after it's been snowing.'

'Okay, you're right. I guess I got carried away having so much fun.' She dropped the handful of snow she was holding and dusted off her mitts. 'It wasn't snowing so heavily when I started. I'll go back inside now.'

'Make sure to get a hot drink and a heat by the fire,' he called to her as she walked away.

'I will.'

She hadn't intended making him feel like he'd spoiled her fun, but he did feel like a wet blanket. She was only building a snowman.

'Don't give up on your snowman. Just wait until the snow eases off a bit.'

She acknowledged his comment from the front door. 'I won't give up on him.'

'Don't give up on me either, Sylvie,' he said quietly.

'What was that?'

'Nothing.' He waved and started to walk away.

A pang of longing cut through her seeing him leave. She took a chance to ask him about dinner.

'Zack, what do you want to do about dinner at the diner?'

He paused and looked back at her. 'Whatever suits you.' His reply couldn't have been more straightforward. He'd let her decide and abide by that without trying to persuade her to make a date with him.

She shrugged her shoulders and tried to take some of the advice she'd received from Nancy and the other women, including Marla. 'Dinner tonight?'

A rush of relief filled his heart. 'I'll pick you up around seven.'

She nodded at him as flurries of snow swirled around her, and then went inside.

She'd no idea how things would work out between them. Dinner was just being social. She could be friends with Zack without involvement. She liked him, and it had been a while, even when dating Conrad, when she'd felt any man care about her.

She recalled recent comments people had made about him. In essence, Zack really was a nice guy. You didn't intentionally set out to break a nice guy's heart. She had no plans to do that, or break her own.

She spent the rest of the morning drawing new designs and sewing her Christmas quilt. Hand sewing had always relaxed her. The rhythmic method of sewing each stitch was calming even though it was difficult not to feel anxious about her date with Zack. It felt like a date, a first date, despite it being no such thing, and she kept wondering what would happen, what they'd talk about. Would he tell her about his past love? The intricacies she already knew from everything Nancy had told her. She almost wished Nancy hadn't revealed Zack's past because now if he did tell her she'd have to pretend she was hearing this for the first time. She didn't like putting on a false front. It added pressure she didn't need. She already felt the pressure of having dinner with him.

She also wondered what to wear. She'd brought two sweater dresses with her — one gray, a color that invariably suited her, and the other one was red, a nod to the festive season. Wearing a red dress would surely seem like she was signaling for attention, so the grey was going to be her option.

After hand stitching quite a few of her Christmas quilt hexies, she then made a start on her patchwork quilt.

She set up the sewing machine and used the small squares the ladies at the bee had cut for her from one of the bundles of fabric she'd bought. Soon she was sewing the squares together and making great headway with the patchwork. Nancy was right about the machine being reliable and easy to use. She didn't need any fancy stitches for this type of sewing, and whizzed through the little piles of fabric squares, stitching them together into a pretty quilt top.

By midday, Sylvie tidied her quilting away and put the sewing machine back in the cupboard.

Lunch was a tasty bowl of soup. Nothing too filling as she wanted to leave room for the diner meal. If it was anything like the last time, she was in for a substantial treat with generous portions. Besides, there was barely any room available in her tummy even for soup as she was already filled with butterflies.

In the late afternoon Jessica dropped by with a roll of quilt batting for Sylvie.

'I closed my shop early today due to the snowstorm. I wanted to give you this batting.' Jessica handed her the soft, white filler that gave a quilt warmth and substance between the top and bottom layers of cotton fabric. 'There's enough to make your patchwork quilt. You mentioned you wanted to sew one. Or you could keep it for the Christmas one. This batting is lightweight and works great with all types of quilts.'

Sylvie offered to pay, but Jessica wouldn't hear of it.

'Think of it as a Christmas gift from me.'

Sylvie gave her a hug. 'Thank you, Jessica.'

They sat in the kitchen and Sylvie made coffee, and they chatted for almost an hour about quilting and romance.

'I hear that Greg stepped out of line last night,' said Jessica.

'Did Nancy tell you?'

Jessica nodded. 'I hope it doesn't affect things between you and Zack.'

'Actually, I'm having dinner with Zack tonight at the diner. I'm using the ticket I won at the sledding.'

Jessica sounded delighted. 'Oh, that's wonderful. I hope you have a great time and maybe enjoy a bit of romance?'

'It's not a date. It's just dinner as friends.'

Jessica smiled. 'I think you need to practice that denial in front of the mirror, because it sure doesn't look convincing to me.'

Sylvie blushed. 'I'm trying to keep an open mind, take in the advice from you and Nancy, but I really have no plans to get involved with Zack.'

Jessica put her coat on to leave. They stood for a moment at the front door.

'Well, whatever happens, I'm sure you'll have a nice time tonight.' Jessica gave her a cheery wave, ran out into the snow, got into her car and drove off.

Sylvie put the batting in the cupboard with the sewing machine. Then she figured it was time to shower, wash and dry her hair, and start getting ready for her night out.

She wore the gray sweater dress with warm black tights and boots. Her hair was smooth and silky, worn down around her shoulders. She kept her makeup natural but added a slick of her favorite rich red lipstick that always made her feel more confident and vibrant.

She'd let the log fire burn itself out to a cinder. The house had retained the heat and the sweater dress was comfy cozy. She checked the time. Zack was due in fifteen minutes. She'd managed to keep a lid on her excitement. Now that it was nearly time to go it had notched up into the red zone.

'Calm down,' she told herself. Zack knew exactly where she stood when it came to wanting a relationship. She sensed he wouldn't come on to her. If she didn't encourage him either, then dinner would be just fine.

A knock on the front door startled her. Zack was early.

She hurried through to the hall, smoothed down her dress and opened the door.

He wore an expensive winter jacket and looked like he'd stepped straight off the cover of a magazine. He looked so handsome — and as nervous as her but hiding it well.

'I know I'm early, but I wanted to check whether you'd like me to drive us to the diner? If so, I'll go get the car ready.'

'No, I'm happy to walk if you are.'

'Suits me.' He glanced at her dress and boots, giving her a polite but appreciative glance.

'I'll get my coat.' Sylvie grabbed her coat from the closet and put it on as she walked through to the hall. She added a scarf and gloves for warmth and pulled up her hood. 'Okay, let's go.'

They walked together along the sidewalk towards the diner. Snow continued to flutter down around them.

'So, what have you been up to?' he asked.

'Apart from building a snowman in a blizzard and having some sense talked into me by this friendly, neighborly guy?' she teased him.

He laughed. 'Apart from that, yes.'

'Sewing my Christmas quilt, and a patchwork quilt. Jessica also dropped off some batting for me.'

'Batting?'

'The soft stuff that creates the warmth of the quilt between the layers of cotton fabric.'

'Right.'

'And I made a start on my new fabric collection — putting the pencils and paper you gave me to good use.'

'I'm glad they've been useful. Remember, if you want to use my studio, drop by.'

'I hadn't forgotten your previous offer, and I do intend to take you up on it,' she said.

'Bring your designs round anytime I'm in.'

She nodded up at him.

They walked in step together and she started to feel pleasantly excited. 'What did you get up to?'

'I spoiled a young woman's fun when she was attempting to build a snowman and felt guilty about it for hours. Then I worked in my studio until it was time to come and pick you up. I also called the diner and asked them to keep a table for us. It's not usually the type of place where you need a reservation, but at this time of year they get pretty busy so I booked a table for two at the window.'

Chapter Six

Sylvie and Zack were seated at their table and selected the festive meal that was the diner's special that evening.

Ana served up their meal, smiling as she placed down plates of honey baked ham with delicious winter vegetables including golden roast potatoes and sweet peppers with a scoop of redcurrant jelly. This was accompanied by two glasses of classic red wine.

Before they started their meal, Zack held up his glass. Stunning blue eyes locked on to her. 'I'd like to propose a toast.'

Sylvie picked up her glass of wine as he continued.

'A toast to friendship far from home.'

A tug of endearment pulled at Sylvie's heart. Zack's toast was so simple yet sincere.

She tipped her glass against his and they smiled at each other over the rims. Light from the little table lamp shone through the rich burgundy tone of the wine, creating a feeling of warmth and Christmastime. This may only have been the town's local diner, but everything from the welcoming ambiance, to the homely decor with tables set with festive covers and multicolored twinkle lights around the room, made her realize she couldn't have asked for better. This was perfect. And so was the company.

They started to tuck into their meal when Santa, the guy who had suggested she try sledding, ambled past the diner window and gave them a cheery wave. Moments later, Nate went by carrying his Santa outfit, heading to a rehearsal for the Santa sleigh ride. He gave Sylvie and Zack a broad grin and a double thumbs up before continuing on his way.

Sylvie paused from eating her food. 'Call me paranoid, but I get the feeling word has got around about us having dinner together tonight.'

'Santa always knows what folks are up to,' said Zack.

She was sure Zack's lips were trying to refrain from smirking.

'Besides,' he continued, 'Nate knows Nancy. And Nancy knows everyone's business. If you ever want to keep a secret, don't tell Nancy or Jessica. I went into the grocery store today to pick up my Christmas cake order, and Nancy was advising me about things to talk to you about during what she referred to as our dinner date.'

Sylvie felt a blush start to rise in her cheeks. 'I sort of mentioned about our dinner to Jessica.'

Zack shrugged.

'What did Nancy advise you to talk about?'

'It was more like a list of what not to talk about.' He started to reel them off. 'Don't mention the weasel guy, Conrad. Avoid making a big deal about Greg.'

Sylvie nodded, agreeing with Nancy's choices.

Zack continued. 'And don't try to kiss you on our first date.'

Sylvie almost spilled her glass of wine. 'What?'

'Unless of course you try to kiss me. Then she said I should go for it.'

Sylvie stared at him in disbelief.

'Oh and she's put a Christmas cake aside for you. You can pick it up anytime.' Zack tucked into his meal, as if he hadn't stirred up thoughts in her head that she wouldn't have considered.

Sylvie sat back in her chair. 'Is it always like this around here?'

'Pretty much, especially when it comes to romance. I think with you being a fabric designer and the ladies loving their quilting, there's a bit of extra interest in you.'

She loaded part of the responsibility on to him. 'And in you, Zack.'

He conceded that point. 'I'm what they call an eligible bachelor. There are a few of us in town, but obviously with this being a smaller population than the city, we tend to get noticed.'

'Did Nancy give you any other advice?' If so, she wasn't sure she wanted to hear it. Her heart was still pounding from hearing the list so far.

'No, that was about it.' He took a sip of wine. 'I've known Nancy and Nate for years. They're like extended family.'

'Nancy really does seem to care about you.'

He nodded. 'I think she just wants me to be happy.'

'Especially after all the heartbreak with your ex–girlfriend.' The words were out before she could stop herself.

Zack stared across the table at her, then he looked down and shook his head.

'I'm sorry, Zack. I wasn't supposed to tell you that I knew.'

He shrugged his broad shoulders. 'What's done is done.'

'Do you want to talk about it?' Sylvie offered.

'No. I reckon Nancy told you everything worth knowing.'

Sylvie reckoned that too, and didn't push for further answers. Raking over the details of something so raw wasn't going to help anything.

They were quiet for a moment as they ate their food, then Zack added a couple of details about his relationship with his former girlfriend. 'I'm over her. I've been over her for a long time now. For a while I used to wonder what she was up to. I don't do that these days.'

There was something in his tone that made her totally believe him.

'I'm over Conrad. I know things are fresher for me, but I'm done with him.'

Ana came over to their table. 'Can I top up your glasses?'

Sylvie held up her glass. 'Definitely.'

Zack did the same.

Ana smiled gently and left them alone.

Sylvie made a toast this time. 'To a happy Christmastime.'

Zack tipped his glass against hers. 'Happy Christmastime, Sylvie.'

They drank a toast and ate their dinner without further discussion of past break–ups.

Ana was serving up their slices of chocolate Yule log when Sylvie noticed Nate dressed as Santa waving over at them. She peered out the window at him. He was standing across the road and seemed eager to attraction their attention.

'Santa is waving at us,' Sylvie said to Zack.

Zack peeked out, nodded acknowledgment to Nate, and then spooned up a mouthful of chocolate log with buttercream.

Nate gave Zack the thumbs up and continued on his way.

Sylvie frowned. 'What was that about?'

Zack made light of it. 'He was just letting me know everything is okay.'

'What is okay?'

'Nothing important.' Zack pointed his fork at the cake. 'This is really good.'

Sylvie agreed about the cake but wondered what was going on between Zack and Nate. Before she could question this further, Zack asked her about her quilting.

'You're making a Christmas quilt. Will you have it finished in time for Christmas or do these things take a while to sew?'

'I won't have it finished. It does take a while to make an entire quilt especially as I'm sewing the quilt top by hand. But that's the fun of it, enjoying stitching it. I find it very relaxing, and that's something I want to try and do while I'm in town. So far I've been sledding, carol singing, building a snowman and joining in the quilting bee.'

'And I thought I was busy.'

'I'm sure you are with all your architectural work and helping out with the festive events.'

'I've had quieter times,' he admitted. 'No complaints. That's what I love about living here, being part of the community and able to work from home.'

'I prefer working from home too. At times when I find the world overwhelming, or I feel lonely in the city, my work makes me feel happy. I get lost in it. It's like my reliable friend. I always feel okay, even when I'm alone, when I'm steeped in my design work.'

'Have you ever thought about moving to a small town?' His tone was tentative.

'No, I haven't. This is just my Christmas adventure.'

'Then you'll definitely go back home to New York?'

'I'll have to. That's where my life is right now. This is a vacation. I have an apartment, and meetings in the New Year with Marla at the home decor company I work for. She phoned me with news — my new fabric designs are going to be the company's leading line for their forthcoming summer collection.'

'Congratulations.'

'Thanks. My career is important to me, Zack. I've worked hard to get to where I am now. It's what I've always wanted.' Or was it? Was it really what she wanted her life to be? Ambition had driven her on, and a need for financial security, but what about the flip side of all this? What about having someone to share it with? Old wounds from her past that had never quite healed ached for a close family life that had always eluded her. Even the thought of an extended family, like Zack had with Nancy and Nate, had never been part of her world. Did that mean it never could be?

She started to feel the pressure weighing down on her, not only from Zack's questions but from her own answers. It was becoming harder to reconcile the benefits and drawbacks in her own mind.

She had no family, no one left. After losing her parents at an early age when she couldn't even remember them, she'd been brought up by her great uncle, a businessman with no time or inclination to raise a little girl. He'd paid staff to do this for him, and she'd left as soon as she was old enough. He hadn't tried to discourage her leaving, and she'd had no further contact with him. They were never close and he'd passed a few years ago. She really was on her own.

Having no family didn't mean she didn't want to raise one of her own. She did, but life hadn't worked out in favor of that, and the few romantic relationships she'd had never nurtured her hopes. Sometimes she doubted herself, thinking her hopes were nothing more than a pipe dream, a happy ending that belonged in someone else's story.

Zack saw the distress in her expression. 'I'm sorry. I didn't mean to pressure you. Let's leave it at that. Let's talk about something else.'

Sylvie let out a sigh. 'Anything else.'

'Well...' he began, 'I've planned a surprise for you this evening.'

She brightened. 'A surprise? I love surprises. What is it?'

He gave her a cute grin. 'All will be revealed — after we finish our meal.'

Sylvie scooped up a mouthful of the sweet chocolate log, eager to see what he'd planned.

After dinner they left the diner and she buttoned up her coat. Zack zipped up his jacket. Their breath filtered into the cold night air.

She put her scarf on. 'Okay, what is it?'

He pointed over her shoulder.

She looked round and saw a horse–drawn carriage waiting further along the road.

Zack ushered her towards it. 'Your carriage awaits.'

She walked towards the vintage carriage. The driver sat up front and a beautiful chestnut horse stood calmly waiting for them.

'You arranged this for me?' She couldn't disguise the delight in her voice.

'I had a couple of Santa guys help me out,' Zack admitted.

They reached the carriage. Zack held her hand and helped her in. The touch of his strong, elegant hand in hers sent a wave of excitement through her. She wasn't sure if he sensed it too, though she caught a spark of shared attraction in his eyes as they momentarily looked at each other up close.

She sat down on the upholstered seat, a thrill of anticipation charging through her. It had stopped snowing and the hood of the carriage was folded back, presenting a full view of the festive scenery.

Zack climbed in and sat beside her. They wrapped up warm, sharing a couple of blankets, tucked in cozy together.

The driver glanced round and Zack gave him a nod to set off. The clip–clop of the horse's hoofs were muffled by the snow underfoot and the large spindle wheels provided a smooth ride for the carriage. An old fashioned coach lamp hung from the edge of the buggy, swinging gently with the rhythmic movement of the ride.

Sylvie gazed all around her. 'This is amazing.' Her open smile touched his heart.

He'd surprised her with the carriage ride, no doubt about it, but he'd surprised himself even more. Seeing the sheer delight on her face changed something deep inside him. Whatever feelings he'd had for her notched up into the no going back zone. Maybe this was the exact moment he knew he loved her, truly loved her.

Whatever heartbreak this lovely young woman had endured was forgotten in her awe of being in the buggy with him, looking at the town all lit up in the snow. More than anything he realized something else. His happiness came from seeing her happiness.

They traveled along the first part of the main thoroughfare, under the boughs of the trees lining the street. The Christmas lights that were draped across the road from the street lamps looked close enough to touch. The reds, golden yellow, green and blue bulbs cast a colorful glow over everything. The decorative trees outside the stores and buildings sparkled amid the evening light, and the store windows made her want to gaze at everything that was lit up. She felt herself catch her breath several times just looking around her.

She gazed round at Zack and smiled. 'This is the first time I've ever been in a horse–drawn carriage.'

'Mine too,' he admitted.

Her gray eyes widened. 'Is it? I thought you'd have done this lots of times.'

'No, this is something that's popular with the tourists and other visitors. I've never actually been in one. Until now. With you.'

'A first time for both of us.' There was no disguising the delight in her voice that she'd experienced this with him.

He pointed to the sleigh being set up outside the community hall as they went by. Nate and the other Santa were practicing their arrival for the forthcoming event.

'Is this part of Santa arriving on his sleigh?' Sylvie asked.

'It is. There's always a back–up Santa,' Zack explained. 'One on the sleigh and one helping in the hall. Often there are others as well.'

'Nate suits being Santa.'

'He does. I think it's his turn to be on the sleigh ride this year.' He motioned to the route they were taking. 'The sleigh is a carriage like this one done up with lights and tinsel. It comes down the main street and stops at the community hall. Everyone cheers as Santa arrives, then there is the opening welcome on stage, followed by a buffet dinner, music and dancing.'

'Nancy said there's dancing there tomorrow night after the chestnut roast. She invited me to pop along. I think I will.'

'You'll enjoy it,' he said.

The carriage took them on a tour of the main parts of the town.

'I love all the decorations,' said Sylvie. 'Everything is so magical.'

'When I was younger I used to feel sad when the Christmas trees and decorations had to come down. Then my father reminded me that we were only halfway through the winter and that there were lots of fun things to do in the New Year until the spring. Just because the decorations were gone, there was still plenty of snow for sledding and building snow houses.'

'Snow houses? You were a budding architect even then?'

'I've always loved to design and build houses. I'd make them out of packed ice, logs and pieces of timber. Often they'd be frozen solid right through to the spring. The seasons here are great. I enjoy winter with all the snow, then one morning I'll wake up and half of it has melted and snowdrops are popping up. You know the grassy verge near our houses?'

Sylvie nodded.

'It's covered in snowdrops in early spring. Then up comes the crocus, and the whole scenery is a mass of white, lilac, purple and yellow with buds shooting through the trees. The days become brighter and longer. I always get an extra urge to design when this happens. It's like a fresh start and a renewed type of energy. I get a heap of work done in springtime.'

'It sounds wonderful.'

'Maybe you'll come back for a spring adventure.'

She didn't confirm or deny that she would.

'If you thought Nate looked good dressed as Santa, you should see him as the Easter bunny. We have Easter egg hunts and the town is all done up for spring.'

'The summers must be beautiful too,' she said.

'They are. There's a cove near here that's great for swimming. The water is the clearest blue. Folks spend an entire day there, cooking up barbecues, lazing in the sun, swimming... '

She became thoughtful, picturing all the things she could enjoy here, but how could she? Her whole world was in the city.

'The trees are spectacular in the fall,' he said, filling the gap that had occurred in their conversation.

'I saw the pictures in Nancy's photo album. The trees in the garden were really beautiful, and I've based my new color range on some of them.'

'That's a great idea. The fall colors here are incredible.' He glanced around at the festive decorations. 'Then of course Christmastime rolls around again and — here we are, on nights like this.'

'The town seems to be the ideal place for you to work, to create your house designs.'

'The seasons mark time nice and slow here. I don't like the fast pace of the city. When I worked there, everyone needed their designs tomorrow. A month could go in like that.' He snapped his fingers. 'Here a month feels like a whole lot of time, but in New York, a week was over so fast and before I knew it, a month was over as well. I found myself wondering, where has the time gone? And no one had ever achieved a fraction of what they wanted.'

'I know how that feels,' she agreed with him.

'I'm now in the fortunate position of being able to pick my clients carefully. I've learned never to get involved with people who

74

are constantly chasing their tails. Even if I try to help them catch up, they won't change, and I end up having to chase my own tail because of my involvement with them. Now...' he shook his head. 'I just say no thanks.'

'You're also lucky to be able to design in the moment, like when it's spring and you feel like creating new designs.'

He nodded. 'Very lucky, but my house designs aren't dependent on one season. They have to suit all seasons. What will you be working on this spring?'

'A winter collection probably. I'll have this town for inspiration though.' She took her phone from her coat pocket and snapped a few pictures of the snowy scenery.

'Would you mind if I took a photo of you?' she asked Zack.

'Of me? You're not intending putting me on one of your fabrics are you?' He was joking.

'No, this is just for me. To remember you by.'

He nodded, but looked the saddest she'd seen him all evening.

She clicked off a couple of pictures, then went to put her phone away.

'Take one of us,' he urged her quickly before she put it back in her pocket. 'Send me a copy, so I have something to remember us by.'

She noted he didn't say — remember her by. It was them, together.

She snapped a few as they snuggled close so she could get both of them in the picture. She checked the photos on her phone and held it so he could view them.

'Great,' he said.

She sent him a copy.

He brought out his phone. 'Got them. Thanks.'

'Would you like me to circle round again?' the carriage driver asked Zack.

Zack glanced at Sylvie. She nodded.

'Yes, thanks,' he told the driver.

They settled back, tugging the blankets up for warmth and sat together taking in the ride. They didn't fill the air with chatter this time, but she felt closer to him than ever.

This trip she noticed many of the other stores, including the art store Zack had talked about. She'd definitely pop in there sometime during her stay. For a small town they had a comprehensive range of stores. Everything a person could need in one main area.

Peering beyond the trees and gaps between the shops, she saw lights in the distance from houses and lamp–lit streets. She imagined what it would be like to stay here, to feel settled.

They eventually went past the cafe, the grocery store and the diner. A full circle trip. Zack had pointed out several other things of interest including where the chestnut roast evening was going to be held the following night.

'Can you drop us off at my house?' he finally asked the driver.

'Sure thing, Zack.'

The carriage trundled down the road and came to a gentle stop outside Zack's house.

Zack jumped out and helped Sylvie step down.

'Thanks again,' he said to the driver.

'Yes, thank you. That was wonderful,' she called to the driver who tipped his hat to them as the horse and carriage ambled away.

They stood together and she wondered if Zack would invite her in, but no, he gestured towards her house.

'Come on, I'll walk you back.'

'It's only two houses along.'

It didn't matter to Zack whether it was one house or several, he was set to walk her to her door and bid her a proper goodnight.

As they walked up the garden path he glanced at the snowman who looked worse the wear for all the extra snow that had fallen on and around him.

'He needs a bit of work,' Sylvie admitted.

'A lot of work,' Zack corrected her.

'I'll tackle him in the morning.'

'Want a hand to tackle him now?' he offered.

'Now?'

'You got something else you need to do?'

'Eh... no.'

'Okay then.' Zack cupped a large handful of snow and started work on the snowman's body.

'I'll reshape his head.' Sylvie scooped up two handfuls of snow and pressed them on to the face.

She stood back. 'I think he's slightly wonky.'

Zack smirked. 'Wonky?'

'You're doing that smirking thing.'

'Sorry.' He pretended to sweep his smirk into a smile. 'That better?'

'Much better.'

Zack viewed the snowman. 'He is kind of leaning to one side.'

'I'll stuff a bundle of snow at the base. That should straighten him up.'

She crouched down and formed her hands into a scooper, gathered a load of snow and tried to force it under the snowman.

'No, Sylvie. You'll hurt yourself.'

Before he could stop her, she exerted a huge effort, tumbled and face planted into a soft drift.

Trying not to laugh, Zack grabbed her, lifted her up and helped wipe the snow off her. She was covered in it.

'Laugh and get it over with,' she told him.

'I'm not laughing,' he said, trying to contain it. 'I'm not even smirking.'

'Inside you are.'

'Me? Would I smirk at a human sugar cookie?'

'Sugar cookie, huh?' she scooped up a handful of snow and started to form it into a ball.

Zack held his hands up. 'No, Sylvie, put it down.'

She threw it and he ducked. 'Missed me. You throw like a girl.'

'I am a girl.'

Zack pressed his lips together and tried not to laugh.

By now she'd made a second snowball and this time her aim was on target. The soft flakes hit him in the face. He spluttered and wiped it off.

'How does it feel to be a sugar cookie?' she asked with a note of triumph.

'One hit does not make me a sugar cookie.'

She quickly grabbed another handful and hit him a second time.

This kicked off a snowball fight between them. Amid the squeals of laughter she had more fun than she'd had in ages.

They ended up in fits of giggles, rolling around in the snow as Zack tried to wrestle the last snowball from her determined grip. She managed to throw it in his face before submitting to being overpowered and pinned down. His features were covered in the powdery flakes but with his face now so close to hers, she had to force herself not to gaze at his lips and those stunning blue eyes that saw only her.

Her breathing was thick and fast from all the excitement, and the reaction he caused within her.

'Okay, Zack, you win,' she conceded.

He focused on her face, her lips and for a second she thought he might kiss her.

At that moment the snowman fell over, jolting them from their all too intimate moment.

Zack stood up, brushed the snow from himself, extended his hand and pulled her to her feet. He held her hand for a second longer than he'd intended. Something in him didn't want to let her go, but he did.

She stepped back, breathless and brushed strands of her snow sprinkled hair back from her face. Her cheeks were flushed and her heart was alight with the feelings she had for him.

'Thank you for taking me as your friend to dinner,' he said, getting ready to walk home.

'You're welcome. Thank you for the carriage surprise.'

He smiled and walked away, glancing at the snowman lying prone on the ground. He paused, lifted him up and straightened him into position. 'Less wonky?'

Sylvie gave him the thumbs up.

He grinned and continued on his way.

Her heart gave that ache again as she watched him walk away.

She breathed in the cold night air, then went inside and changed into her comfy night clothes. Curling up on a chair at the bedroom window, she gazed outside. The snowman stood straight, if unfinished, in the front garden. She planned to get up early the next morning to complete him. She loved the feeling of the quiet mornings here and didn't want to miss a single one of them.

She sighed and thought about the events of the evening. And about Zack. Flicking through the pictures on her phone, she paused when she saw the photos of them together. She gazed at Zack. She couldn't risk falling in love with him. Her plan for a Christmas adventure in Snow Bells Haven hadn't included meeting someone like him, and certainly not becoming romantically involved.

She looked again at his handsome face, fabulous blue eyes and his firm lips. In the picture he wasn't smirking, he was smiling, and yet... there was a hint of sadness in him. She sensed it too, as if they both knew their lives were too complicated to fit together easily. Holiday romances rarely worked out.

She thought about Jessica and her husband. He'd been prepared to drive back and forth from New York to give their relationship a chance, and it had paid off. He was now the sheriff and they were happily married. But she couldn't contemplate driving from the city on a regular basis, even if it was to see Zack. That type of set up had no reasonable conclusion unless she changed her career, and she didn't want to do this. Her design work was part of her and always had been. She needed to be in the hub of the company's design work and that was in the city.

It seemed even less feasible that Zack would up sticks and move to New York. Everything he loved was here in town. Everything she was starting to love was right here too.

She swept her hair back from her troubled brow. Some things just didn't have a happy ever after solution. If she was to enjoy the remainder of her vacation she'd have to settle for a happy for the moment situation. It wasn't a perfect solution, but few things in her life were ever perfect.

Sylvie clicked the phone off and went to bed, snuggling under the patchwork quilt for warmth and comfort, trying not to dwell on thoughts of Zack that would've kept her awake all night.

She pulled the quilt around her, gazed out the window at the flakes of snow falling gently, and finally fell sound asleep.

Chapter Seven

Winter sunlight streamed through Sylvie's kitchen window. The aroma of fresh brewed coffee filtered out of the kitchen when she opened the back door and stepped outside to breathe in the early morning air. She wore a cream sweater, pink knitted hat and matching pink scarf, with charcoal gray pants and boots.

It had snowed overnight. She gazed up at the trees whose brittle branches looked like they were made of ice, and squinted against the sunshine highlighting every crystallized detail.

The effects of the previous night lingered in her thoughts. When she'd woken up at dawn, she'd jumped in the shower, letting the warm water wash some of the surplus tension away. By the time she'd eaten her cereal and fruit for breakfast, she was feeling perky and was determined to enjoy the beautiful bright morning.

She was exploring a corner of the garden near the little frozen pond when a familiar friend came bounding over to her, tail wagging and eyes bright as chocolate buttons.

'Hi, Cookie.' She bent down and gave him a welcoming hug and was rewarded with doggie kisses and snuggles.

She ran her hands over his soft, velvety fur and nuzzled into him. Cookie lapped up every second of it.

'I'm really going to have to tell Zack about us.'

The dog tilted his head to one side at the mention of Zack's name.

'I'm sure he'll be happy that we're friends, but I don't want to keep it a secret any longer. Okay?'

Cookie snuggled into her and then ran over to the gap in the fence where he'd left his chew toy. He picked it up in his mouth and came running back to her.

'You came prepared, huh?'

Cookie dropped the toy and got ready to play their game of throw and fetch.

Sylvie threw the toy and Cookie ran to retrieve it. She gave him plenty of praise every time he brought it back.

'Yay! Good boy, Cookie.'

The garden gave the dog plenty of space to run around, and the two of them ended up chasing each other, going one way, then the next, causing flurries of snow to gust around them.

She tumbled a couple of times, and Cookie ran over to make sure she was okay, resulting in further high jinks and playfulness between the two of them.

Her laughter rang out clear in the fresh air and she totally forgot about keeping a lid on their activity. She gave that dog a good run for his money, and they both bounded around having fun.

She even made a few daring slides and spins on the icy pond, and cartwheels in the snow. It had been years since she'd done a cartwheel, something she'd been good at as a teenager, but the technique came back easily and the snow provided a soft landing when she overshot the last move. Being covered in snow was becoming a regular occurrence. She brushed it off and continued enjoying herself.

She finally flopped down on the garden bench. Cookie sat at her feet with his smiley mouth grinning up at her.

'That was fun, eh?'

He barked, sounding happy and enthusiastic.

She put her finger up to her lips. 'Shh! We don't want to alert Zack, not until I have a chance later today to explain that you've become a regular visitor.'

Cookie didn't bark again. Instead he bounded off to fetch his toy for her to throw.

'Okay,' she said, standing up. 'Then you'll have to head back home.'

She played fetch with Cookie for a few more minutes, then clapped his silky head and gave him a hug. Her face was close to his and she looked right into his adorable eyes. 'You'll have to go back home now.'

Cookie did as she asked. He squeezed through the fence and she watched him run back home. She stood on her tiptoes. There was no sign of Zack this morning.

Exhilarated from all the activity, Sylvie went inside, grabbed her purse and walked down to the grocery store to pick up her Christmas cake and fresh milk. She also expected to be quizzed about her dinner with Zack. Then again, Nancy probably knew everything that had happened.

Nancy smiled at her from behind the counter. 'Morning, Sylvie.'

'Hi, Nancy. I came to collect my Christmas cake.'

'It's right here. It's a traditional fruit cake with marzipan and white icing.' Nancy lifted it from a shelf and put it down on the counter. It was in a white cake box.

'That's ideal. I'll also take some fresh milk.' Sylvie paid for the cake and milk.

Nancy put the items in a bag and grinned at Sylvie. 'I heard your dinner date with Zack was a real success.'

'The meal was delicious.'

'And he took you on a horse and carriage ride around the town.' Nancy sounded very impressed.

'He did. It was a great surprise.'

Nancy kept her voice low. 'Nate helped to organize it.'

Nate came ambling through from the stockroom. 'Are you girls talking about me?'

'I was just telling Sylvie about you helping Zack with the carriage ride.'

Nate brushed aside taking the credit. 'Zack hoped you'd enjoy it. I thought it was a great idea.'

'It was and I did enjoy it. I saw parts of the town all lit up that I hadn't yet seen. Everything looked so lovely. It was fun.'

'So romantic,' Nancy added.

Sylvie hesitated and a blush rose across her cheeks.

'Oh, I knew it,' Nancy beamed. 'I knew you'd both get along.'

'We do get along,' Sylvie agreed. 'Still just friends though.'

Nate gave her a knowing grin.

'We are, Nate,' Sylvie insisted, trying not to smile.

'I'm sure you are.' Nate sounded unconvinced.

'No more than friends,' Sylvie emphasized.

Nate looked at her. 'That I'm not so sure about.'

Sylvie didn't deny it. She wasn't so sure about that either.

'Are you still coming along to the chestnut roast tonight?' Nancy asked her.

'Yes, I love roast chestnuts. There are so many delicious temptations in this town.' Including one who was tall, handsome and helped her build a snowman last night.

'Have you thought about what you'll wear to the dance afterwards?' Nancy rightly assumed that Sylvie was going to that too.

'Not yet, but I'll certainly keep in mind what you said about wearing shoes I can dance in.' Sylvie had packed a couple of pairs of shoes she thought would be suitable.

Nate served a customer while Nancy continued chatting to Sylvie. 'There's a little dress shop along from Jessica's quilt shop that sells the sweetest dresses if you're looking for one.'

Sylvie liked that idea. 'I'll pop by there later.'

'The shop is owned by Virginia, a young woman around the same age as yourself. She's making a real go of her business.'

More customers came into the store and Sylvie left Nancy and Nate to get on with their business.

Outside she squinted against the sunlight to where the dress shop was situated. It wasn't far and she had the urge to do some retail shopping. However, the Christmas cake was heavy and she was carrying milk, so she decided to drop these off at the house first and then go back out.

As she walked past Zack's house she noticed the lights were on inside. She couldn't see him and didn't want to look like she was spying on him or trying to attract his attention. They'd parted last night on a light note of non–committal friendship. No second dinner date planned. No pressure to do anything.

She walked straight ahead, feigning interest in the contents of her grocery bag, while casting a sideways glance at his house. Despite almost kissing, he'd more or less abided by her rule of not becoming romantically involved. She couldn't fault him on that score. He hadn't put his arm around her when they were sitting together in the carriage. He hadn't invited her into his house for coffee. The snowball fight was fun, and when he had her pinned down, she doubted he would've actually kissed her. He'd hesitated even before the snowman took a tumble and startled them out of the moment.

No, Zack was trustworthy. He wouldn't pressure her. So why did she feel she was standing in her own way of happiness? She shook the frustrating thought from her mind and continued on her way.

The snowman was frozen solid in her front yard. He glittered in the sunlight. As she walked up the path towards the house her imagination started working overtime. His stone cold eyes seemed to glare at her as if she was a fool for not letting a nice handsome guy, a successful architect, into her life.

'What are you staring at?' she muttered. 'Careful, buddy, I might just turn you into one giant snowball.' Then she hurried on inside the house feeling even more foolish.

Zack had slept in. He never did this. By nature he was an early riser and often got a lot of work done before the sleepy town had yawned into daily action. But today he was running late. He blamed himself. It wasn't Sylvie's fault he'd been awake half the night thinking about her.

Sylvie was so upfront about things and honest with him. Her honest attitude was something that he greatly admired. Women he'd known had tended to have a secretive side to their characters, hiding things from him. But Sylvie was honest and open. He'd forgotten how good it felt to put his trust in a woman again.

He'd never pressurize her into dating him, but that didn't stop him from wondering if he was doing the right thing. What if he was letting the potential love of his life slip through his fingers just because he was reluctant to speak up? What if she got a call from Marla and had to pack up and go back to New York right now because of her work? What if she didn't stay for Christmas?

He ran a frustrated hand through his hair as a hundred what if scenarios tormented him.

He slumped down on a chair.

Cookie padded over to him, sensing Zack needed comforting, and rested his head on his lap, soulful eyes gazing up at him.

Zack ruffled his fur, then he remembered...

He reached for the miniature video camera he'd attached to Cookie's collar. He'd bought it yesterday from one of the local stores. He'd suspected his dog was visiting other neighbors' gardens. Cookie was definitely up to something. His dog was tuckered out the past two mornings and today he looked like he'd had an active time while Zack had overslept. He knew his dog well enough to sense mischief. Cookie was free to let himself in and out the house via the dog flap in the kitchen door. Until recently he'd never thought that his dog would use it for anything other than a trip into his own back yard.

84

The collar seemed like a good solution to see the world from Cookie's eye view. If his suspicions were unfounded then so much the better.

Zack detached the camera from the collar and set up his laptop to watch what his beloved pet had been up to that morning. He inserted the camera's memory stick. The laptop monitor showed Cookie sniffing around the kitchen, doing no harm, then nosing his way out of the dog flap into the snowy day.

It was interesting in itself to see the world from the dog's perspective, and Zack found himself quickly engrossed in looking at the things Cookie seemed to check on in his home territory — the log pile, Zack's garden chair, his favorite play ball that was frosted with ice.

Satisfied his garden was in order, Cookie ventured over to a gap in the fence and squeezed through. Zack hadn't even noticed the gap, but it was obvious the dog had used this regularly. He nosed the fence slats aside and shimmied through.

The video included audio and Zack heard the snow crunch as Cookie padded across the next door yard without stopping. Nothing here seemed to interest his dog.

Zack leaned forward to study the screen as he realized Cookie was headed for a gap in the next fence leading to Sylvie's garden.

So this was the beginning of his route, Zack mused to himself, wondering where Cookie would go next. However, it soon became apparent that this was where he was headed all along.

Sylvie's chirpy voice sounded clear on the audio. 'Hi, Cookie.' Then her smiling face lit up the screen as she gave his dog a welcoming hug. From the sloppy doggie kissing noises his pet was delighted to see her.

Zack leaned back in his chair reeling from the surprise. His stomach flipped when he realized that the two of them were best buddies.

Cookie's tail wagged whenever he heard her voice.

'I'm really going to have to tell Zack about us.'

'Oh I think that boat has sailed, Sylvie.' Zack's tone was dry.

He continued to watch the footage. 'Where did you learn to fetch like that?' he said. It had taken him weeks to train Cookie how to fetch a ball and here he was doing it like a pro.

The snuggles and cuddles between his dog and Sylvie were heartwarming.

Zack shook his head in dismay. 'How come you get all the hugs and kisses from Sylvie?'

Cookie offered up a velvety paw.

'Awe, no,' he said in an exaggerated tone. 'Giving me a paw now just won't work.' Of course it did, and Zack accepted his dog's paw. 'We're still best buddies too, aren't we?'

Cookie gave Zack an adoring look and snuggled close as Zack watched what happened next.

Sylvie walked past Zack's house heading for the dress shop in the main street. Her hair hung down below her woolly hat and as she tucked wayward strands aside she had a sneak peek at his front window. It was still lit up and no sign of Zack. Maybe he was a sleepyhead this morning?

She strutted on, wondering what type of dresses would be available. She hadn't been dress shopping in ages and was really in the mood to buy something pretty for the dance parties.

Zack rewound part of the video. Watching Sylvie's cartwheels in the snow merited a second viewing.

'Cartwheels? Seriously? In the snow?' What was she thinking? She could've hurt herself. Luckily she'd only mistimed one of them and had a soft landing in a snow drift.

Then there was the ice sliding. Oh boy! He held his breath watching those daredevil moves.

She was certainly living up to her determined claim that she wanted a Christmas adventure. He kept thinking she was going to face plant into the hard packed ice. But no, twinkle toes skipped happily down the garden having skimmed the surface of the frozen pond several times without incident.

She also attempted pirouettes on the ice. Apart from an initial few wobbles, she managed to do them smooth and calm. He couldn't say the same for his heart rate. He wasn't sure if it was racing wildly because he was worried she was dicing with trouble or that he was falling deeper in love with her with every daring move.

He finally closed the laptop. He felt twice as exhausted as she must've been. She'd looked perky and rosy cheeked as she'd waved and kissed his dog goodbye. He felt drained of color and bereft of the will to make himself a cup of much needed coffee.

He had to decide what to do, though this was proving difficult as his mind was filled with images of Sylvie doing extraordinarily energetic things in her garden. And it was her garden. His dog was doing the trespassing. But as a sensible adult it was her neighborly duty to tell him that his dog had become a visitor. What did she think he would do — ban Cookie from visiting? He sighed heavily.

Cookie gazed up at him, sensing his uneasiness.

Okay, so that's what he would've done. He would've put a stop to it right away. He'd have nailed and mended the gaps in the fences and put paid to any further trouble.

But had there been any trouble? The folks next door were friends of his and were often away on business. No harm had been done to their back yard. And they liked Cookie.

No, it was the fact that she'd kept it a secret that niggled at him. She hadn't even hinted that she knew his dog. That was sneaky. No getting around it. And if she was hiding this from him, what else could she be hiding? He'd thought he could trust her. Now he wasn't so sure.

He pushed up from his chair feeling heaviness weighing him down and went through to make that cup of coffee.

The dress shop was one of the prettiest stores in town. Twinkle lights were draped along the edges of the canopy and a Christmas tree stood beside the front door. Sylvie went inside.

The shop was small but the rails were fit to burst with lovely dresses.

The owner, Virginia, served two customers while Sylvie browsed through the selection. Spotlights highlighted the rails and many of the designs were clearly geared for the party season. Sequins sparkled, layers of chiffon and silk shimmered beautifully, and the richness of the fabrics from satin to soft velvet accommodated all tastes from dazzling to classic.

Sylvie was spoiled for choice, but managed to pick out three dresses she particularly liked.

'Can I try these on?' Sylvie held up the dresses.

'Sure. The changing room is through there.' Virginia pointed to a small room curtained off at the back of the shop.

Sylvie hung the dresses up on a hook, pulled the curtain shut, and changed into the first one — a green velvet dress. It had long sleeves and sparkling beadwork details at the neckline. She looked at herself in the full–length mirror. It fitted well and the hemline skimmed just above her knees.

'Are you getting on okay in there?' Virginia called through to her.

Sylvie stepped out from behind the curtain, smoothing the velvet down.

'There's a slight stretch to the velvet,' said Virginia. 'It creates a comfortable fit.'

'It's very comfy for something so fitting. I like it.'

'It suits you, but try the other two on before deciding,' Virginia advised her.

Sylvie felt she'd already decided that the green dress was going home with her as she hung it back on the hanger.

She then changed into a midnight blue dress covered in sparkles, like someone had thrown handfuls of glitter over the top layer of chiffon.

'This is gorgeous,' Sylvie said to Virginia.

One of the other customers peeked in and nodded enthusiastically. 'That blue dress really flatters your slim figure.'

'Thank you,' said Sylvie, unused to complete strangers commenting, but welcoming the friendliness.

'Is this for the festive parties?' asked Virginia.

'Yes, I brought a red sweater dress with me and thought I might wear it for the chestnut roast and dancing tonight. Now I'm thinking the green velvet — and this sparkly blue for the Christmas Eve party.'

Virginia nodded thoughtfully. 'The red sweater dress would be ideal for tonight as it sounds cozy and no one dresses up too fancy this evening. However, I do have one dress that might be a contender for Christmas Eve. It's not on the rails. I've got it in the stockroom. I'll go get it while you try on the next dress.'

Virginia hurried away to fetch it while Sylvie put the third dress on — a pretty amber satin number. Another great fit and she loved the color. She looked at the price tags on all three dresses. Wow! What bargains. The last dress she'd bought in New York cost more than these three put together.

Virginia handed in one of the loveliest dresses Sylvie had ever seen. It was a classy little silver and white dress that sparkled under the shop lighting. The fabric was shot through with silver thread.

'This is beautiful,' Sylvie gasped, grabbing it while pulling back the curtain to show Virginia the amber satin.

'It's going to be a tough choice,' Virginia admitted. 'These neat little dresses flatter your figure.'

'The amber reminds me of the autumn, so I think I'll take it anyway, even if it hangs in my closet until the fall.' Sylvie liked it because it matched the fall colors she was working on for her new designs. Yes, she thought adamantly. This was coming home with her. As was the green velvet and the midnight blue. At these prices? What a bargain. Now if this silver and white dress fitted her...

It did. By now all the women in the shop had gathered to chip in their comments.

'With your hair coloring and skin tone, the silvery white lights you up,' one of the customers remarked. 'That one gets my vote for sure.'

It got Sylvie's vote too.

Virginia carefully wrapped the four dresses while telling Sylvie a bit about her business. 'The dresses are sewn by local seamstresses. The beadwork on that green velvet was done by Ana.'

'Ana from the diner?' Sylvie asked.

'Yes, she's learning dressmaking from the other ladies while working extra hours at the diner. She's saving up to get married in the spring. Then she plans to focus on the dressmaking while they start raising a family.'

'Who designs the dresses?'

'I do, but I use my grandmother's patterns and adapt them for various styles. Classic designs never go out of fashion. Online sales have picked up and we're planning to sew more to keep up with demand. It suits all the women involved as most of them have families to care for and this enables them to work flexible hours from home.'

Sylvie left the shop with four dress in two bags, along with a velvet purse that Virginia had hand made to match some of the fashions she sold.

Buzzing with excitement, Sylvie had to share her delight and popped into the grocery store to give Nancy a peek.

'What do you think?' Sylvie opened the bags to show her the selection of dresses. 'I couldn't resist any of them.'

'They're lovely, Sylvie. I'm so pleased you found them. I love Virginia's shop.'

'What time does the chestnut roast start tonight?'

'Around seven, and the party in the community hall kicks off about eight.'

'Great, see you later tonight,' Sylvie said to Nancy, waving as she left the grocery store.

Across the road Nate was deep in conversation with Zack. Nate didn't see Sylvie, but she thought Zack noticed her and pretended otherwise. A cold shiver went through her. Had Zack just ignored her? No, she must've misread his expression. Obviously he was discussing something important with Nate. They were probably talking about setting up the stalls for later that night. She didn't want to interrupt them and hurried on carrying her bags filled with dresses.

'I don't know whether to confront Sylvie or wait to see if she tells me herself.' Zack sounded annoyed.

'Send me a copy of the video. I won't tell Nancy. This will be just between you and me,' Nate assured him. 'I'll have a look and let you know what I think.'

'I'll upload it online and give you a private link. There's about an hour's worth of footage so there's a lot to pour through.'

'She was doing cartwheels you said?' Nate didn't know whether to frown or smile.

'Yes. If I wasn't so mad at her I'd think it was funny.' It was funny, hilarious in fact, especially watching the expressions on her face up close as she grinned at his dog.

'What was she thinking? That was a foolish thing to do.'

Zack shrugged. 'I thought I could trust her.'

'Did you tell her you had a dog?'

'Yes, I'd been in her garden that first morning looking for Cookie. I planned to introduce them. I guess I should've done it sooner, but not everyone loves dogs.'

'You were worried she wouldn't like him, and then maybe not like you so much?'

Zack's heavy sigh answered that question. Nate had him sussed out.

'Promise me you won't tell Nancy or anyone else until I figure things out.'

'You have my word, Zack.'

'I'll email you with a link to the video once I've uploaded it.'

Nate gave him the thumbs up, then they both went their separate ways.

Sylvie hung her new dresses in the bedroom closet and then decided to sketch some designs before lunch.

She used Zack's pencils again and opened the photo album that showed detailed pictures of the leaves in the garden. She sketched the designs with an ordinary pencil and then added the tones of autumn with the watercolors, trying to figure out what shapes of leaves worked well together.

As always when she was working the time whizzed by. Two hours later she had the makings of her first fabric design — a selection of autumn leaves in beautiful fall colors on a background of rich cream.

She scanned the artwork into her laptop and checked her email. There was a message from Marla. She read it: Hope you're relaxing, having fun and not working too hard. And how are things with you and Zack?

Sylvie typed a quick reply, condensing what had happened with dinner, the carriage ride, snowman and... she hesitated before adding that he'd almost kissed her. She attached one of the photos of Zack sitting in the carriage with her and sent it along with the email.

She'd started heating tomato soup for a late lunch and cutting a slice of sun dried tomato bread to go with it, when she received a reply on her phone from Marla. It read: Wow! Zack is so handsome. Definitely have fun.

Sylvie smiled and clicked her phone off, then ate her lunch at the kitchen table. The bright sunlight had faded to a pale gold. The afternoon light had a mellow quality to it, and after tidying away her dishes, she went outside to finish that snowman.

The temperature was dropping and the snow was becoming hard packed. Sylvie gazed up at the darkening sky as she scooped up the last handfuls of snow and added them to the snowman. The finishing touch was to create a smile on his face using several small stones. The upturned shape took the edge off those beady eyes of his.

She stepped back and admired her handiwork. 'There. Not bad at all.'

A friendly neighbor passing by gave her a wave and a thumbs up for her snowman. She waved back, then went inside to get cleaned up for the evening ahead.

Nate was sore from laughing. Sore too from having to hide his hilarity from Nancy. He was tempted to show her Sylvie's cartwheels but he'd promised Zack he wouldn't and he didn't.

Trying to find somewhere he could watch and listen to the video footage on his laptop had been difficult. He'd left the stockroom and made an excuse to pop home while she attended the store so he could roar with laughter at Sylvie's antics. He understood that Zack was mad at her, but he could only bust a gut from guffawing. You had to love a woman who would attempt a wobbly pirouette on a frozen garden pond in between playing throw and fetch with a dog.

Not wanting to leave Nancy to handle the customers on her own for too long, Nate went back to the store.

'Everything okay, honey?' Nancy asked him.

Nate smiled at her. 'Yeah, Zack asked me to help him out with something that's all.'

Sylvie wore the green dress. Despite the red sweater dress being ideal, she'd made the mistake of trying on the green one after showering and getting ready for the evening, and was reluctant to take it back off. She teamed it with cozy black tights and low heel shoes.

Wearing a warm coat and scarf, she walked to the main street, and heard the sounds of lively chatter and activity as she approached the stalls. The aroma of chestnuts roasting wafted through the air. A lot of people were already there queuing up for bags of the roasted delicacy. Sylvie joined one of the queues where Nate was serving dressed as Santa.

'Ho! Ho! Ho!' Nate greeted her as it became her turn to buy a bag of chestnuts.

'A big bag for me, Nate.' She smiled at him. He seemed extra happy to see her, or perhaps he was just practicing being in character. Even with his white beard on, there was no disguising his wide smile. He looked like he was bursting with joy.

He scooped the chestnuts into a bag and handed them to her. 'There you go, Sylvie. These should help keep you going, especially with all the energy you've expended today.' He stifled a snicker behind his beard.

Sylvie took the bag of chestnuts, paid her money and frowned at him. 'Energy? What energy?' She sounded curious.

'The eh...' he fumbled for the right words. 'The dress shopping. Yes, shopping for lots of lovely dresses.'

She smiled. 'Nancy told you I suppose. There are no secrets around here.'

'Nooo, definitely not.' Nate's tone was edged with laughter.

Sylvie grinned as she walked away so others could buy from the stall. Nate was certainly extra cheerful this evening.

In stark contrast she looked over and saw Zack standing near the large Christmas tree staring at her. What was wrong with mister glum tonight? Zack was acting so strange towards her. Whatever had gotten into him?

His warm jacket was zipped up to the neck, and it looked like he'd zipped his lips into a firm line too.

She wondered whether to approach, or leave him alone until his frosty attitude had melted. Before she could decide, a man's voice spoke over her shoulder.

'Can I tempt you with my sweet potato fries?'

She turned around to see Greg grinning at her. He motioned towards a nearby stall. 'I'm offering an alternative to the chestnuts. Sweet potato fries are one of my specialities.'

'Maybe later, Greg,' she said, walking away.

Chapter Eight

Sylvie circled around the stalls, tactfully avoiding Greg and Zack. She ate some of her chestnuts but her appetite had been dulled by Zack's attitude. All her instincts were firing up, warning her to tread warily, causing feelings from the recent past, bitter experiences she'd swept aside, to resurface. Top of that list of angst was her split with Conrad. It had been a few weeks now since their break–up. Despite her bravado of calling him a weasel and agreeing with Marla that she was better off without him, that wound still sizzled, like someone had cut her with a burning blade.

Dating Conrad had been a double–edged sword experience. On one side he'd been handsome, successful, fun to be with, and their New York lifestyles worked well together on a surface level. They didn't have deep conversations where they discussed making a real commitment. They were just a fun loving couple.

On the other side he'd never cared about her work, her career. She doubted he even knew what she wanted. She'd tried telling him, but he just wasn't that interested. She often felt like she was talking into the void.

Maybe that's what she liked about Zack. From the first time they'd met he'd seemed interested in her. Yes, he was handsome, but it felt nice to talk to a man who cared to listen.

By now she was standing alone beside the large Christmas tree whose branches smelled of wonderful fresh pine and were adorned with shiny baubles and lights.

She'd been so deep in thought she hadn't noticed that Zack had gone. She glanced around her. He wasn't near the Christmas tree or the stalls. Music was starting to filter from the community hall and people were heading over there after eating their fill from the stalls.

She reckoned she'd go there too. The lights from the hall cast a glow across the snow and it looked warm and welcoming. She tugged her scarf up around her neck. The night had a really icy bite to it, or perhaps she was still sensing the cold shoulder Zack had given her earlier.

Her low heel shoes navigated the icy ground just fine, and a sense of anticipation of a party night and dancing swept aside her unsettled thoughts.

Inside the busy hall the tables that had been used for the quilting bee were pushed to the far side and set up as a buffet. Bowls of punch were available to those wanting refreshments, along with plates of sandwiches, snacks and potato chips. The deep red wine punch tempted her, so too did a cup of hot coffee.

The hall itself was decorated with garlands entwined with twinkle lights and colorful party balloons. The music was cheerful and couples were dancing in the center of the floor in front of the stage area.

Santa sat at the entrance of a grotto on stage where parents brought their kids up to meet him and receive a small gift. The delight on the children's faces was heartwarming.

Sylvie had hung her coat and scarf up before walking in. Her green velvet dress didn't look out of place and she was glad she'd worn it. She looked around at the people, searching for Zack but he wasn't there. Her heart sank a little.

Everyone seemed to be part of a family group or a couple. She was the only one on her own. Before she had a chance to feel self conscious, Ana hurried over to her, smiling and admiring Sylvie's dress.

'It looks great on you,' Ana beamed.

'Virginia told me you did the beadwork. It's really lovely.'

'Thanks. It's always nice to see our dresses being worn.' Ana held out the skirt of the pretty dress she was wearing. 'This is one of Virginia's designs. It's hard to resist her bargain rail.'

'Tell me about it,' said Sylvie. 'I bought four dresses and this purse.'

Ana laughed.

'I also heard you're getting married in the spring. Congratulations.'

Ana turned and pointed to a man standing near the buffet table pouring two glasses of punch. 'That's my guy over there. We're busy getting our new house ready for the wedding. He's a painter and decorator by trade.'

'Very handy,' said Sylvie.

'It sure is,' Ana agreed, then glanced around. 'I thought you'd be with Zack.'

'No, we're just friends, and I haven't seen him since earlier.'

'Zack's delivering some of the Christmas packages out to the homesteads,' Greg said, overhearing their conversation. 'There are storm warnings forecast for Christmastime and with it being only three days until Christmas Eve, Zack and several others are making sure the folks receive them. I'd have helped, but I was tending to my stall. He should be back later for the dancing.'

'Christmas packages?' Sylvie wondered what those were.

'They're mainly items for the kids, donated by the community,' Greg explained. 'It's a town tradition.'

'I remember being so excited to open my town package on Christmas morning when I was a kid.' Ana still sounded happy. 'I got a beautiful, hand sewn rag doll. It was made by Jessica's grandmother from scraps of pretty fabric. Her hair was pink yarn pleated into pigtails and tied with ribbons. I loved that doll and wanted to make one just like her. Her grandma taught me how to do it. It's what got me into sewing. I've been sewing ever since.'

Sylvie thought it must be wonderful to be part of a community. 'This town certainly knows how to look after its own.'

'That's what I love about small town living.' Ana motioned over towards her fiancé. 'And falling for guys like him.'

Ana's fiancé held up a glass of punch, indicating he'd got one for her. Ana nodded that she'd be right over. 'See you later, Sylvie, and come join us for a dance.'

Ana went back to her fiancé leaving Sylvie standing with Greg. He didn't have a partner so she wasn't the only one.

'You could always dance with me.' Greg gave her a sheepish grin. 'Unless you're still mad at me for stepping out of line recently.'

Any tension towards Greg faded. She nodded her acceptance to dance with him. 'I'm sorry I didn't get around to trying your sweet potato fries.'

He thumbed behind him towards the buffet.

Sylvie saw that fries were being served up.

'There's a kitchen through the back of the hall. The elves are busy cooking fries as we speak.'

'Shouldn't you be in there helping the elves?' she said.

'They let me out for good behavior to enjoy the dancing. I did all the prep work.'

People were keen to purchase the fries. Again, donation tins were set out rather than standard payment.

'Your fries seem popular, Greg.'

'It's all in the baking and making them caramelized. Sprinkle with salt and pepper. Maybe we should go get some before they're all gone, then we can dance.'

'Sounds fine by me.' As the tension in her eased, her appetite took over. She'd barely touched the roast chestnuts and hadn't eaten dinner before getting dressed for going out. Those caramelized fries looked so tasty and she enjoyed sweet potatoes. With a full night of dancing ahead of her, she figured she needed fuel to keep going.

Sylvie accompanied Greg over to the buffet. He insisted she take a seat at a table nearby while he collected their fries and coffee. He'd remembered how she liked her coffee from the one time she'd been in his cafe.

Greg brought the food and drinks over to her table, expertly balancing everything, used to serving in the cafe. He'd even brought napkins.

'There you go,' he said, placing her coffee down.

She took a sip. 'Just the way I like it.'

He sat opposite her. 'I have a good memory for people's tastes.'

'I was in your cafe once, Greg.'

'A good memory for important customers,' he corrected.

She took another sip and then ate one of the fries.

'What do you think?' he prompted her.

'Delicious.'

Smiling, he tucked into his fries and they sat together eating and chatting.

'The quilting bee members, including me, are making a wedding quilt for Ana.' Greg emphasized his inclusion.

'Lovely. I won't say a thing.' Sylvie kept her voice low.

'Ana knows, but she's pretending she doesn't, and we're pretending we don't know that she knows.'

Sylvie squinted at him. 'I think I get that.'

'Ana understands we would never let her get married without making her a special quilt for the occasion. We stitched an engagement quilt for her. It included hand appliquéd hearts and roses. So there was no way we were missing out on creating a bridal quilt.' He leaned across the table. 'It has white work embroidery in the center block and gold work on the wedding rings design. Totally gorgeous.'

'It sounds like a masterpiece.'

'We hope so. It's less practical than most of the quilts we've made at the quilting bee. We think Ana will keep it as an heirloom quilt. However, it could adorn their bed for years. I'm making her a quilted cushion to match. I love making cushions. They're easy to make and a lot quicker than a full quilt. I like playing around with the designs. I wish I was as good at art as you, but making cushions is like creating small pieces of fabric art that you can sit on your sofa and admire. At home, I have too many cushions.'

'You can never have too many cushions.' She didn't have enough in her apartment.

Greg seemed pleased with her attitude. 'A woman after my own heart. I'm liking you more and more.' His tone was light without any insinuation.

'You really must have a lot of quilting projects to sew. Nancy mentioned that you were making table runners for Christmas.'

Greg nodded. 'Loads of projects. But that's what's fun about sewing and quilting. It's nice to sew as a hobby and we all love fabric like crazy, but there's nothing quite as exciting as having a project that's wanted or needed rather than making something just because we like to sew.'

She told him about her Christmas quilt. 'I've made some progress with it, but I've been so busy recently trying to relax.'

'Busy trying to relax?' he summarized, giving her a grin.

'There's something wrong with that plan,' she admitted.

'Way wrong.'

She found herself laughing in Greg's company and was beginning to see what the ladies of the quilting bee liked about him.

'I'm glad we're getting along now.' She didn't want to keep her thoughts to herself.

'I'm an acquired taste,' he said.

'The quilting bee ladies seem to like you.'

'We have shared interests. Others, like Zack's ex, didn't care for me at all.'

Sylvie took the chance to ask about her. 'What was she like?'

He sighed and pondered his reply. 'I'm trying to be tactful here. She was... standoffish and fickle. Very beautiful though. Almost as tall as me with auburn hair and brown eyes. I'm not saying she was a tease, and I'm not saying she wasn't. She liked to be admired. If you didn't admire her, she found a reason to dislike you.'

'I assume from what you're telling me that you didn't admire her?'

'I did not. I thought she was a cold beauty. She'd done some modelling and made no secret that this town wasn't big enough for her. She wanted to move to California, Los Angeles to be precise.'

'I heard she moved there after splitting up with Zack.'

'Yep, she told him she'd decided she didn't love him anymore, without giving him any warning. As I say, she was fickle. Apart from her looks, none of us understood what Zack saw in her.'

'Nancy thinks she'll never come back here.'

'I agree with Nancy,' said Greg. 'She used to come into my cafe and be so picky. She found fault with everything. I think she did it just to annoy me. Shame on me that it worked every time.' He took a slug of coffee and shrugged off the memory of Zack's ex.

Sylvie had heard enough about her.

'How long have you had the cafe?' she asked, pulling the conversation back to a happier vibe.

'A few years. My grandfather started it up when he was around my age. Then the cooking gene skipped a generation. My father works as a ranger for one of the parks further north. I spent a lot of time hanging out here with my grandfather and loved learning to cook. I thought it was fun. I still do. It's not like work. I took over the cafe when he retired, but he still helps with the accounts. I hate paperwork.'

As they finished their fries and coffee, people started to form small groups for circle dancing. Ana waved over to them.

'Want to join in?' Greg asked Sylvie.

'I don't know how to do this type of dancing. Maybe I'll sit this one out, but you go ahead.'

A firm but friendly hand took hold of hers and encouraged her to have a go. 'Don't worry, Sylvie,' said Greg. 'I have two left feet and no sense of timing. Stick close to me and I'll make you look good.'

Laughing, she let him lead her into the dancing and made up the steps she didn't know as she went along. No one cared to correct anyone else. Everyone was simply having fun. Somewhere along the line Nate and Nancy had joined their circle. Holding hands between

99

Greg and Santa, Sylvie whirled and laughed around the dance floor to lively Christmas music.

As the pace of the dancing quickened, Sylvie thought she caught a glimpse of Zack standing near the stage watching her. On the next time around, he'd gone. She wondered if she'd imagined seeing him. He was wearing a blue open neck shirt and no recognizable jacket. Was it him? And if it was, had he disappeared again this evening?

Amid the hilarity of the dancing, especially when she realized that Greg had been telling the truth about his lack of ability, she didn't want to shout to him or Nate to ask if they'd seen Zack.

Instead she continued whirling around until she was almost out of breath. Luckily that coincided with the change of pace to a slow waltz that allowed everyone to calm down before another circle dance began.

Sylvie waltzed with Greg. 'I never could figure out the rhythm of a waltz,' he said, counting the steps and smiling at her. 'One, two, three...'

She laughed along with him.

'This is such a fun party.'

'I'm glad you're having a good time. This party is geared for everyone, for families to bring their kids,' he explained. 'The Christmas Eve party caters for kids too, but many people are at home tucking their kids in bed, ready for Santa arriving in the morning. This gives most folks the ability to enjoy at least one of the parties.' He looked at her. 'You'll be coming to the Christmas Eve party I hope.'

'Yes, definitely. I've even got a dress.'

'Well then, no excuses for you young lady.'

She was relieved he didn't pressure her into accompanying him. She liked his company but felt no special spark of attraction towards him. She knew that some relationships were slow burn and took time to ignite into something more. Right now, she didn't feel that it would. However, she was keeping that open mind she'd be advised about when it came to giving love a chance. Then again, wouldn't this put her slam dunk in the same position she felt she was in with Zack? Greg wasn't going to give up his grandfather's cafe and move to New York.

Greg's words jolted her. 'Nancy says you've rented the house until a couple of days after Christmas.'

'Yes, then I'll be heading home.' She said the words yet deep inside didn't feel at ease with them. Home. Her apartment. She'd hadn't missed anything about it. Not a single thing. But wasn't that the purpose of coming here on vacation, to leave work and the city behind and just enjoy a small town Christmas?

'Do you think you'll come back? I mean, you could rent the house for a spring break, maybe even go to Ana's wedding. She's getting married around Easter time. The town looks great that time of year, and Nancy I'm sure would be happy to have you stay again. It's a great house, isn't it?'

'It's lovely. Perfect in fact.'

'The house belongs to Nancy's side of the family, but Nate and her have their own home, so rather than sell the property when it fell into Nancy's keeping, they decided to lease it out to holidaymakers.'

'Do you live in the town?' she asked him.

'I have a house with a bit of land near Jessica and the sheriff. I grow a lot of my own vegetables there. I use them in the cafe. This time of year everything is frosted over, but it produces a good yield in the warmer months.'

'You're quite a busy man.'

'But not too busy to relax.'

She smiled remembering what she'd said earlier.

He leaned close and whispered as they danced. 'Don't look now, but Zack is glaring at us from behind the grotto.'

Sylvie immediately looked up at the stage.

'I said don't look,' Greg hissed.

Sylvie looked away. She spoke to Greg through a tight smile. 'Is he wearing a blue shirt?'

'A blue shirt and a white–lipped expression,' Greg confirmed.

'I thought I saw him watching us earlier.'

'Would you like me to waltz us over to the buffet out of his direct view?' he offered.

'Yes.'

Greg made a clumsy move as he waltzed them away. 'Sorry, I'm so clumsy.'

'Don't worry about it. Since I arrived in town I've tripped and fallen into a few snowdrifts and face planted near a snowman.'

'Why does that sound exciting?'

Sylvie chided him playfully. 'You're incorrigible.'

'Is that a good sign or not?'

'I'm not sure,' she said, trying not to laugh.

They stopped dancing and stood beside the buffet.

'What is Zack doing up at the grotto?' she asked Greg.

'Pretending to sort the stage lighting. If he tightens those light bulbs any more he'll go up like a beacon.'

Sylvie had a peek. Zack's body language was head to toe frustration.

'What's up with him tonight?' said Greg. 'Have the two of you quarreled?'

'No, we parted last night on... friendly terms.'

'Very friendly from what I've heard.'

Sylvie accepted a glass of punch from Greg. 'Nothing happened.'

'Nothing except a cozy dinner for two, a romantic horse and carriage ride around the town — twice, and a snowball fight that ended with Zack pinning you down on the front lawn.'

'Is there anything you don't know?' She couldn't be angry at him.

'Did he kiss you, or was it an almost kiss?'

'Did your sneaky source miss that bit?'

'Neighborhood watch. They saw everything. They told Nancy, Nancy told Jessica and she told me.'

'No, he didn't kiss me. Okay?'

'Shh! Zack's heading over here — and he's not smiling.'

Sylvie's tummy tightened into a knot. 'What do you think I should do?'

Greg linked his arm through hers and swept her away. 'Let's see how the elves are getting on in the kitchen shall we?'

Zack blinked and Sylvie had gone.

From his vantage point on stage behind the grotto he'd been able to glimpse her having a great time with Greg. Then people had crowded around them, obscuring his view, so he'd decided to jump down from the stage and go over to where they were seated. It was probably better for everyone that he wasn't near the grotto. Having a face like thunder wasn't conducive to a happy time with Santa. And every time he'd heard someone tell Santa what they wished for Christmas, he'd found himself mentally answering that he'd settle

102

for having things smoothed over with Sylvie and that she'd go with him as his date to the Christmas Eve party. He was sure if he'd admitted this, Nate would've told him those wishes were within his own grasp if he wasn't so stubborn.

Zack made his way through the couples dancing, and headed towards where he'd last seen her with Greg. She'd been smiling and chatting happily. He'd seen that smile before when she'd grinned at Cookie, so it was clear that she liked the guy.

Zack glanced over at the buffet table. Perhaps Greg had taken her there to ply her with more sweet talk and potato fries?

Under other circumstances the delicious aroma of those fries would've tempted him, but the churning in the pit of his stomach vetoed eating anything.

Unable to figure out where they'd gone, he decided to ask Nancy. If she didn't know, all was surely lost.

'I don't know where Sylvie is, Zack. The last time I saw her she was sitting chatting with Greg, eating fries and then they were waltzing.'

'That's the last I saw her too, Nancy. Then they disappeared.'

Nancy didn't seem to know about the video, so that was some consolation. Nate had kept a secret from Nancy. Zack owed him a gold star.

Zack looked around them. 'They have to be around here somewhere.'

'I doubt they'd be canoodling backstage,' a quilting friend of Nancy's commented passing by on her way to refill her glass with punch.

Zack's eyes widened. The thought hadn't crossed his mind. Now it did, causing even more churning inside him.

Nancy rested a reassuring hand on Zack's arm. 'She'll be doing no such thing. We all know who she likes.' She gave him a knowing look.

'She certainly seemed happy with Greg.'

'They're just friends,' Nancy assured him.

That's what Sylvie and him were supposed to be.

'I heard them talking about quilting,' Nancy added, hoping this would make him feel better.

Zack could no more sew than he could fly to the moon, but right now he'd be prepared to give quilting a go if it meant he'd be on the same wavelength with Sylvie.

'Greg was also talking shop with her, telling her about his cafe and cooking.' Nancy's comments were well–meaning, but piled more pressure on to Zack's shoulders. Quilting and cooking. A double pincher movement that was a winning way to a woman's heart if ever he'd heard one. Zack could cook okay. But it wasn't his forte. He couldn't compete with Greg whose culinary expertise had made a success of the cafe.

Zack enjoyed the food at Greg's cafe. He had sometimes taken his ex there, though she preferred to dine in fine restaurants. She was a finicky eater and Greg had always gone out of his way to accommodate her whims without a word of complaint. Greg hadn't tried to make a play for her either, like some other guys in town. Zack had Greg figured for a charmer with the ladies and he invariably seemed to have women buzzing around him, but when it came to Zack's ex–girlfriend, there'd been no hint of that from him.

Greg had appeared to understand the rules between guys and the women they were dating. Unwritten rules. There were lines that were never crossed. Stealing another guy's girl from under his nose was one of them. Unless he was prepared to face the consequences and put his own nose in jeopardy.

When it came to Sylvie, Greg seemed to have forgone those rules. Okay, Zack admitted, he wasn't actually dating Sylvie, but everyone knew there was a slight possibility things were heading that way if she hung around town long enough. Greg understood that and had chosen to flaunt the rules in Zack's face tonight, charming her with talk of sewing and tasty food. Those were the types of things that women admired in a man, they created a warm fuzzy feeling. His architects drawing board couldn't compete with those.

Zack looked around and ran a frustrated hand through his hair, pushing it back from his troubled forehead. Since he'd first met Sylvie, his hair had never been more ruffled in his entire life.

'Why don't you have a glass of punch?' Nancy suggested.

The only punch Zack felt was the one in his gut from having seen Sylvie with Greg. The way she'd smiled at him...

Nancy didn't wait for Zack's response. She poured him a glass whether he wanted it or not. It was in his hand, and he found himself slurping it in one gulp and handing it back for a refill.

Nancy held the empty glass and rested a hand on Zack's shoulder. 'On second thoughts, why don't you go and look for her outside. They could've gone out to gaze at the stars or the Christmas tree lights.'

Zack nodded firmly and walked away. He'd check outside. Maybe that's where they were.

Jessica came over to Nancy. 'What's up with Zack? He seems wound up about something.'

'He's riled that Sylvie was having a fun time with Greg. Now we don't know where they are. I sent him outside to look for them — and to cool off.'

The sheriff was with Jessica. 'Temperatures are falling and there's a warning of a blizzard heading our way. We're hoping it'll blow over. If not, we'd better get ready for a whiteout.'

Nancy shivered at the thought of it.

Jessica commented to Nancy about Sylvie's dress. 'Sylvie looked so pretty in that green velvet tonight. No wonder she's setting guys hearts alight. It's just not like Zack to look so mean. I haven't seen him frown like that since he last got his heart broken.'

'I think he's worried that Greg is wriggling into her affections before he can tell her how he feels,' said Nancy.

Nate came over and joined them. 'I thought Zack was still mad at her.' The words were out before he realized.

Nancy frowned at Nate. 'Mad at her? Why would Zack be mad at Sylvie?'

Nate tried to hide his guilt, but Nancy knew him too well.

'There's trouble brewing for these young people. If you know something, Nate, you'd better speak up,' Nancy told him firmly.

Nate tugged anxiously on his Santa beard. 'I promised Zack I wouldn't tell anyone.'

'I'm not anyone. I'm your wife. There are no secrets between us,' Nancy reminded him.

Nate squirmed on the spot. 'I promised him...'

Before Nancy could question him further, a mother approached them with her seven year old daughter.

The little girl was clutching a letter. She gazed up at Nate and gave him a shy smile. 'Hi, Santa.'

'She wants to send a letter to Santa,' the mother explained to him. 'But she doesn't know the exact address at the North Pole.'

'Well, let me help you out there,' Nate boomed cheerfully. 'We've got a special post box beside the grotto. I collect all the letters and read them personally later. Want to mail it there?' He pointed to a shiny red mailbox on the stage.

The child nodded. 'Yes please, Santa.'

Taking the opportunity to deal with the little girl's request, and evade further quizzing from Nancy, Nate led the child and her mother away.

Nancy leaned close to Jessica. 'I'll wriggle the truth out of Nate later.'

'Let me know what he says.'

Nancy nodded at Jessica. She couldn't begin to think what type of secret Zack had told her husband. And why had he revealed whatever it was to Nate? When two guys were in cahoots about something foolhardy it usually meant one of two things — there was a woman involved and one of them wanted advice about romancing her. Or, there was definitely a woman involved and one of them really wanted advice about romancing her. Nate wasn't a two–timer, so that boiled down to Zack and whatever had happened between him and Sylvie.

Chapter Nine

'And that's how to make sure your sweet potato fries are never soggy.' Greg smiled at Sylvie after explaining his technique to cook the perfect caramelized fries.

The community hall kitchen was busy with helpers dressed as elves rustling up food and refreshments for the party. A snowman was doing the washing up, while someone dressed as a Christmas pudding whipped up the hot chocolate drinks.

'I'll try that, Greg. Thanks for the advice.' Sylvie had never attempted making anything with sweet potatoes, but if she ever did, she now knew how to avoid cooking soggy fries.

Greg grinned at her as the organized chaos swirled around them. 'I guess my hope is to meet someone who shares my interest in cooking. To have a relationship like Nate and Nancy.'

'They certainly are a prime example of togetherness in business and as a couple,' Sylvie admitted. She just couldn't picture herself helping Greg harvest his pumpkins and then making them into pies for customers at the cafe. No doubt there was a woman out there somewhere, even if she'd yet to arrive in town, that would be Greg's ideal partner. It simply wasn't her, though it felt good to have a friend like him.

Greg was astute enough to pick up on her vibe. 'Come on,' he said, 'let's go and enjoy the dancing.'

As they walked back through to the hub of the party they met Nate on his way to the kitchen.

'Ah, there you two are,' said Nate. 'Everyone's been wondering where you'd disappeared to.'

Sylvie spoke up. 'Greg was giving me cooking advice.'

'But you're missing out on all the dancing.' Nate smiled at Sylvie. 'I do believe you promised me a dance.'

Sylvie blinked. 'I did?' She couldn't remember any such promise, then she saw the direct glare Santa was giving her and changed her tone to the affirmative. 'I did.'

Nate held out the crook of his arm and she linked her arm through his.

At that moment, a six foot elf came hurrying out of the kitchen. The bobble on his hat wobbled from the effort to catch up with them.

'Greg. We're running out of your savory sprinkle mix for the fries. Is it three parts cayenne and two parts garlic with one part pepper?' the man asked. He worked part–time at Greg's cafe and was helping out with the party catering. 'Or is it two parts garlic with one part pepper and three parts cayenne?' He paused, confused. 'Hang on a minute.'

'I'll be right there,' Greg assured the elf who ran back to the kitchen with the bobble on his hat bouncing like crazy.

Nate smiled at Greg. 'I'll take Sylvie back through to the dancing while you handle the catering crisis. Oh and, we're running short on the little snowball cakes for the kids. That's what I was coming to get.'

'Leave it to me, Nate. I'm on it.' Greg nodded to Sylvie and hurried away to the kitchen.

Sylvie let Nate escort her back through to the dancing. She gave his arm a squeeze. 'Thank you.'

'One of the elves tipped me off that Greg was teaching you to chop and blanche sweet potatoes.'

'Santa to the rescue.' She smiled up at him and kept her promise of that dance.

Zack stood outside the community hall listening to the carol singers and gazing up at the stars. There was no sign of Sylvie and Greg. He figured they were inside enjoying the party.

The icy air whipped around him, cutting through the fabric of his shirt, but the cold didn't bother him half as much as the thought of going back inside and seeing Sylvie and Greg together.

'What are you doing out here in the cold, Zack?'

He glanced round and saw the sheriff approaching.

'I, eh... I was just looking for someone.'

The sheriff nodded thoughtfully. 'Sylvie's inside dancing with Santa if that's who you're looking for.'

Zack gazed down and smiled. The sheriff knew fine what was going on.

'Can I ask you something?' said Zack.

'Sure.'

'When you used to drive back and forth from New York to see Jessica, before you were married, did you ever think maybe this isn't going to work out?'

The sheriff's jaw set into a firm expression. 'Never. Not once. That first time I met her in New York when she came to the quilt event, I thought... I've just met the woman I'm going to marry. And that didn't make any sense. We didn't know each other. I worked as a security guy in the city, and she came from a small town I hadn't even heard of. But I knew, I just knew. There was something about her, and I had this feeling like I was looking at what I'd always hoped for, what I needed, what would make me happy.'

'Did Jessica feel the same way?' Zack asked him.

The sheriff nodded. 'She told me later that she got anxious every time she thought that she'd nearly cancelled her trip to New York. She's never been one for the city, but she sure does love her quilting, and that's what had encouraged her to make the trip. It made her anxious to think we'd never have met.'

Zack took in every word as the sheriff continued to tell him what happened.

'I needed to reassure her. I told Jessica that we would've met. I'd have visited the town sooner or later and we'd have got together.'

'Is that true?'

The sheriff grinned. 'Nope.'

Zack smiled.

'During those drives back to New York I got to do a lot of thinking — and listened to baseball games on the radio,' the sheriff added with a chuckle. 'But I soon realized that I wasn't driving home any longer. Home was where Jessica lived. The city was where I happened to rent an apartment and worked as a security guard, but it wasn't home. And you're talking to a guy who was born and raised in the city.'

'Is this small town enough for you?'

'Are you kidding me?' The sheriff gave Zack an incredulous look. 'Snow Bells Haven has everything a man and his family could ever wish for.'

Zack nodded his appreciation. 'Thanks for the talk.'

The sheriff patted him on the shoulder. 'I'm not one for giving advice. I think everyone has to make their own decisions. However, if I had to give you one piece of advice tonight, it would be to go back in there and ask that lovely young woman to dance with you.'

'That's good advice,' Zack confirmed.

'You're tootin' is it. And don't be moping because she was dancing with Greg. Get in there and fight for her. Do you think I'd have let a Greg sweet talk my Jessica away from me?'

Zack didn't think so for a second.

'Because if you do, you don't know me very well.' The sheriff gave Zack a confident wink and then continued on. 'I'm going to check on the weather situation, but I'll be back to do some more dancing with Jessica.'

The grin the sheriff gave him made Zack smile broadly, and boosted his determination to take that piece of advice.

Sylvie and Nate danced to the slow beat of a traditional festive song.

'There's something I'd like to tell you,' Nate began hesitantly.

'What is it?' Sylvie asked.

'I was supposed to keep it a secret, and I did, then I let slip a hint about it and now, well, Nancy figures I know something and I'm not telling.'

'You know something and Nancy doesn't?'

Nate gave a resigned shrug as they danced. 'She's going to find out, and I just wanted you to know that—'

Zack tapped Nate on the shoulder. 'May I cut in?'

Nate stopped dancing and relinquished his hold on Sylvie. Although surprised to see Zack, she fell into step with him and allowed him to lead her in a slow dance around the floor.

'Your hands are cold,' she remarked softly.

'Sorry, I was outside.'

'What were you doing?' She tried to sound casual while her heart beat a fast rhythm. Feeling his hand hold hers and his other hand touch the small of her back sent excited shivers through her. Even though she was protected by the velvet of her dress she felt his touch burn through her like hot, white fire.

The blue of his shirt intensified the color of his eyes, and with the top two buttons of his shirt undone, she felt herself unravel. She was drawn to his strength and stature. His masculinity up close had a potent effect on her. Part of her wanted to step back from him and breathe. The dominant part of her refused to let go of him. All sensibility gave way to the urge to enjoy every heart pounding second of this dance with him. It would end when the music stopped, but she was certain the memory of dancing with Zack under the

110

Christmas lights to one of her favorite festive songs would burn bright in her thoughts forever.

His words drifted through to her as he answered her question. 'I was talking to the sheriff and doing a lot of hard thinking.'

His intense gaze didn't falter. He looked at her, only her.

No man had ever looked at her like this before. His direct gaze said more to her in that moment than words ever could. It said everything both of them hadn't dared express these past few days.

Her breathing became ragged, but she still wouldn't let go of the moment.

She'd never seen Zack look so handsome, strong and yet vulnerable. It was a potent mix she found hard to resist. In that long, lingering gaze he was telling her how he really felt about her.

As they continued to dance around the floor she was vaguely aware of the reaction of others nearby. Nancy smiled warmly, happy for them. Jessica nudged Ana and they exchanged a smiling nod. Ana's fiancé put his arm around his bride to be and gave her a squeeze, as if seeing Zack and Sylvie reminded him how lucky he was to have Ana. And Greg gave Sylvie a friendly but resigned smile and then asked another young woman to dance with him.

Zack wished he was as charming as Greg when it came to talking to women, or as warm natured as Nate, even as confident as the sheriff. But he couldn't think how to explain to Sylvie about his recent behavior, his gruff manner, the way he'd cold shouldered her earlier... The thoughts beat him up inside. He just wanted to pull her close and apologize for every stupid second of his foolhardiness.

That was the moment he decided he wasn't going to mention about the video. In the grand scheme of things, it didn't really matter. What mattered was being here with Sylvie. What a stubborn fool he'd been. He'd let his feelings override all common sense. Standing outside in the cold had given him a taste of what his life would be like without her.

Tomorrow morning he'd take Cookie along to Sylvie's house to meet her. Then there would be no need for secrets.

The music stopped and changed to a different beat. People seemed to recognize the song and started to get ready for more lively circle dancing.

Zack held Sylvie's hands and looked straight at her. 'I have to talk to Nate for a moment. Don't go anywhere. I'll be right back for the circle dance.'

Sylvie smiled and nodded as Zack ran over and up on to the stage to talk to Nate at the grotto.

'Nate!' Zack's tone was urgent. 'Forget everything I told you about the video. I've decided to let it go. I'm not going to mention it to Sylvie.'

Nate agreed with this decision. 'I didn't tell anyone, but Nancy knows there's something I'm keeping a secret.'

Zack looked concerned.

Nate stood up from the grotto. 'Leave it with me. I'll deal with Nancy.' He sounded confident.

Zack took him at his word. 'Thanks, Nate.'

As Zack ran back to Sylvie, Nate hurried over to Nancy and pulled her aside for a moment. 'Zack told me a secret. I promised not to tell anyone. Now he wants to forget about the whole thing. I'm concerned if I tell you, then everyone's going to know. It could ruin things for Zack and Sylvie.'

Nate couldn't have been more upfront with Nancy. She nodded firmly, and linked her arm through his. 'Well, let's dance then, honey. There will always be more secrets in this town that's for sure.'

Nate gave his wife a loving kiss on the cheek, and then they joined the others for the circle dancing.

Nancy held hands with Nate and Zack. Sylvie held hands with Zack and the sheriff. The atmosphere in the hall felt like it had lifted, and as the upbeat music started, Sylvie geared up for a fun night of party dancing.

During a break, Zack went to get Sylvie a glass of punch. Nate sauntered over to her.

'That thing I was going to tell you about — forget it. It doesn't matter,' Nate said to her.

'Are you sure? I don't mind if you want to talk,' she offered.

The kindness in her voice made him smile. 'No, it's fine. But there is something I wanted to ask you. I always try to buy Nancy something special for her Christmas. I've got a few things put by and wrapped under the Christmas tree. She's figured out what every gift is.'

Sylvie laughed. 'It's not easy keeping secrets from Nancy.'

'Tell me about it!' He then confided in her. 'She loves fabric. I have no idea what type of fabric is suitable for her quilting. Obviously I could ask Jessica's advice, but those two... it still wouldn't be a surprise. So I thought maybe you could buy fabric from Jessica's shop for me. That way, it would be the first gift I've given Nancy in years that would surprise her.'

'I'd be happy to do that for you, Nate. Would you like me to buy what I think she'd like, or do you have any suggestions.'

Nate put his hands up. 'I'll leave it entirely to you. I'll give you the money tomorrow.'

'I'll buy it, then you can settle up with me,' she suggested.

'You're a sweetheart.'

'I'm happy to do that for you.'

Nate nodded his thanks and went back to Nancy.

Zack brought two glasses of punch over and handed one to Sylvie. 'Everything okay with Nate?'

'Yes, we were just talking about Christmas stuff.' She didn't elaborate and Zack didn't pry further. He'd had his fill of secrets for one night.

'I'd like to propose a toast,' he said, raising his glass. 'To a night of great dancing and wonderful company.'

'And I'd like to add to that toast. To one of the happiest Christmastimes I've had in years.'

They tipped their glasses together and smiled warmly at each other.

Another slow dance started.

'Shall we?' said Zack.

Sylvie took his hand and let him lead her on to the dance floor. As he held her close she hoped he didn't feel the pounding of her heart against his chest. No man had ever affected her as intensely as Zack. Dancing with Conrad had never felt this special. Conrad was a smooth dancer and an even smoother talker. They'd been quite the social couple in New York, but most of the parties they attended were linked to his career on the stock market. She hadn't known anyone personally, and sometimes neither had he, but attending was part of the social scene they circulated in. She didn't miss a minute of it. She'd never felt like she'd belonged in that world. Now here

113

she was welcomed into a small town party where she felt comfortable and at home, dancing with Zack.

They enjoyed a couple of dances then the evening was brought to an abrupt close.

The sheriff came hurrying in and made an announcement from the stage. 'The blizzard warnings have increased folks. It looks like it's going to hit the town later tonight. So if any of you want to get going, now would be the time to head back home before you get caught in the snowstorm.'

People started to say their goodnights and leave. They organized giving rides home to those who'd walked to the party, making sure no one was left on their own.

'Cell phone reception is down,' the sheriff said. 'And some of the lines have been affected, so take care out there. Keep an eye on each other folks.'

Sylvie tried to access her phone. 'I can't get a signal,' she said to Zack. Not that she needed it, but she wasn't used to feeling cut off from things because of the weather.

'Don't worry,' Zack assured her. 'I'll make sure you get home safe. My car's outside. I'll drive you there.'

The sheriff approached Zack. 'Your name is on the list of volunteers to help out if needed, but if you want to take Sylvie home that's okay.'

'I'm going to drive her home and then I'll be right back,' said Zack.

The sheriff nodded. 'Thanks, Zack.'

'I'll get my coat.' Sylvie hurried to pick up her coat and scarf.

Zack grabbed his jacket and they left together.

Outside the community hall was busy with people heading home in all directions. Snow swirled around and an icy wind blew along the street.

'I'm parked over there.' Zack pointed to his car nearby.

Sylvie wrapped her scarf around her neck and made a dash for the car. Zack shielded her and helped her into the vehicle, then ran round and jumped into the driver's seat.

'What is it you've volunteered to do?' she asked as they drove off.

Zack turned up the heater. 'The town always asks for volunteers, capable people to help out the sheriff's office and other local services during emergencies. Nate is a regular volunteer. Often we're not needed, but it makes sense to have us on stand by. If someone's car gets stuck in the snow, or they become stranded and in need of a ride to safety, we'll pick them up.'

The snow was becoming heavier. Luckily it wasn't far to her house and she was grateful for the ride especially as she hadn't worn her boots.

He drove up to her house and pulled over, but kept the car engine running.

'I'll wait to see you get inside safely. Make sure to keep warm. Get some sleep. The worst of this may have blown over by the morning.'

'Will you be okay?' she asked him.

'The community hall remains open,' said Zack. 'It provides a base for the emergency workers to take a break from the cold and grab a hot drink. And it gives shelter to anyone caught out in these conditions.'

She felt like she should somehow be helping too, but sensed she was more of a hindrance to Zack if he had to look out for her as well as himself and others.

'Be careful, won't you?' She sounded concerned.

'I always am. Now go inside and stay safe. You know how to light a log fire now don't you.'

'I do.'

'Then light it and get some heat into the house in case the power lines are temporarily affected by the storm.'

'I'll do that,' she said firmly.

'And call me if you need anything.'

She had a grip on her cell phone and held it up. 'No signal.'

His lips pressed into a firm line. 'There's a landline phone in the house, but you wouldn't be able to contact me unless I was at home.' Then he had an idea, and reached into the car's glove compartment. He pulled out a couple of two–way radios. 'Do you know how to use one of these?'

'A two–way radio? I haven't used one of those since I was a kid.'

He clicked one of the buttons. 'Press this to transmit, then let go of the button to receive my reply.' He handed her one of the radios.

'So if I press this you'll pick up?'

115

'Yeah. I'll keep mine in my pocket.' He put it in his jacket pocket to reassure her it would be on him at all times when he was out.

She felt better knowing she had some way of contacting him, though she really had no intention of doing so.

'Do you want me to help you up to the front door?' he offered. 'That wind is a fierce one.'

'No,' she said quickly, trying to appear capable and not wanting to delay him any longer.

He leaned across her and opened the door for her against the force of the wind.

For a second their faces were close enough to touch. His lips were a breath away from hers.

Taking a calming breath she jumped out of the car and made a run up the garden path to the front door. She opened it and stepped inside, turning and waving to him.

Through the flurries of snowflakes, she saw him wave back to her, then he drove off.

As the snow blew down the road, she watched his car tail lights disappear into the night, then went inside and closed the door against the biting cold.

The first thing she did was build the fire, adding extra logs as it started to burn. The Christmas tree lights gave a warmth to the lounge, and she set the radio down beside her laptop.

The lines must have been affected already because she couldn't access the Internet. The connection was patchy and timed out when she tried to go online.

She closed the laptop, changed out of her dress into cozy nightwear, and made herself a hot drink.

Wearing warm socks and slippers, she sat beside the fire, cupping her coffee and gazing into the flames. What a night it had been. Nothing like what she'd expected. First Zack was standoffish, then he seemed jealous of Greg, but later he'd asked her to dance and they'd ended the night on a note of possibility. She hadn't read the signals she was receiving from him wrong. She was attracted to him and she was sure he felt it too.

She wondered how the night would've ended if the storm hadn't cut it short. Would they have taken a romantic stroll along the main street, following the route they'd taken during the horse and carriage ride?

She would never know, and guessing only sent her thoughts into a tailspin.

She had to get a grip on her emotions, she told herself firmly. She either had to stop now before she got involved with him, for things were surely heading that way. Or she had to take a chance and risk a broken heart if she got to like him too much and missed him when her vacation was over. The third option was a tricky one. Was there a way for them to be together, despite the distance on the map? Was there?

It was difficult to reconcile the issues. They lived different lives in different parts of the country. One of them would have to compromise and give up their lifestyle in favor of the other.

As the flames burned bright in the fire, she put the guard up to contain any sparks and went to bed.

If only the spark of attraction she felt every time she was near Zack could be so easily contained. Maybe she needed to keep her guard up a little longer, just to see where their friendship would lead, and then make her decision whether or not to become involved with Zack.

She climbed into bed and watched the storm increase in pace until the garden was a complete whiteout. She kept the radio on the beside table within easy reach, surprised at the comfort it gave her knowing he was there if she needed him.

Zack drummed his fingers on the steering wheel as he drove away from Sylvie's house. She'd never know how much it pained him to leave her alone under these treacherous conditions.

He was fine about keeping his word to the sheriff and wanted to help out. No question about that. However, he hoped Sylvie built that log fire and kept herself safe indoors. He didn't take her for a fool, or incapable of looking after herself. Certainly not. But she wasn't used to conditions like this in a small town. When a storm hit them it often hit them hard. Those with experience knew what to do, but would Sylvie be tempted to go outside?

Those cartwheels in the snow still flickered through his mind. And the ice sliding. Despite the wobbly spins, those were the daring traits of a woman who would throw caution aside in favor of fun.

He shook his head. What if she was watching the snowstorm out the window and thought it would be fun to venture outside, even if only in the garden?

Visions of a frozen solid sugar cookie flashed across his thoughts, causing his heart to lurch. She surely wouldn't be so foolish as to go out in the snow. However, he'd known holidaymakers do this a few years ago. Thankfully, the sheriff had been alerted that they were in trouble and so they were rescued before any harm came to them. But people from out of the town, especially those from the city, often didn't have enough respect for how dangerous conditions could become.

Zack bit his lip, and for a moment he was tempted to turn the car around and go check on her. Then he remembered — the radio. He could call her, remind her to stay safe, if only to help him keep a clear head to deal with the stormy night.

He picked up the radio and then hesitated. Would this make him look like an overprotective guy? Some women, especially independent ones like Sylvie, might not like that. He was still getting to know her. Did he know her well enough to make that decision?

His finger hovered over the call button. It would be reasonable to check up on her. And yet... he'd only just left her. She was probably still trying to get the fire to light or tucked up in bed asleep. If he called he could wake her.

He withdrew his finger from triggering the call, hoping he'd made the right decision.

Chapter Ten

Sylvie couldn't sleep. She kept watching the snowstorm swirling outside her bedroom window — and thinking about Zack.

Despite being warm and comfy under the covers, the sound of the storm whipping against the houses and the trees outside sent shivers of concern through her.

Throwing back the patchwork quilt, she climbed out of bed, stepped into a pair of slippers, pulled a sweater on over her nightwear, picked up the radio and padded into the lounge.

The fire was still burning and she topped it up with a couple of logs. The scent of the Christmas tree seemed more intense when the fire was lit, and she liked how the aroma from the logs mingled with the pine, filling the room with a real festive fragrance. There was nothing to beat it on a cold, wintry night like this.

She went over to the window and peered out, but there was no sign of Zack's car parked anywhere nearby. He wasn't home yet. The other cars parked in driveways and outside the houses were already covered in snow. The outdoor lights on the Christmas trees and decorations glowed warmly amid the frozen landscape. Most people were asleep for the evening with only a few nightlights shining from the windows. It made her feel that she was the only person up and pacing around watching the storm instead of being sensibly tucked up in bed.

As she walked over to the fire she thought she heard the sound of a car driving past, but by the time she hurried back to the window to peer out it had gone. Most likely it was one of the emergency vehicles or someone from the sheriff's department checking up on the road situation. It certainly wasn't a night to be outside, even though that's where Zack was. Or maybe he was in the community hall on standby?

She flicked a glance at the radio and bit her lip. If she called him now, perhaps he'd think she required his help and would come to her rescue only to find she'd been worrying about him unnecessarily. Zack was needed to assist others in jeopardy from the storm. To call him was selfish.

She heated her hands at the fire and listened to the comforting sound of the logs crackling in the stillness of the lounge as the blizzard blew outside the window.

There would be no venturing out to build a snowman in these conditions, or dressing up in warm layers of clothing to stand outside in the garden for a few minutes to experience the energy of the elements. Nope. Even though this thought had occurred to her and been instantly dismissed.

The warmth of the fire brought a rosy glow to her cheeks. The lounge had a cozy, Christmassy atmosphere with the tree all lit up. She thought herself lucky. But this didn't stop her feeling edgy.

Whenever she was unsettled at home, work always soothed her frayed nerves or eased whatever thoughts were bugging her. She had plenty of wayward thoughts this evening, the majority involving Zack. Although she could've done some sewing, stitching a pile of pretty hexies for her Christmas quilt, she knew it wouldn't take her mind off Zack. Work was a reliable option.

She set up her artwork supplies on the desk beside the fire. A few design ideas had crossed her mind recently, so she decided to paint them using the watercolors and the gouache Zack had given her. The thoughtful extras he'd added came in handy, including a selection of paint brushes in an assortment of sizes from the finest tip for detailed work to a flat brush, and a fuller brush that was ideal for creating washes of color.

After sketching the designs in pencil, she set to work painting them.

Chestnuts were one of the first things she painted using various shades of russet, bronze and gold tones. She thought about the chestnuts roasting earlier in the evening and tried to capture the rich colors and the shiny texture.

Some of her top designs had been created late at night or in the early hours of the morning in her apartment in New York. She could work for several hours without any interruptions and emerge tired but triumphant having finished a number of designs. These bursts of creative energy helped her meet the constant deadlines for her work.

It also helped that her designs were part of a collection. This gave her a theme to focus on. Each design had to complement, match or blend with the others in the collection. The fall theme of this new collection was one she was keen to draw. Autumnal tones were a delight to work with and she envisaged that this particular palette would make a lovely collection of fabrics. The warm bronzes and coppers offset with calming green tones would create the perfect balance of nature, and hopefully some beautiful designs. Within the concepts, she had to picture what would work commercially, so that Marla and the home decor company could use them on bed linen, table covers, curtains and cushions. This was one element Sylvie loved — creating designs for items that people would use in their homes. And then there was the adaptability of her designs to be suitable for prints on quilting fabric. She enjoyed the challenges her work presented, and felt these kept making her push herself to create fresh ideas.

She completed the first design by adding details to the chestnuts. It wasn't quite to a botanical level, but the detailing created a striking pattern on different colorways from pale cream to burnished gold. The second version of this design had copper tone leaves added to the chestnut artwork. She continued to work on variations of the theme, including a scattering of small leaves in muted greens that gave movement and interest to the pattern.

As always when she was on a roll with her designs, she lost track of the time. She hadn't even stopped to make a cup of coffee. It was only when she noticed that the fire was burning low and if she wanted to keep it going she'd need to throw more logs on.

Satisfied she'd made good progress with her design work, she cleared away her paints and let the fire flicker its last.

Zack sheltered from the storm at the entrance of the community hall. He gazed out at the snow covered street and drank a cup of coffee alongside Nate.

Zack's jacket was zipped up to the neck and he cupped his hands around the coffee for warmth. Nate still wore his Santa outfit as it provided a padded buffer against the cold.

'The sheriff says there's no sign of anyone else needing assistance tonight,' said Zack, thankful everyone was safe. 'He thinks we should go home now and get some sleep. He'll contact us if things change. It's looking like the storm will blow over by the morning and the roads into town will be cleared by the afternoon.' He gazed up at the sky. It certainly looked like the worst of the storm was over.

'I'll be heading home then. Nancy will be waiting up for me.'

Zack drank the remainder of his coffee, thinking it must be nice to be going home to someone he loved who cared enough to wait up for him. He'd never had that type of close relationship, but he hoped one day he would.

'I think you've made the right decision to forget about the video,' Nate told him. 'Some things are better left in the past. Confronting her about Cookie isn't going to help build your relationship with her.'

Zack nodded, agreeing with everything Nate had said, especially about not confronting her.

'Thanks for keeping quiet about the video and smoothing things over with Nancy. As for Sylvie, I don't have a relationship with her yet.'

'You could've fooled me. From the way you two were dancing together, I assumed you were going to become a firm couple.'

Zack knew that people would be looking at him dancing with Sylvie and sensing the spark of attraction between them. 'I'm still taking things easy with her.'

Nate laughed. 'Is that why you drove past her house at least twice tonight?'

Zack smiled at him. 'You noticed?'

'I think everyone from me to the sheriff noticed.'

Zack looked down and scuffed his boots in the snow. 'The sheriff said a bunch of stuff tonight that got me thinking what to do about Sylvie. It boils down to the fact that one of us would have to give up their lifestyle in favor of the other.'

Nate nodded his acknowledgment about the predicament. 'I like Sylvie. I felt comfortable with her the first time she walked into the store to buy groceries and looking for logs.'

Zack smiled at the thought of how proud she was that she could light a fire. 'She's got the hang of building a log fire now.'

'She isn't like most city folks I've met. I keep forgetting she's from New York. It's the same with the sheriff. I forget he was once a city guy. He seems like he's always lived here in town. And I think Sylvie's like that, or has the potential to be like him, settled here rather than in the city.'

'I wish it was feasible to do that without jeopardizing her career.'

Nate put a friendly arm around Zack's shoulder. 'It's Christmastime, the season when wishes can come true.'

Zack sighed deeply. His Christmas wish this year was an easy one. There were always new people on vacation in the town, but he hadn't anticipated meeting a woman like Sylvie during the holidays. He wanted a chance for them to be together. This was his wish.

Zack and Nate waved each other goodnight, got into their cars and drove off in different directions.

Zack turned the heater on full to warm himself up during the short drive home.

The streets were empty of people, and he looked at the houses with their festive decorations lit up as he drove along. The architect in him loved the structure of the buildings in town, and all the houses near where he lived had classy designs with Sylvie's house being one of the prettiest.

He noticed the lights were still on in Sylvie's lounge as he pulled up in front of his home.

He peered out the window. There was no sign she'd been out building snowmen in her garden or anything else for that matter. The snowman on her front lawn had been frosted over with an extra layer of snow, but apart from that, he was undisturbed.

Zack got out of his car and walked up to his front door, casting a glance at Sylvie's lounge window. He hoped she'd taken his advice about lighting a fire and staying safe and warm.

Kicking the snow from his boots, he hung his jacket in the hall and went through to the bedroom, taking the radio with him.

He received a great welcome from Cookie. The dog had been snuggled up in his basket with his blanket and two soft toys.

Zack picked up the toys. 'Two toys tonight?'

Cookie was just happy that Zack was home. He padded around, tail wagging.

'Come on, let's get you tucked back in bed. In you go,' Zack encouraged him.

The dog got into his basket and settled down, allowing Zack to get ready for bed. He changed into a thermal top and sleep pants.

Zack eased the tension in the muscles of his broad shoulders, shrugging off the effects of a freezing night outdoors.

Getting into bed he looked at the radio on the dresser beside him and wondered if he should call Sylvie. What if she was asleep? Just because her lights had been on it didn't mean she was awake. She hadn't called him so he assumed everything was okay.

Sylvie was snuggled up in bed under the patchwork quilt that had become like a welcoming comforter to her. Having just peeked out the lounge window and seen that Zack's car was back safely, she'd turned the lights off, secured the house and gone to bed.

She was no expert on snowstorms, but from gazing out the window it appeared to have eased off. The wind that had buffeted the house had ceased, as if the storm had blown its worst and then swept on past the town. It was still snowing, but lightly, and the flakes were no longer swirling around like miniature vortexes.

If Zack was now home it also indicated that the worst of the storm was over. Apart from a double helping of snow scattered over everything, the town would be back to normal soon. She hoped he hadn't had a tough evening out there, and suddenly had the urge to contact him.

She picked up the radio. Her finger itched to press the call button, but then she changed her mind and put it down. Obviously, Zack was okay. He was home, probably tired and wanting to get some sleep. He didn't need a call from her, especially at this late hour.

She fluffed her pillow, pulled the quilt up around her and settled down.

Zack had let his imagination get the better of him, something he didn't do very often, but he'd made a habit of it ever since Sylvie had arrived in town. Imagining new architectural designs was fine, however, he'd noticed a recent tendency to over think things whenever Sylvie was involved.

Reasoning with himself rarely worked when she was on his mind. That's why ridiculous scenarios formed in his thoughts and were difficult to shake off.

Worry gnawed at him. Maybe Sylvie's lights were on so late because she'd gone outside, perhaps to pick up logs for the fire, tumbled in the snow, which she had a tendency to do, and was now lying frozen in the back yard.

Yes, his thoughts had taken a worrying turn and now he couldn't settle without calling her to check she was safe. If she labeled him an over protective worry wart, it didn't matter. There was no way he was going to get a wink of sleep without knowing she was okay.

He pressed the call button and waited to see if she picked up.

Sylvie jumped when the radio buzzed. She wasn't asleep, but the unexpected sound jarred her. She lifted it up and took the call.

'Hi, I just wanted to check in with you to see you were okay.' He tried to sound pleasant and not like a guy who'd envisioned all sorts of unreasonable scenarios.

'Yes, I'm fine.' It was her turn to hide her reaction to his call. The excitement, relief, heart pounding joy of hearing his voice, and that he'd actually called her, took some suppressing, but she thought she'd managed to sound calm.

The relief of knowing she was okay washed over him, but the effect of her soft voice sent waves of deep emotion through him. He strived to keep his tone level. 'The storm looks like it's going to blow over by the morning.' Unlike the feelings he had for her. 'Obviously there will be minor disruption with some of the roads needing cleared, but that will be all done by the afternoon.'

'That's great to know.' She heard the nervous excitement in her tone, not from the good news about the snowstorm, but from listening to his deep, manly voice. There was something intimate about a late night call, especially via a two–way radio. It had an element of secrecy between two people. Unlike a cell phone, they both couldn't speak at the same time. This somehow made her listen intently to every word he said, waiting to respond to him.

'I hope I didn't wake you,' he said.

'No. I couldn't sleep earlier, so I worked on my new fabric designs. I've only just gone to bed and wasn't asleep. I noticed your car was parked outside so I knew you were home.'

His heart melted that she'd cared to keep a lookout for him. 'I'd love to see your designs, unless of course you don't want anyone seeing them until they're finished.'

'I'm happy to let you see them.' She almost invited him over for coffee the next day, but hesitated. Maybe he'd invite her to his house to see his study and she could bring her artwork with her?

The pauses between transmitting and receiving via the radio emphasized the hesitation in her voice.

It was his turn to speak. 'Excellent. I'm always interested in seeing other artists and designers work.' He was particularly fascinated in Sylvie's work. If he could learn more about it, hopefully he could think how to encourage her to stay in town while not jeopardizing her career progress. He admired that she'd attained her current level of success through her talent and sheer hard work. He'd no intention of standing in the way of her continuing to reach her full potential.

'I'd be interested in having a look at your architectural work,' she said, picturing his studio would be as organized as Zack appeared to be, and filled with wonderful detailed drawings of the houses he designed.

He held back from setting a time to invite her over to his studio. He wanted her to meet Cookie like he'd planned. When that was all smoothed over, he'd ask her round to his studio. 'Yes, I'll show you sometime.'

She didn't take his casual response as a rebuff. 'I used the paints you gave me, and I'm going to buy more artwork supplies from the art store in town. I'd like to have a look around it, and I remember what you said about it being really tempting.'

'It is.' But not as tempting as wanting to ask her to have lunch with him the next day, or dinner the following evening. 'I guess I'd better get some sleep and let you do the same.'

'Yes, it's really late, but thanks for calling, Zack.'

'Goodnight, Sylvie.' He released his finger from the transmit button and listened to her final response.

'Goodnight.'

She put the radio down on the bedside table and snuggled under the quilt, thinking about Zack. She felt the tiredness take over now that he'd called and she knew everything between them was okay.

Zack was more settled now too. He set his alarm so he wouldn't sleep in. It had been quite a night. He planned what time to take Cookie round to Sylvie's house in the morning. After breakfast would be good. Not too early, but early enough so that she hadn't gone out shopping for art supplies.

He lay in bed thinking everything through. Even if she told him she'd met his dog before, he wouldn't tell her about the video. He'd make light of the whole issue and they'd take things from there. At least he knew she liked dogs, and Cookie was crazy about her. He glanced at his mischievous buddy sleeping sound in his basket. That dog had great taste in friends. He also snored like a trooper.

Zack smiled to himself and pulled the covers up around his shoulders feeling the most content he'd been in a long time. Perhaps it was the sense of hope he had of working things out with Sylvie.

Snow was piled up outside the kitchen door when Sylvie opened it the next morning after finishing her breakfast. Dazzling sunlight caused her to cup her hand and shield her eyes as she gazed at the back yard. The blizzard had created a wonderland and she couldn't resist stepping out into it. She loved the feeling of the snow beneath her boots. A sense of happy anticipation filled her heart at the thought of how much fun she could have here. She was on her own, but not lonely. Not in a place like this.

The beauty of it was amazing. Long crystals dangled from the branches of the trees as if someone had draped them there overnight. The facets scintillated in the morning sunlight. Precious jewels could barely compare to their clarity and white fire. And that was only the trees. Her eyes widened in awe at the magnificent aftermath the storm had created. From its fierce passing the blizzard had left behind a glistening reminder of how incredible nature could be.

She stepped carefully into the garden. Her black pants were tucked inside her boots and she wore a comfy cream sweater on top of two layers of long sleeve thermal vests. A pink woolly scarf was wrapped around her neck and matched the hat she was wearing. If Zack saw her he wouldn't be able to scold her for not dressing for the weather. She was kitted out for the elements, and planned to head to the main street to do some shopping once the stores were open.

However, the first thing on her agenda was to explore the garden before it melted a little and faded from its breathtaking height. There was no real warmth in the sun that she could feel, but she imagined the ice crystals hanging from the trees would start to drip as they began to defrost during the day.

Taking her phone, she snapped numerous pictures, being extra careful not to have a repeat performance of what happened to her when she'd photographed the town's road sign. No tumbling into snowdrifts today.

Satisfied she'd captured the trees and scenery from all angles, she put her phone away safely and let the playful side of her nature

127

take over. Pictures like this were priceless and would be very handy when she was designing her next winter fabric collection. But at the moment there was a wondrous garden of fresh snow waiting for her to have fun in.

Although being adventurous had been one of her top priorities during this vacation, sliding the entire length of the icy pond wasn't sensible. Then again... all around the edges were mounds of fluffy snow, nature's pillows, to soften her fall if she happened to take a tumble.

She would've bet that she was the only person within the town's radius who was brushing the snow off an icy pond with the sole intention of sliding on it for sheer glee. This had to count as a ten on the adventurous scale. At least in her world.

Zack would never approve. In her imagination she pictured the look he'd give her if she even suggested attempting such a mildly daring feat.

Never one for being good at doing as she was told, she still found herself glancing furtively in the direction of Zack's garden, checking to see he wasn't watching her.

The radio was sitting on the kitchen table where she could hear it if he called. There was still no signal on her cell phone and no online access when she'd opened her laptop earlier.

Putting the brush back near the log pile where she'd found it, she ventured over to the far end of the pond. This would give her a slight run up to it, picking up enough momentum to skim the full length of the surface.

Although she was accountable only to herself, there was something wonderfully mischievous about doing this. The garden backed on to a field and the trees on either side of the house shielded her from being seen in her back yard by her neighbors. Unless they were out in their own back yards, and snooping over at her, she was hidden from prying eyes.

There was no sign of anyone, especially Zack. Due to the late night he'd had he might still be asleep in bed, or sitting by the fireside with Cookie curled up beside him. Zack was the sensible type. Sylvie on the other hand...

Checking again that no one was watching her, she decided to give the slide a go.

128

Throwing caution aside, she took a long breath, and made a clear run at the icy pond.

Chapter Eleven

Zack should've been tired but he wasn't.

Despite having only slept for a few hours, he was feeling energetic and all fired up on scrambled eggs, hot buttered toast, coffee and excitement.

Fresh from the shower, he'd smoothed his hair back from his clean shaven face, and dressed in smart, warm clothes that looked casual but classic. Adjusting the collar of his white shirt underneath his rich cream sweater, he tightened the belt on his dark pants and evaluated his appearance in the mirror. If he'd had to guess his own profession from the clothes he was wearing, he'd have nailed himself as a well heeled architect.

Cookie sat watching him.

'It's okay for you, buddy,' said Zack. 'You've got a coat that resembles silky, chocolate velvet. Guys like me have to work at it.'

The dog continued to watch him, amused by the extra effort Zack was putting into his attire. Zack wasn't a messy dresser and took care of his appearance, but although his visit to Sylvie wasn't a date, it sure felt like one. If it had been a dinner date, he'd have found it easier to dress for the occasion. Finding the right thing to wear on a freezing winter morning wasn't straightforward.

Zack shrugged his ski jacket on, leaving it unzipped and open. There was no point in dressing smart and then hiding it under a jacket, even if it did look expensive. He picked up his keys from the hallway along with a scarf that he wore stylishly around his neck. His only hope was that he hadn't overdone things and now resembled a guy who'd stepped off the cover of a menswear brochure.

He opened the front door and headed outside accompanied by Cookie. 'Okay, let's go visit Sylvie.'

At the mention of her name the dog's attention perked up, but he kept at heel as they walked the short distance to her house.

'Remember to behave yourself,' Zack reminded him.

The dog eyeballed him sideways.

'Yeah, me too, buddy.'

The road was quiet and hardly anyone was about, which suited him fine. There was enough talk circulating about him and Sylvie without him being seen going to her house this morning. He wanted to properly introduce Cookie to her. He also wanted to chat to her.

He'd been thinking about her work, her career, and wanted to talk to her about it. He pictured they'd sit by the fire, drinking coffee, and he'd ask her whether she was at a crucial point in her career, and really get to understand her work process. He hoped to find a way for them to be together without affecting her prospects.

'Right, here's the plan,' Zack said quickly as they walked up the path to her front door. 'I'm going to knock, Sylvie will answer, and then I'll introduce the two of you. At least try to pretend you don't know her. She'll invite us in, so no jumping up on the furniture. And don't do that crazy thing where you get a wild notion to chase your own tail.' He'd done enough of that for both of them. In his case it was called trying to make right what he'd done wrong.

The dog eyeballed him again.

'I'm serious. Save those antics for home.'

Zack cleared his throat and knocked on her door. He stepped back, expecting her to open up. His heart drummed inside his chest. He needed her to be home. He hoped she hadn't gone out shopping. There was no response. He knocked again in case she hadn't heard him. Still no response.

He sighed heavily and glanced down, disappointment draining him to the core. After all this effort, working himself up, bringing his dog along...

Wait a minute. What was Cookie trying to tell him?

His dog never ran off when he was out with Zack. He was very well behaved in that respect. However, Cookie was crouching down in the snow at the side of the house, hitting his front paws off the snowy ground, the way he did when he was ready to play games. The dog's expression urged Zack to understand.

'What is it? Where's Sylvie?'

Cookie ran towards the back yard and then back again. He stared at Zack expectantly.

'Is Sylvie out back? Go find her. Go find Sylvie.'

This was all the encouragement the dog needed to hear. He bounded off down the side of the house to the back yard, closely followed by Zack who almost kept up with him.

The dog reached the back garden seconds before Zack did.

Sylvie was mid–slide. It was one of her faster efforts as her confidence on the icy pond had increased. Unable to stop herself, she saw Cookie running towards her, his tongue lolling out of that smiley mouth, clearly happy to see her.

The dog misread her sliding towards him as a gesture of welcome and bounded at her full pelt.

The clash as Sylvie and the dog met on the icy surface was one that Zack was sure would be burned in his memory forever. Neither of them could stop themselves. Cookie pressed his paws hard on the ice in an effort to slow down and skid to a halt.

Sylvie was already committed to sliding fast, and the look on her face was worthy of being in a comic cartoon.

Zack ran towards her, but couldn't prevent Cookie from flattening her. She ended up prone on the ground. Luckily the momentum pushed her away from the ice and she had a soft landing in the snow.

Although she almost had the breath knocked out of her, the slobbering, wet kisses quickly revived her senses. Cookie was so pleased to see her.

'Are you okay?' she heard Zack ask, feeling like her world had gone full circle. This is what he'd said when they first met. Here she was still falling into snowdrifts and being rescued by Zack.

'Yes, I'm fine.'

Cookie's wet nose sniffed around her face. He was doing his own checking to see that she was okay.

Sylvie smiled and smoothed his fur.

She glanced up at Zack as he reached down and hauled her to her feet. She thought he looked great this morning. Zack always looked great, but there was an extra stylishness to his clothes that was particularly attractive.

Sylvie brushed the snow from her pants, shook the flakes from her hair and waited on the reprimand from Zack. It wasn't forthcoming. Instead, he took her aback by sweeping aside her daring antics and introducing his dog.

'I thought I'd bring my dog round to finally meet you. This is Cookie.'

She went along with the pretence. 'Hi, Cookie. Aren't you a sweet guy.'

Oh if only she'd paid him the same compliment, Zack thought, his morning would've been pretty much perfect.

'I'm sorry if his over enthusiasm got the better of him.'

Sylvie refused to blame the dog. 'No, I'm happy to meet him. He must've been the cutest little puppy.'

'I got him from the rescue center two years ago. He was already way past the puppy stage by then.' He patted the dog's head. 'But I bet he was a cute puppy.'

Cookie welcomed all the attention he was getting, however, he was in a playful mood and started to bound around the garden, trying to encourage them to have fun with him.

'I think he's hinting that he wants some fun,' said Sylvie.

Zack pulled Cookie's favorite red play ball from his jacket pocket and handed it to her. 'I'll give you the first throw.'

There was a challenge in his voice that made her smile.

'Are you sure you want to give me an advantage?' she asked.

He noticed the mischief in her eyes. 'I'm having second thoughts.'

'Too late,' she shouted and threw the ball for Cookie to fetch while running to the bottom of the garden.

Cookie kicked up a flurry of powdery snow in his effort to fetch the ball.

Zack patted his hands on his thighs. 'Here, boy! Bring the ball here.'

Cookie had other ideas and ran straight for Sylvie.

She laughed as she accepted the ball from Cookie's mouth and held it up triumphantly.

Zack put his hands on his hips. 'Like that, huh?'

She gave him an impish grin.

Zack rubbed his palms together, ready to grab the next throw.

Sylvie went to throw the ball to the far side of the garden, then spun around and threw it in the opposite direction. Feigning a throw didn't fool Cookie, but Zack fell foul to her trickery and started to run in the wrong direction before realizing she'd thrown him a mock.

While Cookie retrieved the ball and ran with it to Sylvie, Zack took his jacket off and put it down on the frozen bench.

Sylvie giggled. 'Was the jacket slowing you down, Zack?'

'Fair warning,' he joked with her. 'The gloves are off. I'm taking you and your sidekick down.'

If she'd thought he was handsome with the ski jacket on, he now appeared twice as attractive in his white shirt and manly cream sweater that showed the breadth of his shoulders tapering down to a slim waist and taut torso. If he was using this as a distraction tactic, she secretly conceded it had worked.

He stood tall and ready for action with his long, lean thighs encased in slim fitting pants. His boots were expensive and rugged. Two words she'd happily tag Zack with.

Sylvie threw the ball and watched Zack and Cookie run to catch it.

'My money is on the dog,' she shouted to Zack.

Zack gave her a playfully menacing glare, then continued to search around in the snow for the ball. It had landed in a deep snowdrift under one of the trees. She laughed as she watched them. Zack found it first then dropped it when Cookie jumped up and knocked him aside.

'Hey, that's cheating, buddy!' said Zack.

Cookie nosed around in the snow and found the ball.

Sylvie applauded. 'Go Cookie!'

Zack pretended to complain to her. 'He's not playing by the rules.'

As Cookie ran to give her the ball, she grinned at Zack. 'What rules?'

Zack pointed at her. 'Okay, you asked for it.'

From that moment on, there was a free–for–all as the three of them played around in the snow.

Sylvie wasn't sure who threw the first snowball, probably her, though no way was she admitting to that.

Zack defended himself by throwing a barrage of snowballs at Sylvie. She tried to run for cover behind the bench, even using his jacket as a shield, but unfortunately she couldn't beat him while laughing so hard.

The two of them ended up tussling and rolling around in the snow near the icy pond, while Cookie searched for the ball further down the garden near the trees.

The dog had sussed out the correct location and picked up the ball.

Meanwhile Sylvie had resorted to stuffing a snowball down the back of Zack's sweater, causing him to yell with laughter.

She still had another handful of snow in her clutches, and Zack used his strength to overpower her, pinning her wrists down until she released her grip on the last snowball.

Zack rolled over on to his back, and they lay together breathless in the snow.

'I win,' Zack gasped.

'No you don't,' she argued, smiling over at him.

Their faces were so close she could see the clear blue of his eyes, and the temptation to kiss his confident grin was overwhelming. In one wild moment she almost leaned in to kiss him, and he moved in to kiss her too.

In the second that they both hesitated, Cookie pushed his happy face between the two of them, dropped the ball and covered them with doggie kisses.

Sylvie hugged the adorable dog and then stood up. 'I think Cookie wins.'

'You'll get no argument about that from me.' Zack got up, brushing the snow from his clothes, but no amount of surface brushing was going to clean up the mess he was in.

Sylvie grinned at him. 'I feel guilty. Your clothes are such a mess. You'd been so well groomed when you arrived.'

'Well groomed? I don't think I've ever been called that before.'

She gestured towards her house. The kitchen door was still wide open. 'Do you want to come inside and get cleaned up?' She glanced at Cookie. 'Both of you?'

'Nooo, you don't want this guy in your house when he's dripping with snow. If he decides to chase his tail, your lovely pristine lounge is going to get real messy.' He shook his head. 'No, we'll be heading back home to get tidied up.'

'I don't mind,' she said.

'I do. We've caused enough chaos to your back yard without trailing it inside.'

Sylvie smiled at the state of the garden. 'It looks like a whirlwind hit it.'

'I wouldn't call you a whirlwind.'

'I was meaning you,' she countered.

He grinned at her and picked his jacket up from the ground where she'd dropped it. He shook the excess flakes off.

'Sorry about your nice jacket.' She winced at the state of his sweater and pants. 'And your sweater. And you hair.'

He lifted his hand and touched the top of his hair, realizing it was sticking up. 'What was that you were saying about me being well groomed?'

She laughed. 'Thanks for coming round. That was fun.'

Cookie was sitting down patiently waiting in the snow.

'We've tuckered him out,' said Zack.

'I don't even want to think how sore my muscles are going to feel later.' She eased off her shoulders.

'What muscles?'

'Ha!'

'Okay, we'd better get going before we freeze solid like that snowman out front.' Zack gave her a heart warming smile, then trudged round to the front lawn, closely followed by Cookie.

Sylvie kept pace with them, intending to wave them off.

Zack paused. He couldn't simply walk away, he thought, without inviting her over to his house. 'I guess you'll be going shopping now?'

'Yes, I've a couple of things I want to buy.' Including fabric for Nate to give to Nancy. If there were any more blizzards, perhaps some stores would close early for the holidays. She didn't want to risk not having bought the fabric.

'If you're not busy later, maybe you'd like to pop round this afternoon. I'll show you my studio.'

Her heart soared at his invitation. 'Yes, I'd like that.'

'Bring your artwork with you. I really would like to see it.'

'I will,' she confirmed.

Waving Zack and Cookie off, she felt a surge of elation. Everything was starting to feel so right.

Zack came running back as she was about to close the front door. Her heart lurched. Was something wrong? Had he changed his mind about inviting her?

'I have to ask you a question,' he began, sounding serious.

'Okay.' Her tone was dubious.

'It's about your work, your career.'

She nodded, giving him the go ahead to continue, though why he couldn't wait until later to talk to her about her work she couldn't fathom.

Zack hadn't been given a chance to talk to her due to their fun in the snow, but he wanted to know a few things so he could think them through before she came over to his house that afternoon.

'You told me that you work on one fabric collection and then straight on to the next.'

'I do.'

'And when you're not working, you work to relax?'

Sylvie bit her lip. Put like that it sounded like she was a workaholic.

Zack gazed right at her. 'I know how my early career depended on getting people familiar with my work, with my name, during the first few years. I'm surmising that your career is similar, and that this is a crucial point in your life when you have to work extra hard to push through to the next level where your name, your brand of fabric designs, is better known. Am I right?'

'You are. Marla says my designs are popular, and each new collection increases in sales. I'm lucky that the company has a wonderful sales team and they approach various clients whenever I bring out a new range of designs. Many of the buyers are businesses, including hotels who purchase a whole range of my designs. But Marla says the main problem is that we have to reach other potential customers, not just the ones we're regularly dealing with.'

'You have to become known to a wider audience?' said Zack.

'Exactly. That's why I've now got a website, and I update that with news and pictures of my new designs, to hopefully increase sales.'

'So my question is really... this wouldn't be a good time for you to up sticks and leave New York to work somewhere else, even if you could still continue creating your designs?'

'No, Zack. It wouldn't.' Her truthful reply hurt her as much as him. She saw the disappointment in his eyes.

Cookie barked, urging him to leave.

'We'll talk more about it later.' He smiled and the warmth in those blue eyes of his made her heart squeeze.

They both knew what he was talking about, where things between them were heading. But finding a solution to everything was going to be hard. However, she still had hope, especially as he wanted to find a way for them to be together. Suddenly her heart lifted again. He really did care about her. He really did.

He walked away to his house, turned around and waved to her. She waved back and smiled, then got ready to go shopping.

Cookie was all cleaned up and cozy.

'I think that went well with Sylvie,' Zack said to him, sitting by the fire, drinking coffee. He'd changed into dry clothes and dealt with his hair. He wasn't particularly well groomed but the closest he could manage.

Cookie was content to stretch out on the hearth rug. He'd had a great morning.

'She's very competitive though, isn't she? She was determined to beat me.'

Cookie glanced at him.

'Yes, I know, you beat both of us.'

Zack reached over and grabbed his laptop. He opened it up and tried to log online. 'I want to check out her website. I didn't know she had one.' The connection was patchy and kept timing out. He persisted anyway.

'As a career woman I suppose she benefits from having a competitive streak in her,' Zack reasoned. 'Succeeding as a designer in the city is no mean feat. It's a competitive business, so I'd say she's got that element nailed.'

The dog gave a relaxing sigh and was starting to fall asleep in front of the fire. Zack could've happily joined him, but he needed fresh groceries. He planned to pop out to Nate and Nancy's store for milk and cake and anything else delicious to serve up to Sylvie that afternoon.

'No connection,' he said, finally giving up and closing the laptop. 'Remind me to check her website later.'

But Cookie was snoring.

Zack smiled to himself, threw on a jacket and hurried out.

Jessica's shop was very busy, so Sylvie decided to go to the nearby art store first.

The store appeared small from the outside, but once she stepped inside she was amazed how big it was. It stretched all the way back to an area that was set up for teaching art and crafts during the evenings and weekends.

There was a counter near the middle of the store, and a handful of customers.

A tall, dark haired, attractive guy with green eyes smiled acknowledgment to her as she went over to the watercolor paper supplies. He was with two other men and the three of them were discussing the quality of oil paints. Further along from the watercolor area, a couple were selecting wedding stationery and Sylvie was tempted to buy one of the lovely floral notebooks on display. She loved stationery. She also loved everything she saw in the watercolor range of products and cherry picked new colors to add to the ones Zack had given her.

Zack had been right — this store was a total temptation. She picked two pads of the types of paper she wanted for her artwork, and was gazing around at all the items when the man with the green eyes approached her.

'Can I help you with those?' He referred to the armful of products she was holding.

'Thanks, but I can manage,' she said, thinking he was a customer.

He could tell from her reaction that she didn't know he was the owner of the store.

One of the guys he'd been talking to called over to him. 'Luke, are these oil paints available as a set? I'd like to buy them as a Christmas gift.'

'Yes they are,' said Luke, striding over to assist the customer. 'I can gift wrap them for you if you want.'

'That would be great,' said the customer.

Luke flicked a glance at Sylvie as he went past on his way to the counter to serve the customer.

She pretended not to notice. How was she supposed to know he owned the store?

While Luke was busy, Sylvie continued to wander round, adding little bits and pieces, resisting almost everything she wanted to buy as she didn't need them. She did succumb to picking up the floral notebook and a really pretty tin for keeping her pencils in.

Luke finally approached her again. 'Allow me to take these items over to the counter for you.'

She handed them to him. 'Thanks.'

139

He gestured towards the back of the store. 'Feel free to take your time and have a look around.'

He had a pleasant manner and a voice to match, setting her at ease in his store.

'I could get lost for hours in a store like this,' Sylvie commented to him.

He pointed to a table set up with paper cups and hot coffee ready to pour.

'You're kidding,' she said, smiling. 'Do people really stay in here that long?'

'They certainly do, and they're welcome.' His reply sounded genuine. 'Help yourself to a coffee. That pot's fresh made.'

She thought about where she had to go next — Jessica's quilt shop. She could be in there for ages as well. A coffee seemed like a good idea and would keep her going until she got home.

'I think I will,' she said to Luke. 'And I'll buy all those items,' she added, allowing him to deal with her purchases.

She poured a cup of coffee and wandered over to the counter to pay for her supplies.

'I'm Luke by the way,' he said, wrapping her paints carefully and putting everything in a bag for her.

'Sylvie.' She sipped her coffee and handed over her credit card.

Her name triggered a reaction in him. 'Zack's friend?'

'Yes. I'm here on vacation.' He probably knew everything about her, so she took the opportunity to talk about Zack. 'He recommended your store to me. Is he a friend of yours?'

'We went to school together. We were both in the junior running team.'

'Zack's a runner?'

'Used to be. He was the team leader. We all used to train up near the cove. I don't know if you're aware, but there's a beautiful cove near here.'

'Zack mentioned it. He said it's popular for swimming and fun during the summer.'

'It is. Zack's got a cabin up there.'

This was news to Sylvie. 'A cabin?'

'He designed it himself, so as you can imagine with him being an architect, it's a beauty. He built it along with some of the local guys.'

'He built it as well?'

140

'Quite a bit of it, but local builders and roofers helped him.' He handed her the bag with her art supplies. 'The cabin has a great view of the cove. You should ask him to take you up there, though it probably resembles the North Pole right now.'

Sylvie nodded and took all of this in. 'Well, thanks for your help. Have a nice Christmas.'

'If you're still around, I might see you at the town's Christmas Eve party.'

She smiled, nodded again and left.

Walking the short distance to the quilt shop, she felt quite excited that Zack had a cabin. She pictured it covered in snow beside the cove. Maybe he'd take her up there as part of her holiday adventure?

She went into Jessica's shop and started to browse through the fabric bundles. Jessica smiled to her while serving a couple of customers. This allowed Sylvie to pick the fabrics for Nancy's gift without having to make up excuses to Jessica about why she was loading up on more fabric.

Jessica kept glancing over at her. Sylvie assumed it was because she was piling up four bundles of lovely fabrics that she thought Nancy would love for her quilting. From seeing what Nancy was sewing at the quilting bee, she had a good idea of the colors and types of prints she liked.

However, Jessica was trying to get Sylvie's attention because she had something important to tell her.

Finally the customers cleared from the shop and Jessica hurried over.

'Your boss, Marla, phoned me. She wants to speak to you. It's important.'

Sylvie blinked. 'Marla phoned you?'

'Yes. The shop has a landline phone. She tried to call you on your cell and couldn't get a reply, so she phoned me, hoping I could get a message to you.'

'Did she say what it was that's so important?'

Jessica shook her head. 'No, but I'm happy for you to call her on my phone here.'

'Are you sure?'

'Yeah, help yourself. I'll make myself busy. Go ahead. The phone is through there.' She pointed to the back of the shop.

'Thanks, Jessica.'

Zack went over to the cake display in the grocery store. 'What type of cake do you think Sylvie would prefer — chocolate or one of these with lots of cream?'

Nancy grinned. 'Is she coming over to your house?'

'She is. This afternoon, so I want something delicious.'

'What about the Christmas cake you bought?'

'I want to keep that for Christmas Day.'

'Chocolate cake,' said Nancy. 'We know she loves chocolate. That one over there has chocolate buttercream filling. It's very nice.'

'I'll take that one.'

Nate came hurrying into the store. 'Zack! I have to talk to you — outside.' He eyeballed Zack, indicating he couldn't talk in front of Nancy.

'Christmas secrets, huh?' said Nancy.

Nate nodded and hustled Zack outside as fast as possible. He pulled him out of earshot and away from the store's front window. He didn't even want Nancy to see Zack's reaction when he heard the news.

'What is it?' Zack asked him.

'Before I tell you, I give you my word I didn't tell anyone anything. It didn't come from me.'

Zack had never heard Nate sound so distressed. 'Okay,' he said slowly, giving Nate the nod to continue.

'It's about the video with Sylvie.'

Nancy popped outside and interrupted them. 'If you're looking for Sylvie, I just saw her go into Jessica's shop.' She handed Zack a bag containing the chocolate cake. 'Don't forget your cake.'

'Thank you, Nancy,' said Zack.

Nate glared at her, indicating that he needed to talk to Zack in private.

Nancy went back inside leaving them alone.

'What about the video?' Zack asked him.

'While we've been off the grid due to the snowstorm, something crazy has happened...'

Chapter Twelve

Sylvie phoned Marla and she picked up right away. 'Hi, Marla. I'm calling from Jessica's shop. She said you wanted to speak to me.'

'Yes. I couldn't reach you on your phone and you haven't replied to your emails. I didn't know Zack's full name to contact him, so I called Jessica. I thought she could get a message to you.'

'What's wrong?' said Sylvie.

'You sound cheerful, so I'm guessing you haven't seen the news.'

'What news?'

'The story that's been trending online on social media.'

'I've had no access to anything like that. I was at a party in the community hall last night and then there was this huge snowstorm, but it's blown over now, if that's what you're worried about. I'm quite safe.'

'No, it's not that, but you're the hot topic.'

'Is it my fabric, my designs?' There was a clash of hope and panic in Sylvie's voice.

'Not quite, but I have to say that sales and interest in your fabric designs have gone through the roof.'

'Wow!' This could only be a good thing.

Marla was silent for a moment.

'Come on, tell me what the news is about?'

'Brace yourself, Sylvie.'

Sylvie's whole insides gripped in readiness.

'A video featuring you is trending all over social media.'

It took a moment for this to sink in. 'A video of me?'

'Yep.'

'Doing what?'

'You're outside having a lot of fun in the snow.' This was Marla's downplayed version of it.

'The sledding?' Her fastest sled time was the first thing she thought of.

'No, not the sledding. The highlight of this video, for me, is seeing you doing cartwheels in the snow. One of our company directors prefers the part where your face is seen in close up talking to Zack's dog.'

'Cookie?'

'Yes, Cookie. But one of our main investors says he's impressed that you've got more energy than a chocolate Labrador.'

'How did someone make a video of me with Cookie? Who filmed it?'

'Technically, the dog.'

'The dog?' Sylvie sounded incredulous.

'Cookie was wearing a pet collar camera.'

Sylvie felt emotionally pole–axed. 'Zack put a camera on the dog's collar? Deliberately?'

'That's one smart dog, but I doubt Cookie could fasten it on himself.'

Sylvie reeled back. 'Another weasel. I certainly know how to pick them.'

'Calm down. There's an upside to all of this.'

Right now, Sylvie couldn't see anything except trouble brewing.

Overhearing their conversation and gleaning the gist of it, Jessica opened her laptop in the front shop and managed to log online. She hardly had a chance to type the full heading into the browser because the story was trending so strongly that the search engine was filling in the gaps for her.

Jessica clicked on the video and watched the whole thing while Sylvie continued to talk to Marla. She pressed her hand over her mouth to stifle her laughter and give them enough uninterrupted time to figure out the fiasco.

Sylvie sounded totally exasperated, disappointed, betrayed and just plain mad. As she mentally joined the dots to everything that had happened between her and Zack and Cookie, she formed an upsetting conclusion.

'Zack's been spying on me all along, using his dog to do his sneaky work. How low can a man get?'

'You don't know that. You're jumping to conclusions.' Marla tried to sound reasonable.

'He was acting weird last night,' Sylvie stated flatly, her voiced edged with accusation.

'What type of weird?'

'Standoffish to begin with. A real cold fish. Then later on he was charm personified, asking me to dance with him, and even cutting in on Santa.'

'He cut in on Santa? Who does that?' Marla sounded aghast.

'We started dancing and he gazed at me as if I was the only woman in the world he cared about.'

Marla was beginning to edge towards Sylvie being right about him.

Sylvie gave a disappointed sigh. 'I think he's set me up again.'

'When?'

'This morning. He came round when I was in my back yard. He brought Cookie with him. He said he wanted to introduce us. What a whopper that was. He knew fine I was friends with his dog.'

Marla now didn't sound so convinced of Zack's good intentions. 'If he's made another video of you, what would be on it?'

Sylvie hesitated.

'More cartwheels?' Marla asked.

'No cartwheels, but I did attempt sliding on the icy pond.'

'Would it be considered funny?'

'No.'

'Would it?' Marla repeated.

'It might, depending on your sense of humor.'

'You know what they say, all publicity is good publicity.'

'Unless you look like a dork,' said Sylvie.

'Humor me. I overdid the eggnog cocktails last night, then I got jolted awake with this whirlwind.'

'I'm sorry. I don't want to ruin your Christmas.'

'Ruin it? Sales have doubled overnight. The pressure is off me now to think up a fresh campaign during the usual dip we take after the holidays. If half the interest already shown by companies wanting wholesale deals on your fabric collections plays out, this will be one of our most profitable New Years in a long time. Presales of your new summer collection have shot up overnight.'

Sylvie's response was laced with sarcasm. 'An overnight sensation.'

'Don't knock it. Business is tough. Any edge is a bonus.'

'I've made myself seem like a total nincompoop.'

'Do you remember the last humorous video to trend? We spoke about it over lunch one day last month.'

'No, I'm sorry, I don't.'

'Exactly,' Marla said triumphantly.

'Okay, I get your point. But that doesn't stop me feeling like I'm in the spotlight for all the wrong reasons.'

'We'll make it the right reasons. Our marketing and publicity people are on it.'

'Oh great, I get to upend everyone's Christmas.'

'We hire sharks to deal with our publicity. These guys don't do Christmas. They circle around the business pool continuously.'

Sylvie took a calming breath. 'What should I do about Zack? Should I confront him and get mad? Or should I play it cool?'

'There's no playing cool with this. It's hit the hot zone and is continuing to skyrocket.'

'Should I tell him that he's a weasel? Or should I totally ignore him?'

'I'd go with option A. But I've always been one for speaking my mind.'

Jessica cleared her throat and interrupted. 'I have the video on my laptop, Sylvie, if you'd like to watch it.'

'I'll call you later, Marla,' said Sylvie. 'I'm going to have a look at the video.'

'Okay, we'll speak later.'

Sylvie clicked the call off and took Jessica up on her offer.

Jessica refreshed the video to let Sylvie see it from the beginning.

'On a scale of one to ten, how bad is it?' Sylvie asked her before watching it.

Jessica hesitated.

'Tell me the truth,' Sylvie urged her.

'It's the funniest thing I've seen in a long time.'

'That bad, huh?'

Jessica smiled tightly and pressed play.

Zack paced back and forth. 'Sylvie's going to be mad at me when she sees this.'

Nate frowned. 'I can promise you I never shared the video with anyone, so I don't know how it ended up online.'

Zack was frantically checking his phone, trying to get a signal. 'I thought when I uploaded the video I'd set it to private, but it looks like I didn't.'

Nate gave a resigned shrug. 'And once a video like that is out there in the wild, it only takes one spark on social media for it to catch fire.'

Adrenalin was pumping through Zack's entire body. 'I make one little mistake and now Sylvie's trending all over the media. Did the video have many views when you last watched it?'

'Oh, yeah, and every time I refreshed it, another thousand hits were added.'

Zack felt as if he couldn't breathe. 'I have to talk to Sylvie before she finds out from someone else. I need to explain to her what happened.'

Further along the street, Nate saw Sylvie coming out of Jessica's shop carrying a large bag filled with fabric in one hand and her art supply bag in the other.

'Don't look now, but Sylvie's heading this way.'

Zack glanced round. 'Do you think she knows already?'

Nate didn't sound optimistic. 'Well, I've never seen her glare so angrily.'

'Right.'

'I'll leave the two of you alone so you can tell her the truth.' Nate went to hurry away.

Zack grabbed his arm. 'No. You're my back up.'

Sylvie marched up to them and handed the bag of fabric to Nate. 'I got this for you. I hope it's suitable.' Every syllable sounded tense as she tried to keep a lid on her anger. She wasn't angry with Nate, not yet anyway, but the two of them were together and Nate wore a guilty expression.

Nate accepted the bag and peeked inside. 'This is perfect. Let me know how much I owe you.'

Sylvie was listening to Nate, but casting daggers at Zack. 'The receipt is in the bag.'

Jessica scooted past them into the grocery store. All of them knew what that meant. Nancy was about to find out and then everyone would know. To be fair, Jessica had asked Sylvie if she could tell Nancy, and been given the go ahead.

147

Zack stepped forward and faced Sylvie. 'This is ridiculous. We all understand what's going on here.'

This triggered Sylvie. 'The only thing that's ridiculous, Zack, is that you dared to upload that video of me.' She glared at him. 'You're such a weasel.'

Under other circumstances the weasel insult would've bounced off him. But her scorn cut deep. She now ranked him as low as Conrad.

'I'm not like Conrad,' Zack argued.

'No, you're not like him,' she agreed. 'Conrad would never have put a video of me online for everyone to see.'

'I only uploaded it privately so that Nate could see it,' said Zack. 'Unfortunately, I thought I'd set it to private but I hadn't.'

'Oh well, that makes it okay then.' The sarcasm in her voice didn't disguise how upset she was.

Nate stood quietly, keeping out of the firing line.

Zack spread his arms wide. 'I'm sorry, Sylvie. I'm really sorry.'

She brushed aside his apology. 'You had no right to secretly film me. You're such a sneak.'

He reeled back from the second assault on his character. Now he was a sneak as well as a weasel.

'And a liar,' she said.

The insults were adding up.

'I didn't lie,' Zack reasoned. 'I simply didn't tell you about the video. In fact, I'd decided to forget it ever existed and never mention it to you.'

'It's a bit late for that,' she told him.

'I realize that now.' He sounded exasperated. 'I wouldn't intentionally lie to you.'

'You lied to me this morning when you brought Cookie round to meet me,' she argued. 'You knew I'd met your dog.'

He didn't have a good excuse.

'I'll wait,' she said, eyeballing him.

'Things had become complicated,' he began. 'I thought this was the easiest way to start afresh. To make things how they should've been between us if Cookie hadn't gone into your garden and you hadn't kept it a secret. A clean slate for both of us.'

'You don't start a clean slate with a lie, Zack.' There was no doubt she meant this.

He stepped closer. 'We can wipe it clean now.'

She cast her eyes down. 'No, I could never trust someone who secretly filmed me. You probably filmed me this morning. Is that going to be your next video?'

'No!' He couldn't have sounded more adamant. 'I put the dog collar camera on Cookie because I suspected he was going into other gardens. I sensed he was up to something. The last person I thought he'd been visiting was you. I assumed you'd have told me if he had.'

She glanced up at him, tempted to believe him. 'You didn't put the camera on Cookie so you could film me?'

'No, definitely not. I was shocked when I saw it was your garden he was disappearing into — and that the two of you had become buddies. Without even a hint from you. You can imagine my surprise. He's my dog. I trusted you.'

Nancy tapped on the inside of the store window to get their attention. She jabbed a finger, urging them to glance across the street.

Sylvie, Zack and Nate saw a man, in his thirties, watching them. He was armed with a camera and a curious expression.

Zack and Nate recognized him immediately. Sylvie hadn't a clue.

'Quick, into the store.' Nate hustled Sylvie inside, taking advantage of the reporter's view momentarily being blocked by passers by. He closed the door behind them.

'What's wrong?' said Sylvie.

'He's a reporter with the local newspaper,' Nancy told her.

'The press are after me?' Sylvie's anxious tone caused Nancy to reassure her.

'Don't worry, Sylvie, I'll keep him busy while you guys make a run for it out the back of the store.'

The intended reassurance and furtive plan did nothing to calm Sylvie's anxiety. 'Now I'm on the run from the paparazzi?'

Nancy gave Sylvie's shoulder a firm squeeze. 'No, he's a local reporter. He's okay. The paparazzi won't be here until later.'

'The roads into town are still blocked,' Jessica explained.

'Do you want me stay?' Nate offered to Nancy.

'No, you go help Zack and Sylvie. Jessica and I will bamboozle the reporter. Hurry now, he's coming over here.'

As they disappeared through the back entrance, the reporter walked in. 'Is Zack here, with Sylvie?'

'No, just Jessica and me.' Nancy lifted up a tray of gingerbread cookies. 'Try a cookie, they're on offer this morning.'

'Another time,' he said.

'Okay,' said Nancy. 'Have a browse. See if there's anything else you'd like. The bread is fresh baked this morning.'

Jessica smiled at Nancy as if nothing was untoward. 'I'd like to pick up my Christmas cake.'

'I've got it over here.' Nancy lifted the cake from a shelf and chatted happily. 'I've almost finished my Christmas quilt. Your idea of adding a holly print fabric to some of the blocks really works.'

'That's wonderful. I've got new fabric arriving after Christmas that I think you'll love. Pop round later and I'll show you the samples. There's a snowdrop print that is totally gorgeous.'

Nancy and Jessica kept up the ruse while the reporter eventually decided to leave.

'If you see Zack, ask him to give me a call at the paper.' He pressed a card down on the counter.

Nancy picked it up. 'I'll make sure he gets it.'

Nate checked that no one was outside the rear of the store. A small back yard led on to a sidewalk. He beckoned to Zack and Sylvie. 'Okay, it's clear.'

'I'll take you home,' Zack said to her.

'No, I'd prefer to take care of myself.' She turned away from Zack. 'Thanks for your help Nate.'

Zack tried to insist. 'I'd like to——'

Sylvie held up her hand and cut him short. 'I really don't want to speak to you right now.' She walked away.

Zack felt the weight of his grocery bag containing the chocolate cake increase as he watched her go. There would be no coffee and cake with her this afternoon. No showing her around his studio while she let him see her artwork. Whatever trust she'd had in him was broken. The day suddenly seemed colder.

'Give her time, Zack,' Nate advised him. 'She's got a lot to think about.'

Zack agreed. And so had he.

Sylvie trudged home. She'd never had to keep a lookout for the press before. She found herself glancing around warily.

Once safely inside her house, she put her new art supplies down on her desk, but had no urge to paint or do anything other than think over the things that had happened.

By lunchtime she still wasn't hungry, but she was able to use her laptop to watch the video in its entirety. It was longer than she'd imagined. Every moment of her crazy, fun filled morning with Cookie was captured. Her antics in the snow almost made her smile, so she understood why others found it amusing. Why she'd thought cartwheels in the snow were a good idea, she couldn't fathom.

She dared to read some of the comments people had left, most of them positive, with the majority claiming her madcap video had cheered them up on a cold winter's day when they'd felt the pressures of the holiday season upon them.

But had Zack really put the camera on Cookie's collar because he wanted to see what his dog was up to? Or was it an excuse to secretly film her? The doubt tore her apart inside.

The more she thought about it, the more anxious she became, until she decided to change her clothing into something she hadn't worn in the video, or that morning, so she wouldn't be easily recognized, and headed back out.

Walking was good for thinking things through.

Sylvie's hooded coat shielded her from prying eyes. She hadn't worn this coat since she'd arrived.

In the late afternoon, she walked the full length of the main street without anyone recognizing her. Then she headed back down, occasionally strolling up other streets, exploring the town center area. No one bothered her and she felt great to be anonymous, even if only for a little while.

Someone finally recognized her.

Greg's hands were thrust into his jacket pockets and his expression was tense. He walked towards her. She could tell right away that something was troubling him.

'Are you okay, Greg?'

'I don't want to burden you with my woes. You've got enough issues to deal with.'

'Burden me. It'll take my mind off my problems,' said Sylvie.

'You know what they say, a burden shared is a burden doubled.'

'Hmmm, I don't think you've got that quite right.'

He thought about it. 'I haven't, have I?'

'No.'

He brushed his comment aside. 'Forget I even said it.'

'Tell me what's bugging you,' she said.

'Apart from the horrible, deep, cringing sensation whenever I think about my behavior last night.' He shook his head in dismay. 'It was a party. People were dancing. And what did I do? I monopolized the prettiest girl in the room and insisted on showing her how to cut and blanche sweet potatoes.'

'I learned a lot.'

'You were a star pupil. You didn't complain once. Not even when I bored you with the reasons why your fries could become soggy.'

She laughed.

'You deserve a prize for being continually polite while I rattled on about the perfect caramelized fries. And I fully intend to get you something. A small gift to put under your Christmas tree, from me.'

'No, you don't have to do that.'

'I do. For me, to stop the deep, cringing feeling.' He smiled at her. 'Santa did right in coming to rescue you from my culinary clutches.' He paused. 'I should get something for Nate too.'

They continued walking. He took the same route along the main street as Sylvie.

'Have you been busy at the cafe?' she asked him.

'It's been quite a day. Hearing that the love of my life is coming back to town for Ana's wedding in the spring, and hiding from you.'

'Hiding from me?'

'Yes, I saw you walking by the cafe earlier. I think you were going to Luke's art store.'

'I did go there.'

'I was pinning up the new menu on the cafe window and stepped back out of your view. You didn't see me?'

'No.'

'That's useful to know. I've always wondered if I could be seen from that angle.'

'Why were you hiding from me?'

'For all the reasons I've explained. I didn't want to face you because I was so embarrassed by my behavior last night.'

They'd settled that, so she brought up the other issue that was bugging him.

'Tell me about the love of your life coming back.'

He dropped his guard and told her everything. 'Ana has invited one of her best friends from the past to be a bridesmaid at her wedding in the spring. I'm helping Ana with the catering. She came by to discuss part of the menu, and to tell me she'd invited my ex–girlfriend.'

'The love of your life?'

He nodded. 'I thought she was the one. She told me I was the one for her. We dated for a while and I expected we'd get married once her studies were complete. Instead, she told me she wanted to experience what life was like outside the town. She had friends in New York and had been visiting them more often. The plan was that she'd take a month out, go live with them, get the city hankering out of her system and then come back and settle down with me.'

'And it didn't quite work out that way?'

Greg shook his head. 'At first I thought, it's only four weeks. Give her the space she needs. She worked for the dog rescue center in town.'

'Where Zack got Cookie?'

'Yes. She loved working with the dogs. I never met an animal that didn't love her. Anyway, she started training for more qualifications, and taking extra studies in the city. Then the month was extended to another month, then another few weeks, and it became clear to me that she was never coming back.'

'I'm sorry, Greg.'

He nodded, quite emotional. 'I thought I was over her.' He shrugged. 'Then Ana shows me pictures of her online, smiling like she used to do.'

'She hasn't changed?'

'Yes, she has. She's even prettier than when she left.' He sighed. 'I haven't been able to get my guts to untwist since Ana told me. I like Ana, as a friend, and she wanted to warn me. They were a group of close friends and it's only natural that they'd all be Ana's bridesmaids. There shouldn't be one missing just because I'm a sucker.'

'No, you're not.'

'I am. I let her go. I didn't fight to get her back. I didn't persuade her to come home, because I loved her so much I wanted her to be happy more than anything else. And if that meant her being in New York, then okay. I let her go,' he repeated, tearing himself up about it. 'I didn't want her to come back because of me. I wanted her to come back because she missed the town, and wanted to come home.'

'Is she married, engaged?'

'Still single. I don't want to get my hopes up. It's easier to keep my hopes down on the bottom rung on the ladder for a softer landing.'

'What does Ana think about all this?'

'Ana's too sweet to say. I assured her that I'm over the past and everything is fine.'

'Did she believe you?'

'Probably not.'

Greg suddenly pulled Sylvie close to him and gazed deep into her eyes. 'Smile at me.'

'What?'

He spoke through a clenched grin. 'Smile as if you're besotted with me. The paparazzi are here.'

The speed with which she pasted a fake grin on her face showed the extent of her concern. 'Have they seen me?'

'They checked you out, but because you're standing with me, they're still looking around.'

'Are you sure it's the paparazzi? How many are there?' Sylvie asked.

'There are three guys, all with cameras, and none of them seem like they belong here. They look like photo journalists to me. They're carrying very expensive and professional cameras. I wouldn't mind one of those.'

Sylvie continued gazing up at Greg while tugging the hood of her coat around her face, pretending it was because of the icy weather. 'There's nowhere to hide without them seeing us.' They were slam dunk in the middle of the town. 'If we go into any of the stores, we could get cornered and snapped.'

'I'll hide you.' Greg put his arm around her shoulders and pulled her close.

She rested her head on his shoulder as they walked along and furtively sized up the paparazzi. Greg was right about them not fitting into the town. They appeared to have no interest in anything other than hunting down their objective — Sylvie, and gleaning photographs.

'I'm thinking of making a run for it,' Sylvie whispered to Greg.

'No, you'll only attract their attention, and I doubt you could outrun these guys.'

'Don't bet on it. I'm fast when I'm desperate.'

'Those boots would slow you down,' Greg said lightly. 'On second thoughts, you probably could beat them.' He smiled at her. 'Those cartwheels, Sylvie. Those cartwheels!'

'Shh! They're heading right for us.'

'I'm going to lean in and pretend to kiss you. Pretend. Okay. So don't get any ideas.'

This made her laugh, and he leaned in as they walked past the paparazzi, effectively shielding her face from them.

Her genuine laughter was a great defense, and allowed them to walk right past the three guys without them giving her a second glance.

'If we can reach the cafe, we're home and dry,' said Greg.

The cafe was on the other side of the street and further along. 'Let's go for it,' she said.

'Keep a tight hold of my hand to prevent slipping on the snow.' He clasped her hand in his.

'I won't slip,' she assured Greg.

'I was meaning me.'

Again, she laughed and together they ran to the cafe. Rather than blend into the crowd, they stood out due to their giggling and fast sprinting.

'Did they see us?' Sylvie gasped as they reached the cafe.

'Yes, everyone saw us, but the paparazzi don't think for a second you're you.'

Greg went to the window and peered out. He stood where he'd hidden from Sylvie, assured he couldn't easily been seen.

Sylvie saw the paparazzi split up and go into three different stores, including Jessica's quilt shop.

'They've gone into Jessica's shop.' Sylvie sounded concerned.

155

'That's their mistake. I bet they come out loaded with fabric whether they're into quilting or not.'

Sylvie laughed. 'This is the most horrible fun I've had in a long time.'

'I think there's a compliment for me in there somewhere.'

There was, she thought, liking Greg more with everything he did for her.

Chapter Thirteen

The tall elf from the previous night's party was busy cooking pancakes, while another Christmas elf served customers. The aroma of maple syrup, nutmeg and ginger wafted in the air. If they hadn't been in a hurry, Sylvie would've succumbed to an invitation to sit down at one of the tables and enjoy a serving of freshly made pancakes with syrup, whipped cream and blueberries.

Greg led Sylvie by the hand through the cafe into the kitchen at the rear of the premises. He whispered to the tall elf as they went by. 'Sylvie was never here.'

The tall elf tipped his spatula towards Greg. 'Gotcha.'

'We're one Christmas elf short today due them being snowed in,' Greg told Sylvie.

Elves working in the cafe didn't seem out of place, especially as the festive decorations extended to twinkle lights around the entire room and a Christmas tree at the window that was so pretty, Sylvie would've happily taken it home with her. She liked Greg's taste in decor. Now knowing him better than the first time she'd been here, she noticed the little touches he'd added including quilted wall hangings instead of pictures and quilted placemats and table runners. He'd probably sewn the red and white gingham table covers himself because each one draped perfectly and fitted the small tables for two and the larger family sized tables.

Remnants of the cafe's original styling remained intact from Greg's grandfather's era. Greg had kept the decor fresh, but retained the vintage elements. He'd attained a balance of modern and vintage, and she almost wished she could wrap the whole place up in a box and take it home with her to New York.

They stood at the back of the cafe kitchen to talk in private. He took his jacket off and hung it up on a peg.

Sylvie tipped her hood down but kept her coat on. 'Thanks for rescuing me, Greg. I can evade the press from here.' She intended leaving via the rear door.

'At least have a coffee before you go. It's cold out there.'

'You're busy. I'm fine.' She really hadn't planned to stay.

'Nonsense.' He sat her down in the kitchen and poured her a coffee. 'I feel better having spoken to you about my ex. Thanks for listening.'

'Anytime, Greg.' Then it dawned on her that this wouldn't be true because she'd be leaving soon.

Greg had a knack for reading her expressions. 'We can surely keep in touch by phone and email after you go back to New York?'

She liked that idea. 'Yes, we'll do that.'

'Just as friends,' he emphasized. 'I can call you up as it gets nearer to Ana's wedding and the meeting with my ex.'

'Definitely,' said Sylvie. She pictured giving Greg bolstering talks on handling his first encounter with his ex. She was no expert on relationships, but she was a good listener, and having someone to talk to was what he valued from their friendship. Maybe it would help her too, knowing that when she was home in the city, she still had a connection back to the town, and that not everything from her vacation was gone forever.

'Ana's so excited about the wedding,' Greg said, sounding as exuberant as Ana was. 'Every time she gets an idea for the menu she runs it by me, and we talk about whether it would work with the theme she's planning.'

'It's nice that you make time for Ana.'

'She's a good friend, and I can totally understand her enthusiasm. A wedding is so exciting. We've had a few locally this year. People say it's a great town for romance. There are still quite a few eligible bachelors available. Not that I'm hinting.' He started to give examples of the men available. 'There's Zack, obviously, and me, and Luke from the art store—'

'Luke?'

'Yes, but Virginia loves Luke.'

'I didn't know they were a couple,' said Sylvie.

'They're not. He likes Virginia as a friend, but nothing more than that.'

Sylvie sympathized. 'It's difficult to find the perfect match.'

'It is. Folks used to joke that any woman who wanted to catch Zack or Luke would have to be a very fast runner.'

'Luke mentioned that he was in the local running team and that Zack was the team leader. Were you into sports as a kid?'

'No. I love to swim in the cove during the summer, but I'm not the sporty type. When I was a kid I used to volunteer to make the lemonade drinks for the running team to avoid having to be in it. Even then I enjoyed doing the catering. I had a wonderful method for slicing the lemons to give the maximum flavor.'

Sylvie laughed. 'Well, you seem to have found your ideal career.'

'I have, and it keeps me fit. I probably run a few miles every day working in my cafe. It's a very active job.'

The tall elf came hurrying into the kitchen. 'Greg, a customer wants one of your layer cake specials. Is it chocolate sponge on the bottom, strawberry sponge on top and vanilla sponge in the middle? Or is it strawberry on top, vanilla in the middle and chocolate on the bottom?'

'I'll be right through,' Greg told him.

Sylvie finished her drink. 'Thanks for the coffee.'

'It'll keep you going if you have to hide behind trees, lurk in the bushes or dive for cover into someone's garden to avoid the press.'

'Hiding? Maybe,' she conceded. 'But there will be no lurking or diving into gardens.'

Greg opened the back door. 'Run wild, run fast and don't let the paparazzi get you.'

'Never,' she joked and hurried out. Then she called back to him. 'Greg, have you ever known Zack to be a blatant liar?'

Greg scoffed. 'Mr Blunt? Are you kidding?'

'I'm having trouble believing the things he's telling me.'

'About the video?' Greg asked.

'Yes, he says he didn't upload it to make it public. He says he thought it was private. Nate backs him up on this, but what if he's lying to him too?'

'I'd be inclined to believe Zack. If I were you, I'd trust him ninety percent and give myself ten percent wiggle room in case he has another reason for not being totally upfront with you.'

'Thanks, Greg.' She waved and hurried away.

The stores were all lit up and the main street was abuzz with people doing their Christmas shopping. Jessica's quilt shop was busy with customers, so too was Virginia's dress shop. The carol singers had lit their lanterns and stood amid the hub of things singing their festive songs.

159

With the hood of her coat pulled up Sylvie merged with the townsfolk and walked along thinking about everything that had happened. She felt better having spent time with Greg. Talking to him had made her forget her own troubles, and although she was keeping a watchful eye out for the paparazzi, she didn't feel so angry and upset. Greg had made her laugh and that had eased a whole load of tension. Now it was up to her to stay calm and think clearly what she was going to do about trending on social media.

From anything she'd heard about the paparazzi, they wouldn't hang around town for long just to get photographs of her. She was only newsworthy while she was a trending topic, and that wasn't going to last. Once the interest in her waned, they'd leave her be. All she had to do was avoid them for the time being.

Flakes of snow began fluttering down, so she decided to walk back home.

Her mind rewound the last conversation she'd had with Zack, and his insistence that he hadn't been sneaky. Was he telling the truth? She wasn't sure.

She thought about the things that had happened since she'd arrived in town. Nothing had played out the way she'd imagined. Now here she was still unable to relax and enjoy herself.

It would soon be the Christmas Eve party night. Then after Christmas Day she'd be getting ready to pack her bags and head back to the city.

As she tried not to work herself up about this, she noticed a man standing beside a tree further along from her house. She blinked against the flakes of snow, wondering if he was one of the paparazzi. It was possible. He resembled one of the men she'd seen earlier. He could be waiting for her to come home.

She was approaching Zack's house and had to make a decision. Should she keep walking and hope he wasn't interested in her, turn around and run, but risk him chasing after her, or take advantage of the darkening weather conditions and hide from him?

With every step she took her heart pounded faster. Now level with Zack's house, she decided to hide. If she walked further along to her own house the man was bound to see her. Then she noticed the man was starting to head her way. There was no one else around.

The lights were on Zack's house and she caught a glimpse of him near the front window. Had he see her too? Hopefully not, because she was about to jump over the low fence that bordered his property and hide in his garden.

Without further hesitation she jumped the fence. Unfortunately she slipped in the snow as she dived for cover. She hoped the man hadn't seen her and kept down low.

The click of a door opening alerted her that someone had seen her. A glance over her shoulder made her tense. Zack was running down the garden towards her with a concerned expression on his face.

'Sylvie! I didn't recognize you at first. Then when you did that flying leap over the fence and face planted in the snow I knew it was you.'

'Keep your voice down,' she snapped at him.

'What are you doing?' he whispered.

'I'm hiding. Go away.'

'Hiding from what?'

'The paparazzi.'

Zack immediately glanced around. His eyes panned the whole area from the garden to the street. 'I don't see anyone.'

Sylvie popped her head up and saw the man further along the street. 'There he is, and he's heading this way.' She started to move in stealth mode across his garden.

'Where are you going?' he hissed at her.

'Taking Cookie's route from your back yard and then along into mine.'

'Don't be silly. Come with me to my house.' He pulled her up, grabbed hold of her elbow and hustled her to his front door. Light shone from the doorway and illuminated the porch.

Sylvie didn't resist. She hadn't relished the idea of skulking through the back yards in these conditions. Zack's house would suffice while she thought what to do.

He almost lifted her off her feet to hurry her inside and closed the door behind them.

She sighed with relief and brushed the snow from her coat where she'd been lying in the garden.

'Let me take your coat,' Zack offered.

She shrugged it off.

He shook the excess snow from it and hung in up in the hallway to dry. The warmth from the fire in the study filtered through, and the aroma of something cooking reminded her how hungry she was.

He pushed up the sleeves of his grey sweater emphasizing his lean, strong forearms. The sweater and dark pants he wore accentuated his broad shoulders and long legged physique.

'I'm rustling up dinner,' he said, seeing her react to the delicious smell of a home cooked meal. 'You're welcome to join me. It's nothing fancy, just stew and crusty bread. I've hardly eaten anything all day.'

'It smells temping, but I...' she shook her head, indicating she still wasn't comfortable talking to him after everything that had happened.

'Be tempted,' he said firmly. 'Come on. Cookie's snoring in his basket. It'll give us a chance to talk.'

To refuse would've been petulant. They needed to talk, even though her pulse was racing at the thought of raking over their differences. It was this that caused her pulse to quicken, wasn't it? It couldn't be because Zack's handsome appearance and forthright manner caused reactions within her that she'd rather not have to deal with right now. She had enough to cope with trying to figure out if she could ever trust him again.

She nodded and followed him through to the kitchen, while glancing in at his study. His house bore an elegant style combined with traditional warmth. She thought how much it reflected Zack's classy, masculine taste.

The decor in his kitchen was a prime example of what she perceived a man like him would have. It was functional, fuss free and equipped with the right amount of practical gadgets for someone who cooked for himself, but wasn't particularly into home cooking. Zack's main interests lay in his architecture work and looking after his dog.

Zack stirred the stew on the stove and wondered if she sensed how nervous he was. All the plans he'd had for inviting her round to his house were cast to the wind. The chocolate cake he'd bought for her was untouched. He hadn't anticipated she'd be here now.

'Take a seat.'

Sylvie sat down at the kitchen table that had a setting for one. 'Can I help you with dinner?'

He almost refused her offer then instantly changed his mind. 'Sure. The plates are over there in the cupboard and there's cutlery in the drawer.'

Sylvie got up and went over to the cupboard. She selected a white dinner plate and set it down on the table along with cutlery.

'The stew is ready for serving. I was about to heat the coffee and slice up some bread.'

'I'll sort the bread and the coffee,' she offered, flicking on the coffee pot. She washed her hands and then cut several pieces of bread.

She saw him flick secret glances at her, as if he couldn't quite believe she was in his kitchen making dinner with him. If only he knew she was thinking the same thing. She felt nervous and yet comfortable, at odds but at home, uncertain yet sure this was the right thing for both of them — to sit down to dinner like two sensible adults and discuss the corner they'd managed to back themselves into.

Zack ladled the stew on to their plates then set the pot back on the stove.

'This smells delicious,' she said, and poured two cups of coffee.

They sat down opposite each other.

She picked up her cutlery and began to eat her stew. 'This tastes great.'

'I didn't feel hungry until I started cooking,' he admitted. 'I knew I had to eat something so I could think straight.' He tore a piece of bread and ate it.

'I've barely eaten since breakfast. I had a cup of coffee at Greg's cafe, but that's all I had when I was out.'

Zack stabbed his fork into a chunk of meat. 'Weren't you concerned you'd be seen in the cafe by the press?'

'I was hiding through the back in the kitchen.'

He shook his head in dismay. 'What a trail of trouble we've caused for people in this town.'

His words rang true with her. 'We have caused chaos,' she agreed. 'Nancy and Jessica bamboozled a local newspaper reporter, and Greg embroiled an elf in the subterfuge.'

'Do I even want to know about that?'

Sylvie pursed her lips. 'No.'

'Thank goodness. It's bad enough that I've involved Santa in the mess we've made of things. But I thought I could rely on Nate's opinion when it came to the video. That's why I gave him access to it.'

'Merry chaotic Christmas, huh?'

He smiled and focused on his meal. 'I've no idea how to shake the paparazzi off your tail.'

'They won't chase me for long. The hits on the video are bound to be slowing down. I'm not a celebrity, and it's crazy that they want pictures of me, but I understand when there's a popular story involved, the press are likely to hound me. I won't be newsworthy for long. It'll be old news soon. I just have to avoid them at the moment.'

'Is that what Marla wants you to do?'

'I don't know. I haven't spoken to her for hours. Have you?' She'd picked up on a hint of something in his voice.

He nodded. 'I called her. I wanted to apologize for the trouble I've caused and to make sure it didn't affect your career.'

'You spoke to Marla?'

'Yeah.'

'What did she say?'

'She sounded very happy about the publicity your work is receiving due to the video's popularity.'

'So you really did speak to Marla?' Sylvie didn't hide her surprise.

'Yes, did you think I was lying about that too?'

'I don't know. I keep getting thrown curveballs. Every time I think I've got things under control — bam.'

He gestured around the kitchen. 'I know how you feel. I'm having an issue with this.'

She frowned at him. 'With what?'

'With you sitting here in my home having dinner with me like we're a regular couple.'

'You make it sound like it's something bad.'

'Quite the opposite,' he said. 'I could get used to this.'

She blushed.

'You're blushing,' he told her.

'I'm not. It's the heat from the stew.'

He threw her a disbelieving glance.

164

'And from the harassment,' she said.

'You're harassed eating stew and drinking coffee?'

'No, but I'm still supposed to be angry with you.'

He concentrated on eating his dinner, but a smirk played across his lips.

'You're smirking, Zack.'

'I'm trying not to.'

'Try harder.'

'Okay. I won't tell you that you're cute when you're angry with me.'

'No, that would rile me.'

'I should probably say things like — I wish I'd never uploaded the video or shared it with Nate.'

'That would be a good start.'

'And that I'm really sorry for causing you to trend on social media.'

'That would also work.'

'Anything else?' he said.

'Yes, give me another scoop of that stew. It's delicious.'

Zack got up and served her a second helping.

'Are we friends again?' he asked hopefully.

'Help me deal with the press, and I'll consider drawing a line in the sand.'

'Speaking of drawing, I've yet to see your artwork. I'd love to see your work.'

'Unless you have a secret tunnel to my house, I think we're stuck here for now.' She paused. 'Unless...'

'What?'

'You used to be a fast runner.'

'I still am,' he insisted.

She gave him a mischievous grin.

He mentally joined the dots of her plan. 'You want me to run to your house to get your artwork while you hide here?'

'No, I'll go with you. A quick sprint across the back yards, grab my portfolio and then back here.'

'That wouldn't be sensible, Sylvie.'

'When did that ever stop us?'

He stabbed his fork at his dinner. 'We'll finish this and then make a bolt for it, without being caught by the press.'

Sylvie nodded firmly. 'We have a plan.'

A sleepy–headed Cookie padded into the kitchen, yawning and stretching, unaware they had a guest for dinner.

Sylvie smiled at Zack, waiting for the dog to realize they had company. Any moment now...

The wide eyed look Cookie gave her, followed by an enthusiastic welcome made her laugh.

'Hi there, Cookie.' She leaned down and gave him a hug.

Overexcited and not knowing what to do with himself, Cookie started chasing his own tail, round and round, his paws padding on the kitchen floor.

Sylvie applauded and then got up to calm him down with hugs and snuggles. 'Whoa there!'

Zack started to clear the dishes away. 'Are you sure you want to make a stealth run for your portfolio?' he asked her.

'I'm having second thoughts. It would be a silly, crazy thing to do.'

Zack nodded, then thumbed towards the hallway. 'I'll get my jacket.'

'Can you see anyone?' Sylvie whispered, tucking in behind Zack as they made the first part of their run from his back yard to the neighbor's garden next door.

Zack's eyes panned around the area. It wasn't as dark as he thought it would be. The gardens were lit in patches of shadows and light, illuminated where the street lamps shone through the gaps between the houses into the back yards. He'd also forgotten how many houses were aglow with Christmas lights.

'I don't see anyone,' he said, helping her step over the fence.

She wore her coat with the hood up. 'You're a bad influence on me, you know that, don't you?' she whispered.

The look he gave her.

'Okay, so maybe it works both ways,' she conceded.

They'd left Cookie in Zack's house, snuggled up by the fireside, as they didn't plan on being out for long.

Flurries of excitement made her glad they'd decided to do this. She wondered if Zack felt the same.

They ran across the neighbor's back yard and stopped at the fence leading to her garden while Zack assessed the situation. 'I can

166

see why Cookie enjoyed doing this,' he said, unintentionally answering her question.

'It's fun, isn't it?' she said.

'With you it is.'

Her heart squeezed as he gazed at her. His handsome features were accentuated in the glow of the street lights. His eyes were the deepest blue she'd ever seen them.

They gazed at each other for a moment as they crouched down out of view of prying eyes. For a second she thought he was going to kiss her, but he didn't.

'I'll help you over the fence,' he said, taking her hand in his strong grasp, steadying her as she stepped over into her own back yard.

She fished her keys from her coat pocket and they entered the house via the kitchen.

'Don't turn the lights on,' he reminded her. 'It'll alert anyone watching the house that you're home.'

She pulled her hand back from the light switch in the kitchen. There was enough ambient glow filtering through from the lounge where the Christmas tree was still lit. She hadn't thought to turn it off when she'd left earlier, and it helped illuminate the lounge.

She lifted her portfolio from her desk and tucked another couple of pieces of artwork in it.

Zack was right behind her, leaning over her shoulders, eager to see her work.

Not realizing he was so close, she turned quickly and bumped right into his chest.

He put his hands on her shoulders to steady her, and again there was a moment of closeness where she thought he was going to kiss her.

She snapped into efficient mode to stave off the intimacy. 'Okay. Let's get out of here.'

He followed her through to the kitchen, and took the portfolio from her as she locked up.

They made their way back, taking the same route, running and hiding, climbing the fences and scurrying back to the safety of Zack's house.

He closed his kitchen door and leaned against it. 'Phew!'

'Will I make the coffee?' she offered, shrugging her coat off.

'Yes, please.' He hung her coat and his jacket in the hallway.

Cookie came running through, giving them a great welcome. Zack patted the dog's head, reassuring him they were home and that he could settle back down.

'I'll put more logs on the fire.' Zack walked through to the study.

'Okay,' she called to him. While making the coffee she viewed his kitchen. Was that a chocolate cake over there?

'I bought a chocolate cake from the grocery store earlier,' Zack said from the study.

'Two coffees and two slices of cake coming up.'

Zack piled the logs on the fire and watched them spark into life. He breathed deeply. Maybe now they could relax and enjoy some calm, quiet time together.

Sylvie carried the coffee and cake through on a tray and set it down on a table near the fireside. Cookie was curled up cozy on one of the scatter rugs.

Zack lifted a slice of cake and bit into it.

Sylvie stepped around his study. 'This is really nice.'

He let her look around. She walked over to his desk and studied his latest project — a detailed architectural structure.

'I'm working on a new house design,' he said.

She leaned close, fascinated by the level of detail. 'This is amazing. So precise.'

He put his coffee down and went over to the desk. 'I'm trying to figure out a better way to allow light to filter in through the skylights above the hallway. Light is always a deciding factor for me.'

She gazed at his design. Part of it was drawn in pencil and other parts had been finished in ink.

'Where's your portfolio?' He sounded enthusiastic.

'It's in the kitchen.'

He went through, picked it up, came back and handed it to her at his desk.

She unzipped the portfolio and showed him her latest designs. 'I painted these with the watercolors and gouache you gave me.'

'May I?' he asked before touching any of them.

'Yes.' She trusted he'd know how to handle artwork.

He held each piece carefully and studied them. 'These are beautiful.'

168

She searched his face for any hint of false flattery and happily found none.

'These are the first designs for my new autumn collection.'

'I love the chestnuts, the colors, the way you've created movement with the leaves. Do you draw them in pencil and then color them?' He held her work under a desk lamp. 'Do you use illustration pens to ink some of your designs?'

'I do. I use a mix of techniques depending on what type of print effect I want for the fabric design. Some flowers are soft edged watercolor, others are drawn like illustrations in pen and ink and then colored.' She pointed to one of the pens on his desk. He had a whole load of pens, but she recognized one in particular. 'In fact, I use this type of pen.'

He smiled, happy their work had something in common.

'My designs are nowhere near as detailed as yours,' she said. 'Only in my dreams could I achieve your level of precision.'

'We're different types of artists. I don't even think of myself as an artist. I'm an architectural designer.' He admired two of her drawings. 'Now this is the work of an artist. I create what will exist. You paint what could exist. An artist's vision of flowers and nature is something I've always loved.'

He led her through to the hallway and pointed to a painting on one of the walls. A floral painting. The only watercolor. Everything else was a framed piece of architectural design. The colors of the painting stood out amid the monochrome art.

'This was painted by my grandfather. It's one of my favorite pieces of art. I love the transparent quality of the watercolor, the soft edges, how it creates an impression of petals and leaves.' He paused, admiring it. 'I'd love to be able to paint like that, but it's not my style. I've tried, but precision is my thing.'

They went back into the study and he poured through the contents of her portfolio as she explained each piece.

'These are some of the watercolor flowers that are part of my summer fabric collection. A few of them are complete paintings, but I don't use an entire painting for a design because the pattern has to work as a repeat on the fabric. I select parts of the painting by scanning it into my computer and then begin piecing it into a workable pattern.'

He held up one of the watercolor roses. 'This is beautiful, so soft and delicate.' He cast a glance at her. 'Very beautiful, really lovely.'

She blushed, but he made no comment this time.

She tried to remain calm while being aware of how his closeness affected her. He'd pushed up the sleeves of his sweater again, and she noticed how strong his forearms were, and he had the elegant hands of an artist.

'This is one of my personal favorites,' she said, showing him a cornflower painting. 'I love the colors in this. I love these tones of blue.'

His blue eyes were gazing at her. Their clarity shone under the desk lamp. She held her breath, and for one unforgettable moment, all she could feel was the connection between them. If ever there was a moment when her heart took one step closer to his, it was this moment here with Zack.

She blinked and stepped back, brushing her hair away from her flustered face. 'So that's how I create my designs.'

His gaze held on to her, reluctant to let the moment go, but he finally relinquished it, and tried to sound calm while his heart felt fit to burst from the overflowing feelings he had for her. 'What do you do with all your artwork?' He swept his hand over the selection in the portfolio.

'I file them away for posterity I suppose, and for future reference. I've framed several pieces and they're in my apartment.'

'I'd like to buy a few pieces. Everything I have is monochrome. It would be lovely to have some color on the walls of my study.'

She was taken aback and flattered. 'I'd be happy to give you a few pieces, or paint something for you.'

'You'd do that?'

'Sure. What would you like?'

'I'd like anything you'd care to paint for me.'

'Do you have any favorite flowers or colors?'

'I love most flowers — roses, orchids, bluebells, and I do like blue, though I'm happy to have any colors. Really, I'll leave it up to you.' He again admired her artwork. 'Anything you paint I'm sure I'll like. I'd be happy to buy your work.'

She smiled, but had no intention of asking him to pay for her art.

'We should drink our coffee before it gets cold,' he said.

She nodded.

170

They sat by the fireside and enjoyed their coffee and cake. A comfortable silence stretched between them for a few moments.

'This is the first time I've felt truly relaxed since I arrived here,' said Sylvie.

'Are you going to the Christmas Eve party?' His tone sounded level, but tension rippled through him.

'Yes.' She sensed he was leading up to something.

'Anyone asked you to go with them?'

'No. I think it's okay to go on my own.'

'It is, but maybe you'd like to go with me?' He looked over at her to gauge her reaction.

'Are you inviting me to the Christmas Eve party, Zack?'

'I do believe I am.'

She smiled at him. 'Okay. I accept.'

Relief washed over him. 'All we have to do is keep out of trouble until then.'

Sylvie nodded. 'I'll try if you will.'

He raised his coffee cup in a toasting gesture. 'We have another plan.'

Chapter Fourteen

'It's getting late.' Sylvie stood up. 'I should be going.'

She'd enjoyed her evening relaxing by the fire in Zack's study. The sofa had been so comfortable, and the heat from the fire was making her drowsy even though she'd had extra cups of coffee. Between them, they'd decimated most of the chocolate cake while Zack ensured they had plenty of coffee during the whole evening.

Discussing their respective careers had felt good, though neither of them had a workable solution regarding how they could possibly be together if they ever wanted to start dating. Zack didn't want to leave town and she couldn't leave New York. This impasse resulted in Zack making them another round of coffee and chocolate cake. They'd tiptoed around their feelings and attraction for each other, but Sylvie made it clear where she stood when it came to the idea of dating him while she was on vacation. A holiday romance wouldn't work for her.

Zack understood.

They'd chatted again about their work, and she learned that Zack was in the midst of a really lucrative project designing houses for one of the nearby towns. And he'd told her that family was important to him, and that one day, when he found the right woman, he'd love to settle down and have a family of his own. This ticked yet another box for her.

Sylvie put her empty cup down on the coffee table and walked away from the log fire. She stifled a yawn.

'You're welcome to stay here if you want to avoid the press. Have a sleepover. I'll take the sofa. You can sleep in my room.'

'I don't want to impose,' she said, though she sensed his offer was genuine.

He didn't push this further. He hadn't expected her to say yes. 'Or you could take the back yard route home. I could go with you. Keep a lookout.'

'That's an option, but I'm happy to go on my own.' She picked up all the pieces of her artwork from Zack's desk and zipped them safely inside her portfolio.

Zack peered out the study window. Everything appeared calm and quiet. 'It is late. The chances are that the paparazzi have gone and you could walk along to your house via the front entrance.'

'That suggestion gets my vote so far,' said Sylvie. This was surely the easiest thing to do.

Zack had another idea. 'Or how about the one that will please Marla?'

'What's that?' she asked.

'Go out and let the press snap a few photos of you. It'll give you more publicity and then they'll have no reason to hang around.'

'That is some smart thinking.' Marla had wanted her to gain as much publicity as possible. Instead of running and hiding from the press, she should be making sure she was seen.

'Want me to go with you?' he offered.

'Yes, if I'm going to be in the news again, I think you deserve to share the glare.' She gave him a playful grin.

'Can I reconsider my previous offer?'

She shook her head. 'No reneging on me, Zack.'

'In that case, let's take Cookie with us.'

'He's sound asleep. He may not want to go out on a freezing cold night.'

'Cookie always wants to go out.' He went over to the dog. 'Want to go walkies, Cookie?'

The dog's eyes opened although he still lay snug as a bug by the fire.

'Walkies, Cookie, walkies,' Zack repeated.

The dog jumped up, eager to go.

Zack grabbed his jacket. 'Okay, we're ready.'

Sylvie put her coat on and picked up her portfolio. 'Let's go.'

The three of them headed along the sidewalk towards Sylvie's house. The fresh air perked her up, and she relished breathing in the atmosphere of the cold, Christmassy night.

'Typical,' she joked. 'There's never any press when you need them.'

'Maybe that's the secret to avoiding them. Seek them out and they'll vanish.'

They continued walking. Cookie enjoyed being outside in the snow and his tail wagged constantly.

Sylvie thought about the fun they'd all had in the snow that morning. 'It's a shame you didn't put the dog collar camera on Cookie this morning. I would've loved to have watched that video.'

Zack raised his shoulders up and sighed. 'Unfortunately, I didn't.'

She teased him. 'It would've been nice to see you getting beat by a girl and a dog during the snowball runs.'

'I was outnumbered two to one. Besides, you and Cookie had an advantage over me. You'd both been practicing these past few mornings.'

She laughed as they teased each other.

'I had a lovely evening,' he said, 'and I think your artwork is great.'

'Thanks, I had a good time.'

'What are you up to tomorrow?' he asked her.

'I'm not sure.' She smiled to herself. 'I remember what I first told Marla about my vacation. I said I planned to relax, sip mulled wine in front of a real log fire, eat gingerbread cookies, listen to Christmas music and enjoy the whole season.'

'That sounded like a great plan.'

'It was, until I met this guy and his dog. Then everything became chaotic. Now it's almost Christmas and I'm still waiting to have a totally relaxing day.'

'You still have time to do that.'

She nodded. 'I owe myself one of those days.'

'You do,' he agreed. 'You don't want to think back to your vacation here and feel you missed out on things.'

She wondered if that included being with him.

They were so engrossed in conversation that they never noticed the guy sitting in a car opposite Sylvie's house. It was only when they heard the clicking of the camera and saw the flashes that they realized they'd been photographed. Happy he'd obtained the pictures he'd been waiting for, the guy drove off.

Sylvie turned to Zack. 'At least it gets it over with. Marla will be pleased.'

Zack nodded. 'Now you can relax.'

Sylvie paused at her gate and breathed in the wintry night air. 'It feels as if things are going to be different from now on. A fresh start, fresh plans.'

174

He hoped he was included in her plans. 'I'll walk you to your door.'

'No, it's okay.'

'I insist.' The dog nudged against him. 'And so does Cookie.'

She smiled and let them escort her to her door. She opened it and bent down to give Cookie a hug. 'Make sure to keep Zack out of mischief.'

Zack scoffed. 'What about you?'

'I'm going to keep away from trouble. I'll probably have a sewing morning, stitching my quilts. Then I'll get my dress ready for the Christmas Eve party. I know it's not for a couple of nights, but I want to make sure it fits just right. This guy I'm going with to the party is very stylish. I'll have to pull out all the stops.'

'You could wear what you've got on right now and I'd still think you were the loveliest woman there.'

The strength of his comment rocked her back on her heels. She grinned at him.

'Did I just say that?' He sounded self–conscious.

'Oh, yes.'

'Blame it on drinking too much coffee.'

'Or blame it on the town,' she suggested.

'What do you mean?'

'Greg told me that people say this is a great town for romance.'

'It has that reputation. So yes, let's blame the town.'

They laughed, and then he stepped back, getting ready to leave. 'Well, goodnight.'

He started to walk away with Cookie.

'Just one thing before you go,' she said. 'Whatever they do with those photographs or write about us in the media, we agree not to get mad with each other.'

'Deal.'

'Goodnight, Zack.'

He gave her a wave and walked home with Cookie. Out of earshot of Sylvie, he commented to the dog. 'I wish I had filmed our fun together this morning. Even though you did team up with Sylvie to help her beat me. That video would've been one for the archives, but I'll remember the great time we had. Sylvie's not a woman I'll ever forget.' He was feeling buoyant about taking Sylvie to the

Christmas Eve party, while simultaneously downhearted that her vacation was drawing to a close soon after that.

Sylvie went inside and got ready for bed. Tiredness had crept up on her. She snuggled under the covers. The two–way radio sat on the bedside table where she'd left it the previous night. She wasn't tempted to call Zack. Tonight, she felt content. They'd talked all evening and settled their main differences. Zack hadn't filmed her deliberately. She believed him now. He'd only wanted to see what Cookie was up to. Circumstances had messed up his sensible intentions. He hadn't filmed any other videos of her. The only video was the one currently trending online. The hits on it were slowing down when Zack checked on it earlier. It might spike again if new photos were added to it on social media, but it was definitely on the wane. And she was glad. Grateful for the publicity and the attention it had brought to her designs, but also relieved that things would eventually settle down.

She sighed and gazed out the window. Nothing was settled with Zack. She was looking forward to going to the party with him, but how would things work out between them? When she went back to New York, would she keep in touch with him the way she planned to remain in contact with Greg? Tiredness stole away any chance of figuring out what to do, and she slept sound right through until the dawn.

Winter sunlight cast the kitchen in a warm yellow glow as she sat there having breakfast. She loved this kitchen because it always felt cozy even when it was a frosty day outside. Her city apartment kitchen was an extension of the open plan lounge and she preferred the traditional setting of this house.

After breakfast she padded around in thick socks and wore comfy casuals. She enjoyed the morning as planned, sewing her quilts and relaxing by the fire. She hummed along to festive carols while getting on with her quilting and thinking up ideas for her designs.

The Christmas tree lights were on, and it was the first time she'd ever had a Christmas tree without any presents wrapped up underneath it, but then she remembered that the vacation was her gift to herself.

176

At lunchtime, she popped out to buy fresh milk and bread from the grocery store. She'd wrapped up warm, and blinked against the dazzling sunlight glinting off the snow. The town looked so beautiful against the winter blue sky. The excitement of being here hadn't worn off. She snapped a couple of photos of the main street because it looked so picturesque.

She was about to go into the store when the tall elf from Greg's cafe came running up to her clutching a spatula. His face was flushed and he had something urgent to tell her.

'A guy, as tall as me, was in the cafe asking questions about you. I told him nothing. Well, nearly nothing. Nothing that matters.'

Sylvie held her hands up. 'Calm down and tell me what he said.'

'He walked in, real confident. He wanted to know where he could find you, where you lived.'

'What did you tell him?' she asked.

'I said, I'm making cream cheese bagels, bud. I don't know where she lives.'

'What happened after that?'

'Then he started asking me about Zack. What type of guy he is, what does he do for a living? So I told him the truth. I said Zack's a great guy, a successful architect, real smart, always helping out the community. I said I didn't know where he lived either, but that you liked Zack and his dog. I told him I didn't know any more than that and didn't want to get fired for slacking on the bagel making for customers.'

'What was his reaction?'

'He said thanks, and palmed me two hundred bucks.' The elf showed her the cash still clenched in his hand. 'What should I do with the money?'

'Keep it.'

The elf's eyes lit up with glee. 'Really?'

'Yes. Buy something nice with it.'

The elf already had an idea. 'I was thinking of buying my wife a new dress from Virginia's shop for the Christmas Eve party.'

'You should do that.'

The elf thrust the spatula into her hand. 'Thanks, Sylvie. Greg's due back from the bank any second now. Would you please tell him I'll be back in ten minutes.'

Without giving her a chance to refuse, he ran straight for Virginia's dress shop.

Sylvie stood for a moment in the draft of the whirlwind the elf had caused. Life here was definitely way more hectic than New York.

'Why are you standing brandishing one of my spatulas in the main street, Sylvie?'

She turned to see Greg trying to figure out what was going on.

'And was that one of my elves running into the dress shop?' he added.

The cafe's logo was on the handle of the spatula. She gave the utensil to Greg and explained what had happened.

'Two hundred dollars?' Greg was astounded.

'Uh–huh.'

'The press are still hunting you down?' he said.

'So it would seem. One of them got photos of me with Zack and Cookie last night. I thought they'd leave town after that. I guess not.'

'Want to come in for a coffee?' Greg offered.

'Thanks, but I'm trying to have a relaxing day at the house. I only popped out to pick up some groceries.'

Greg smiled at her. 'Enjoy your relaxing day. And don't worry about the press. I'll let the elves handle them from now on.'

Sylvie laughed, and Greg went into the cafe.

Her phone rang as she was about to step into the store. She stood outside to take the call from Marla.

'I got your email about the photos from last night,' Marla began. 'Great pics. Zack is so tall and handsome, and I love Cookie. What a cute dog. You all look so happy together, even though you've got an expression like a jack rabbit in one of the photos.'

'You've seen the photographs? Have they published them already?' Sylvie didn't know what type of time scale the press worked to.

'They're only on social media. And that's all the publicity we need. The hits on the video have jumped up again.'

'Email me a link. I'd like to see them.'

'I'll do that,' Marla said, and then hesitated. 'But there's something I have to tell you.'

The phone connection started to falter.

'What did you say, Marla?'

'He called me and said he wants to talk to you. He said—'

'It's a bad connection. I can hardly hear you. Say that again.'

'He wants to apologize to you, Sylvie. I thought I should warn you. You know what he's like.' Marla's voice was intermittent.

'Marla, I don't know who you're talking about.'

The connection cut out. Sylvie held her phone up, trying to pick up a signal. As she turned around she saw a man standing smiling at her.

'I think Marla is talking about me.'

Sylvie gasped. 'Conrad!'

His blond hair shone in the sunlight and he wore expensive casuals that made the most of his tall, fit build. Conrad looked like money. And this was the only thing about him that didn't deceive.

She was so taken aback seeing him there that she didn't stop him from wrapping her in his arms and hugging her close to him. He kissed her cheek and gave her one of his charming smiles.

'I've missed you, Sylvie. I've been such a fool, but I think the break we've had has made me realize we should be together more than ever.'

She found the impetus to push him away. 'We broke up. It's over. I made it clear I never wanted to see you again.'

'I can tell you're still upset with me.'

She glared at him. 'You think?'

'Don't be mad at me for coming here. I saw you on that video, and I knew I had to see you again, to try and make things right between us.'

'You saw the video?'

'Yes, and I called Marla to find out where you were. She wouldn't tell me, then I found out that you were here. It's a small town, and I figured I could find you quite easily.' He glanced around with disapproval on his suave features. 'A woman like you doesn't belong in a town like this. This place just isn't you. What are you doing here anyway? Marla wouldn't tell me anything.'

Good on Marla, Sylvie cheered inwardly. 'I'm on vacation.'

'You came here on purpose?'

'Yes.'

He seemed to need further assurance. 'You're not here to work?'

'No, I'm here for the holidays, to enjoy Christmas, on my own.'

'What about Zack?' Conrad's tone was condescending.

'It's none of your business,' she snapped at him. Hearing him bring up Zack's name triggered a strong reaction in her. 'How dare you come here and confront me like this. How dare you!'

'Let's not squabble, sweetie.' He went to give her a hug but she pulled back.

Sylvie saw several sets of eyeballs watching them. Nancy and Nate peered out the window of the grocery store, Ana looked out at them from the diner, and one of the elves stared anxiously from the window of Greg's cafe.

'People are watching us,' Sylvie hissed at Conrad. 'Don't make a scene.'

Conrad turned up the charm. 'I don't want to make a scene, babe. I want to make things right between us.' He put his hands gently on her shoulders and gazed down at her with that look of genuine caring he could nail so well. 'We need to talk.'

Sylvie crossed her arms and tilted her chin up. 'Say whatever you have to say and then leave.'

Conrad indicated across the street. 'My car is parked over there. We can talk in private.' He glanced over his shoulder at the people watching them, then gazed at her. 'I drove all this way just to see you.' He put the flat of his hand on his heart. 'Please hear what I have to say.'

Sylvie hesitated. Conrad had always been a master when it came to a game of charm chess. Despite knowing this, she could still feel his moves work on her.

Conrad added a sincere smile. 'I really have missed you so much, but I've been too stubborn to do anything about it, until now. Seeing your beautiful face up close and your smile on the video, it made my heart ache for you.' His gave her a dazzling smile. 'And those daring spins and cartwheels... wow! Just wow!' He gazed at her and stepped close. 'I thought, this is the woman for me, she always was, and I messed things up big style. Give me ten minutes of your time. That's all I ask.'

Sylvie felt herself tilt towards agreeing. She'd been suckered by his charm many times, but she'd never heard him speak so openly to her before.

'We used to be a cute couple. Come home to New York, baby. You're a talented, intelligent, beautiful, kind and caring woman. You don't belong here.'

'I think I do.'

He shook his head. 'This isn't real life, not for you. You're all caught up in the Christmas atmosphere, but this won't last. Once the snow melts and the silly season is over, this will be just another little nowhere town offering no prospects for a woman like you.'

She hated that he'd hit on some of her concerns. Not about the town, because she loved it, and had seen pictures of it during other seasons. It was the worry that perhaps she'd wanted a cozy, small town Christmas so much, she wasn't thinking of the practicalities, especially when it came to her career.

'You've always lived in the city. You can't flip on a dime and suddenly become a small town homebody.'

Conrad was backing her against the ropes and she wasn't armed well enough to totally disagree. Some of the things he said were valid.

'In all the time I've known you, you've never expressed an interest to live in a town.'

'I probably didn't,' she agreed. 'Even if I had, I doubt you'd have listened to what I wanted.'

'The not listening was an issue. I get it. But sweetie, it works both ways. Could you name one deal I made on the stock market?'

She wouldn't meet his gaze, because no, she couldn't. Conrad's work on the stock market wasn't a world she understood, or frankly was interested in. Stocks, shares, trading, shouting about numbers and the market. She let it all wash over her, confident that Conrad dealt with it. She wouldn't know a bull market from one in a china shop.

He threw another question at her. 'Name me one of the companies whose dinners we attended.'

'How should I know? It was nothing but conglomerates, corporations, subsidiaries and mergers. I didn't see the point in knowing any of them because even if I had, they'd merged and become another company.'

'You didn't even try.' His tone was level, without accusation. 'I'm not getting at you. I'm just telling it like it is. You accepted their hospitality, wined, dined and danced at their parties, and didn't know anything about them. At least I know Marla and the trading record of the home decor company you work for.'

She held up her hands in surrender. 'Okay, my bad.'

He pulled her hands down and held them in his. 'I can help you pack your bags and we can go home to New York.'

'No, I'm happy here.'

He upped his game. 'If you really want a cozy Christmas, let's drive to my house in Vermont.'

She tilted her head back and stared at him, searching for any hint of a lie. 'You have a house in Vermont?'

'Yes. See what I mean about the two–way lack of communication?'

'You never mentioned it to me.'

'I did. Remember when we were at that party near the lake, and you nearly fell in?'

She remembered. 'You were talking about someone's beautiful house in Vermont...'

Conrad was shaking his head. 'My house, Sylvie. I was talking about my new house in Vermont. You'd been on the champagne.' He shrugged off the issue. 'It doesn't matter now. What matters is us. Getting back together.' He flicked a glance around. 'And getting out of here.'

'No. You're no good for me.'

He continued to hold her hands, clasping them in his. 'A man can change. I've changed.' He leaned down and gave her a stunning smile. 'You'd love Vermont. It's a beautiful house.'

'I'm sure it is.' Everything Conrad owned, wore and acquired shone with style and panache.

He spoke in a confiding tone. 'I've made a few highly lucrative deals recently. Even if I never earned another dollar, which isn't going to happen, we're set for life, babe.'

'You were already set for life when I met you.'

'I was. Now there's another couple of layers of icing on the cake.' He smiled warmly. 'And you're to blame.'

She frowned at him.

'I've been so fired up inside since we split up,' Conrad confessed. 'I think that made me even more of a tiger on the trading floor. I nailed some sweet deals.'

She pulled her hands away from his. 'I don't care about the money.'

'Don't hate me for my ambition, for being a tiger, because if I didn't have that sort of drive, I'd be dressed as an elf baking bagels.'

She glared at him. 'Don't talk like that about these people.'

'I'm sorry, that was out of line, but you have to understand how frustrated I feel trying to convince you to believe me. I really have changed, Sylvie.'

An elf came hurrying up to them from the cafe. Although the elf wasn't quite as tall as Conrad, he was sturdily built and prepared to confront the interloper.

'Is everything okay, Sylvie?' He eyeballed Conrad.

Conrad didn't flinch.

'Yes, thanks, everything's fine,' Sylvie assured the elf.

The tension in her voice and the disdainful expression on Conrad's face made the elf reiterate his concern. 'Are you sure you're okay?'

'She's fine,' Conrad said smoothly.

'Who are you anyway?' the elf asked him.

'Conrad. I'm Sylvie's boyfriend.'

The elf stepped back. 'Sorry, I didn't know that. Nobody tells me anything right. I thought she was sweet on Greg.'

Conrad frowned at Sylvie. 'Greg?'

'He owns the cafe,' the elf told him. 'I'll leave you two alone now. I have to get back to making a baked Alaska.' He scurried away.

Conrad sneered. 'What's with the elves in this town?'

Sylvie sighed. 'It's Christmas. It's a nice town. People here enjoy celebrating the season.'

Conrad refrained from further derision of the town. 'Come on, let's talk in the car.'

He sounded reasonable and it made her feel unreasonable if she'd refused. Nancy and Nate were on the verge of coming to her rescue too. She didn't want to cause a scene, especially at lunchtime when customers were enjoying a festive break in the cafe and the diner.

Sylvie let Conrad escort her across the street to his sleek, expensive car. He put his arm around her shoulders as he made sure she didn't slip on the snow. He was trying his utmost to be chivalrous by opening the car door and helping her inside. Closing the passenger door, he ran round to the driver's side and got in, casting a glimpse at the faces watching them.

Zack's jacket flapped open as he ran towards the cafe. He opened the door and called to the elf making baked Alaska. 'Who's the guy with Sylvie?'

The elf scooped ice cream into a flan case. 'Her boyfriend, Conrad. I think he's here to take her back to New York for Christmas with him.'

Zack felt he'd been given a sucker punch in the guts. He nodded at the elf and then ran outside just in time to see Sylvie drive off with Conrad. He ran his hands through his hair as the frustration built inside him.

Nate approached Zack. 'You got my message?'

'Yes.' The cold air cut through him, or perhaps it was the thought that he'd just lost Sylvie to her ex–boyfriend. 'I thought she was finished with him.'

Nate saw the tension in Zack's expression. 'I overheard some of their conversation. He saw her on the video and decided he wants her back. He's got all the charm to entice her, and he's dangling a house in Vermont in front of her like a Christmas bauble.'

The defeat in Zack's voice was unmistakable. 'I can't compete with that.'

'You'd better, Zack. And you'd better do it now,' Nate warned him.

Zack nodded at Nate and pulled his phone from his jacket pocket. He tried to call Sylvie but couldn't get a signal. He sighed, even more frustrated. 'I don't even know where they've gone.'

'I'm betting they're driving to her house. He offered to pack her bags for her.'

He slapped Nate firmly on the shoulder. 'Thanks, Nate.'

Zack ran home in record time. There was no sign of Conrad's car. He hurried inside his house. Cookie scurried through to welcome him.

'Keep a lookout for Sylvie, Cookie. Watch for Sylvie.'

Cookie ran to the window and stared out, front paws on the window ledge, alert at the sound of her name.

Zack left Cookie to keep watch and ran through to the bedroom to pick up the two–way radio. 'Please have the radio on you, Sylvie,' he urged her. He tried to call but she didn't respond. He shoved the radio in his jacket pocket and hurried through to the study as Cookie began to bark.

Zack peered out the window. There was Conrad's car. They'd just pulled up and were getting out of the car and going into her house. Zack patted Cookie's head in thanks and to calm him down, while eyeing the competition. Conrad had the winning looks that most women would swoon over, and the money to go with it. Where did that leave him?

He tried but couldn't get through to Sylvie by phone. The cell had no signal and his landline was giving him an engaged tone. And she wasn't picking up via the radio. Maybe she was busy packing, or Conrad was distracting her?

Zack then tried to phone Nancy at the grocery store but that line was busy. He pictured it would be red hot with gossip for the next two hours while Nancy and Nate relayed the details of what had happened to Jessica, the sheriff and others in town.

He sat down on the edge of the sofa to think what to do. If he barged up to Sylvie's door without doing things right, he could push her to leave with Conrad. No, he had to do this properly.

He sighed reluctantly. There was only one option he could think of.

Conrad wandered around Sylvie's lounge while she made them coffee. He viewed the embers of the fire. It had almost burned itself out.

'Does someone come round and build a log fire for you?' Conrad asked.

'No, I learned to light it myself,' she called through from the kitchen.

'Your new found skills will come in handy for lighting the log fire at Vermont. I wouldn't know how to do it. I've barely spent any time there.'

She carried the coffee through and handed him a cup. 'I haven't said I'll go with you to Vermont.'

Conrad pretended to take an interest in her Christmas tree. 'Nice tree.'

'Nancy decorated it.'

'Nancy and Nate are the people who own this house?' He gazed around. 'I like it. It's cozy.'

'I didn't think it was your style, Conrad. You're more the sleek, monochrome type of guy.'

He meandered around, sipping his coffee. 'I can do cozy.'

Had he changed? She eyed him with curiosity. Or was he using his charm to get her to drop her guard?

'I still think you'd like Vermont.'

She didn't doubt it. She'd love it. She just didn't love Conrad.

He pulled out his phone and held it up. 'Still no signal.'

The landline phone rang, jolting Sylvie. She picked up and was happy to hear Marla's voice.

'Sylvie! I've been trying to call you on your cell and on this connection, but I think the conditions are affecting things. I have some great news for you.'

'Great news?'

Conrad's attention swung around to Sylvie.

Marla sounded so excited. 'The company is so pleased with the reaction to your new fabric collection and other ranges you've designed. And... the marketing people have suggested to the board that we capitalize on a new image for you.'

'A new image for me?'

'Yes. We have a plan. We'll focus on the small town quaintness of your floral designs. The company want you to stay where you are. A city image wouldn't gel with this right now. We'll emphasize the town's beautiful flowers and trees and whatever else that creates an image of homeliness and warmth. We think it will be perfect for the fall collection you're working on. Imagine all those trees with the colors of the leaves. It'll look amazing. However, once the fall designs are finished, we want you to work on general themes rather than seasons, so you won't be working ahead of the curve any longer.'

Marla was racing ahead, but Sylvie's mind was rewinding the part where the company wanted her to relocate here. 'If the company wants me to move here, that means...'

'No more problems of you living in New York and Zack in Snow Bells Haven. We'll need you to come to meetings in the city several times during the year. But you can bring Zack and come and stay with Peter and me.' Marla's voice had a lightness to it. 'And I can come and stay with you sometimes, maybe for a weekend if the invitation was there.'

'You'd be welcome,' said Sylvie. 'Bring Peter and the kids.'

'Oh the kids would love it. So would Peter. He was raised in a small town.'

'Yes, he told me about that.'

Marla joked with her. 'A couple of the directors want to visit too. Is there fishing down there?'

'I'm sure there is. There's also Zack's cabin at the cove.'

'I can see the directors considering opening up a company branch in the town.'

'It could work out well for all of us,' said Sylvie.

Marla agreed. 'We can chat by webcam and you can email your designs between meetings. It'll work out just fine. And customers won't be duped. You really will be living and designing there.'

'So I suppose that also means...' Sylvie hesitated and glanced at Conrad. The plan hadn't gone down well with him.

'You can start dating Zack. I think you'll be a great couple,' said Marla. 'I'll email all the details from the company's meeting with the marketing people.'

'This is amazing!' Sylvie enthused.

'Have you heard from Conrad? Did he turn up in town?'

'Yes. I'll talk to you about that later.'

'Okay. Merry Christmas, Sylvie.'

'It is, Marla, it truly is.'

Not according to Conrad. As Sylvie finished the call with Marla, he put his coffee down and sighed. He hadn't heard the whole conversation, but he'd overheard some of the things Marla had said, and sussed enough to know where the chips had fallen. 'Where does that leave us?'

Zack grabbed a pen and paper. He wrote a quick note, rolled it up and tied it securely to Cookie's collar.

'Take this to Nancy at the grocery store. Go to Nancy, Cookie. Tell Nancy.'

Zack opened the front door and the dog didn't hesitate as he urged him on. 'Quick, go tell Nancy.'

Zack didn't even have time to open the gate. Cookie bolted down the garden and jumped the fence. He bounded down the sidewalk, alert to everything, tail up and ears flapping back from the force of the speed as he raced along the snow heading straight for the grocery store.

187

Cookie knew his way to Nancy's store. It was an almost daily route for him and Zack. Cookie also adored Nancy, and not just because she gave him doggie treats that she ordered in specially for him.

Zack waited until he felt enough time had passed, then got ready to take the chance of a lifetime. He knew in his mind the things he wanted to say.

Armed with nothing except a heart full of hope, Zack walked along to Sylvie's house. He saw her inside the front lounge and Conrad was there with her. Seeing them together was like a dagger through him.

Sylvie suddenly locked eyes with him, as if the connection between them was so strong she'd sensed Zack's approach before she actually saw him.

Zack saw the expression on her face. She was tense, and yet hope still bubbled inside him.

Sylvie hurried to the door and opened it. 'Zack.'

He stopped where he was on the front lawn.

Conrad joined Sylvie at the door. While she stayed where she was, Conrad stepped outside in a face off with Zack.

Zack kicked off what needed to be said. He directed his comments straight at Conrad. 'I know you can offer Sylvie a great life in New York, an apartment in the city and a house in Vermont.'

Conrad accepted the challenge being wielded. 'Yes, you got something better to offer her?'

The sound of carol singers approaching filled the air.

'I have something that money can't buy.' Zack motioned in the direction of the singing.

Sylvie stared wide eyed when she saw what was heading their way.

Behind the carol singers were a number of people. She saw Nancy, Jessica and the sheriff, Greg with his elves, Virginia, Ana and Luke, along with others she'd seen around town. There was a reindeer too. She didn't know who the reindeer was, but underneath those antlers was another friend. And Nate was dressed as Santa.

Zack's heart felt fit to burst when he saw them. He'd hoped Nancy and Nate would turn up, maybe with a couple of others, but he hadn't anticipated this strength of turnout of support, especially at such short notice. The townsfolk never failed to amaze him.

Cookie walked at heel beside Nancy and Nate.

Conrad glanced at Sylvie for an explanation of what was going on. She had no idea. Conrad stood his ground against Zack, waiting to see what was going to happen.

Everyone poured into Sylvie's front yard and stopped as a gathering behind Zack.

'I have all these friends who love Sylvie and want her to become part of our community,' said Zack.

Cookie ran up to Sylvie, tail wagging.

'And a dog,' Zack added.

Conrad looked beaten, but was determined not to back down.

Nate stepped forward and directed his comment straight at Conrad. 'I overheard you talking to Sylvie. If you really are a changed guy, do the right thing. I think you know what that is.'

Conrad was quiet for a moment, then seemed to gather all the strength he could muster and stood tall and straight. He gazed at Sylvie one last time. 'Goodbye, Sylvie.' He didn't wait for her response, and walked briskly away, got into his car and drove off.

The lights on the Christmas tree shone brightly outside in the community hall on the night of the Christmas Eve party.

People were gathered, huddled together happily in the cold night to see the arrival of Santa on his sleigh.

Sylvie stood beside Zack, amid all their friends. Everyone was wrapped up against the snowy air, but underneath their warm coats and jackets they were dressed in their party clothes.

The carol singers' voices rang out clear as the sleigh made its way along the main street accompanied by the cheers and waves of the townsfolk.

The sleigh pulled up and stopped outside the community hall. Santa waved, and everyone went inside.

Elves unloaded a heap of gifts from the sleigh and carried them into the hall where they were distributed under the Christmas trees.

Sylvie gazed around the hall. Couples had started dancing to the festive music. She wore the silver and white dress she'd bought, and the fabric sparkled under the lights.

Zack held out his hand to her. 'May I have this dance?'

She smiled at him and they began dancing to a romantic Christmas song under the twinkling lights that decorated the hall and highlighted the dance floor area. They slow danced, and Zack held her close.

'You know I love you, don't you?' he said gently.

'I love you too.'

He smiled, pulled her closer and was about to kiss her when a flurry of shiny red and gold balloons were released down on the partygoers.

Sylvie laughed as their kiss was interrupted, and playfully hit the balloons aside.

They continued to dance.

They waltzed past Nate and Nancy and several other couples, people she now considered to be her friends. The tall elf grinned at her as he danced with his wife. The new dress she wore was lovely. Sylvie nodded to him and he grinned back at her.

'There's something I want to ask you,' Zack said as they danced.

'What's that?'

'Where are we having Christmas Day? At my house or yours?'

'You have two houses, Zack,' she reminded him playfully.

'One house and one cabin.'

'Okay... your house on Christmas morning, the two of us and Cookie. Then maybe we could head over to my house in the afternoon. And later we could venture up to the cove and you can show me the cabin.'

'An adventurous day.' He sounded fine with that.

'Adventure was part of my plan.'

Zack nodded as he gazed at her and leaned in for a kiss.

As their lips were about to touch, both of them hesitated and glanced around. This time there was nothing to stop them. Nothing at all.

Zack pulled her into his warm embrace and kissed her.

He eventually pulled back and they both smiled at each other.

She'd always known that Zack's kiss would melt her heart. She gazed at him and smiled. 'Merry Christmas, Zack.'

'Merry Christmas,' he said, and kissed her again.

End

About the Author:

Follow De-ann on Instagram @deann.black

De-ann Black is a bestselling author, scriptwriter and former newspaper journalist. She has over 80 books published. Romance, crime thrillers, espionage novels, action adventure. And children's books (non-fiction rocket science books and children's fiction). She became an Amazon All-Star author in 2014 and 2015.

She previously worked as a full-time newspaper journalist for several years. She had her own weekly columns in the press. This included being a motoring correspondent where she got to test drive cars every week for the press for three years.

Before being asked to work for the press, De-ann worked in magazine editorial writing everything from fashion features to social news. She was the marketing editor of a glossy magazine. She is also a professional artist and illustrator. Fabric design, dressmaking, sewing, knitting and fashion are part of her work.

Additionally, De-ann has always been interested in fitness, and was a fitness and bodybuilding champion, 100 metre runner and mountaineer. As a former N.A.B.B.A. Miss Scotland, she had a weekly fitness show on the radio that ran for over three years.

De-ann trained in Shukokai karate, boxing, kickboxing, Dayan Qigong and Jiu Jitsu. She is currently based in Scotland.
Her colouring books and embroidery design books are available in paperback. These include Floral Nature Embroidery Designs and Scottish Garden Embroidery Designs.

Also by De-ann Black (Romance, Action/Thrillers & Children's books). See her Amazon Author page or website for further details about her books, screenplays, illustrations, art and fabric designs. www.De-annBlack.com

Romance books:

Sewing, Crafts & Quilting series:
1. The Sewing Bee
2. The Sewing Shop

Quilting Bee & Tea Shop series:
1. The Quilting Bee
2. The Tea Shop by the Sea

Heather Park: Regency Romance

Snow Bells Haven series:
1. Snow Bells Christmas
2. Snow Bells Wedding

Summer Sewing Bee
Christmas Cake Chateau

Cottages, Cakes & Crafts series:
1. The Flower Hunter's Cottage
2. The Sewing Bee by the Sea
3. The Beemaster's Cottage
4. The Chocolatier's Cottage
5. The Bookshop by the Seaside

Sewing, Knitting & Baking series:
1. The Tea Shop
2. The Sewing Bee & Afternoon Tea
3. The Christmas Knitting Bee
4. Champagne Chic Lemonade Money
5. The Vintage Sewing & Knitting Bee

The Tea Shop & Tearoom series:
1. The Christmas Tea Shop & Bakery
2. The Christmas Chocolatier
3. The Chocolate Cake Shop in New York at Christmas
4. The Bakery by the Seaside
5. Shed in the City

Tea Dress Shop series:
1. The Tea Dress Shop At Christmas
2. The Fairytale Tea Dress Shop In Edinburgh
3. The Vintage Tea Dress Shop In Summer

Christmas Romance series:
1. Christmas Romance in Paris
2. Christmas Romance in Scotland

Romance, Humour, Mischief series:
1. Oops! I'm the Paparazzi
2. Oops! I'm A Hollywood Agent
3. Oops! I'm A Secret Agent
4. Oops! I'm Up To Mischief

The Bitch-Proof Suit series:
1. The Bitch-Proof Suit
2. The Bitch-Proof Romance
3. The Bitch-Proof Bride

The Cure For Love
Dublin Girl
Why Are All The Good Guys Total Monsters?
I'm Holding Out For A Vampire Boyfriend

Action/Thriller books:
Love Him Forever
Someone Worse
Electric Shadows
The Strife Of Riley
Shadows Of Murder
Cast a Dark Shadow

Children's books:
Faeriefied
Secondhand Spooks
Poison-Wynd
Wormhole Wynd
Science Fashion
School For Aliens

Colouring books:
Flower Nature
Summer Garden
Spring Garden
Autumn Garden
Sea Dream
Festive Christmas
Christmas Garden
Christmas Theme
Flower Bee
Wild Garden
Faerie Garden Spring
Flower Hunter
Stargazer Space
Bee Garden
Scottish Garden Seasons

Embroidery Design books:
Floral Nature Embroidery Designs
Scottish Garden Embroidery Designs

Printed in Great Britain
by Amazon

16244889R00119